An Outside Chance

The Chances
Book 3

Emily E K Murdoch

© Copyright 2024 by Emily E K Murdoch
Text by Emily E K Murdoch
Cover by Dar Albert

Dragonblade Publishing, Inc. is an imprint of Kathryn Le Veque Novels, Inc.
P.O. Box 23
Moreno Valley, CA 92556
ceo@dragonbladepublishing.com

Produced in the United States of America

First Edition November 2024
Print Edition

Reproduction of any kind except where it pertains to short quotes in relation to advertising or promotion is strictly prohibited.

All Rights Reserved.

The characters and events portrayed in this book are fictitious. Any similarity to real persons, living or dead, is purely coincidental and not intended by the author.

ARE YOU SIGNED UP FOR DRAGONBLADE'S BLOG?

You'll get the latest news and information on exclusive giveaways, exclusive excerpts, coming releases, sales, free books, cover reveals and more.

Check out our complete list of authors, too!

No spam, no junk. That's a promise!

Sign Up Here

www.dragonbladepublishing.com

Dearest Reader;

Thank you for your support of a small press. At Dragonblade Publishing, we strive to bring you the highest quality Historical Romance from some of the best authors in the business. Without your support, there is no 'us', so we sincerely hope you adore these stories and find some new favorite authors along the way.

Happy Reading!

Kathryn Le Veque

CEO, Dragonblade Publishing

Additional Dragonblade books by
Author Emily E K Murdoch

The Chances Series
A Fighting Chance (Book 1)
A Second Chance (Book 2)
An Outside Chance (Book 3)
Half a Chance (Book 4)

Dukes in Danger Series
Don't Judge a Duke by His Cover (Book 1)
Strike While the Duke is Hot (Book 2)
The Duke is Mightier than the Sword (Book 3)
A Duke in Time Saves Nine (Book 4)
Every Duke Has His Price (Book 5)
Put Your Best Duke Forward (Book 6)
Where There's a Duke, There's a Way (Book 7)
Curiosity Killed the Duke (Book 8)
Play With Dukes, Get Burned (Book 9)
The Best Things in Life are Dukes (Book 10)
A Duke a Day Keeps the Doctor Away (Book 11)
All Good Dukes Come to an End (Book 12)

Twelve Days of Christmas
Twelve Drummers Drumming
Eleven Pipers Piping
Ten Lords a Leaping
Nine Ladies Dancing
Eight Maids a Milking
Seven Swans a Swimming
Six Geese a Laying
Five Gold Rings

Four Calling Birds
Three French Hens
Two Turtle Doves
A Partridge in a Pear Tree

The De Petras Saga
The Misplaced Husband (Book 1)
The Impoverished Dowry (Book 2)
The Contrary Debutante (Book 3)
The Determined Mistress (Book 4)
The Convenient Engagement (Book 5)

The Governess Bureau Series
A Governess of Great Talents (Book 1)
A Governess of Discretion (Book 2)
A Governess of Many Languages (Book 3)
A Governess of Prodigious Skill (Book 4)
A Governess of Unusual Experience (Book 5)
A Governess of Wise Years (Book 6)
A Governess of No Fear (Novella)

Never The Bride Series
Always the Bridesmaid (Book 1)
Always the Chaperone (Book 2)
Always the Courtesan (Book 3)
Always the Best Friend (Book 4)
Always the Wallflower (Book 5)
Always the Bluestocking (Book 6)
Always the Rival (Book 7)
Always the Matchmaker (Book 8)
Always the Widow (Book 9)
Always the Rebel (Book 10)
Always the Mistress (Book 11)
Always the Second Choice (Book 12)
Always the Mistletoe (Novella)
Always the Reverend (Novella)

The Lyon's Den Series
Always the Lyon Tamer

Pirates of Britannia Series
Always the High Seas

De Wolfe Pack: The Series
Whirlwind with a Wolfe

Noble titles throughout English history have, at times, been more fluid than one might think. Women have inherited, men have been gifted titles by family or gained them on through marriage, and royals frequently lavished titles or withdrew them as reward and punishment.

The Chance brothers in this series agreed to split the four titles in their family line, rather than the eldest holding all four. It is a decision that defines their brotherhood, and their very different personalities.

Get ready to meet a family that is more than happy to scandalize Society...

Chapter One

September 14, 1812

D ODO LOUGHTY HAD found her mark. Now all she had to do was work out her approach.

The whole thing shouldn't have been difficult. She was actually supposed to be here, at Baron Llyne's party, and that in and of itself was unusual. Dodo never usually managed to get invited to such things. She certainly never came to such occasions without a chaperone—though she doubted her mother, even if she were in the same city, would have approved of her task tonight. Nor had she had any desire to appeal to her new landlady for the job. She had no doubt the solicitous woman would have refused.

When the invitation had arrived in the post at Dodo's lodgings yesterday, she had scrabbled to reply in time, and here she was.

And so, it appeared, was half the town.

Bath was supposed to be quiet at this time of year—that was what Dodo's mother had said. Though Dodo's parents actually thought her to be in York, visiting her aunt. Her parents had hesitated to allow her to travel without a chaperone to begin with, but she had assured them there was no need of their sole maid to accompany her because it was such a short distance. But she had actually gone to Bath—quiet Bath. That description was why Dodo had chosen this part of the world to visit at just such a time. But instead—

"Careful there!" cried a portly, scowling gentleman carelessly as he pushed past her.

Dodo's headpiece, a delicate pink ribbon encircled with lace, was almost knocked off her head as the man shoved her none too delicately toward the wall. It was a fortunate thing, indeed, that her balance was excellent. It was an unfortunate thing, indeed, that she wasn't able to get a good kick at him as he passed.

Not, Dodo reminded herself, *that I should be thinking of doing such things, much less actually doing them.*

No, she was here to make money. That was all. One of Baron Llyne's card parties was precisely the right sort of place for a lady to do such a thing.

Not that I should be doing such a thing, either…

"Ah, there you are!" came the booming voice of a woman who appeared to be half human, half siege engine.

Dodo blinked as a curvaceous woman wearing a crimson, silk gown with her blonde hair full of feathers bore down on her. This couldn't have been—

"I hope you find Baron Llyne's home welcoming," boomed a lady who could only be Lady Romeril as she stopped short before Dodo. "I do not think I have had the pleasure of your company before, Miss Loughty. Forgive my forwardness. I ensured old Llyne invited you, as I was simply desperate to meet you. Your landlady tells me everything that goes on in that place of hers, I'm afraid."

That explained how anyone had even known Dodo was in town—or who she was to begin with. She attempted to smile. It was not something she was particularly good at, and recently, she hadn't had much cause to bother.

As she tried now, moving her face into an approximation of a smile, she saw a flicker of uncertainty in the woman's eyes.

Good heavens, she would have to do better than this…

"Thank you, Lady Romeril, for your gracious intercession on my behalf," Dodo managed, fanning herself slightly with a hand. *When had it grown so stifling in here?* "It was very kind of you to—"

"No kindness meant, I assure you," said Lady Romeril with a stern look down her nose. "You are new to Bath, new to the *ton*, as far as I can make out. I wanted to assess you."

Dodo had been warned about this.

Oh, not by any particular person. She knew almost no one in Bath and had spoken to fewer than five people altogether since she had arrived last week. But that did not matter.

Somehow, everyone knew about Lady Romeril. It was a part of Society that seeped into the skin.

And Lady Romeril was most definitely the sort of person to assess others.

Her roving eye flickered across Dodo's person, which most irritatingly started to heat up with embarrassment as she was subjected to the review.

Well, honestly! This was not even Lady Romeril's home, nor Lady Romeril's card party, nor Lady Romeril's Titian paintings on the wall, and—goodness, the detailed carvings on that golden clock were elaborate.

Still, Dodo thought wretchedly, shifting her necklace in her discomfort, *being Lady Romeril and a terror in Society did not give her the right to examine young ladies as though they were cattle.* Particularly when this specific young lady was here without a chaperone and was wearing a necklace with jewels that appeared at first glance to be sapphires but that any detailed inspection would soon reveal to be glass...

"Hmm," said Lady Romeril with a raised eyebrow. "To whom shall I introduce you, then?"

Dodo almost choked, she spoke so hastily. "I am afraid I do not know anyone here to—"

"All the more reason to introduce you," said her hostess swiftly. "Come on. Play whist with Lady Amelia Zouch."

It did not appear to matter to Lady Romeril whether or not Miss

Doris Loughty—Dodo to the few people with whom she was close—wished to play whist. Or play anything. Her fingers grasped her guest's wrist and Dodo was swept across the room and deposited on a chair opposite a young lady with fine, blue eyes and flaxen hair, and two gentlemen, both of whom seemed bored beyond their wits.

Dodo swallowed, mouth dry. "Lady Romeril—"

But she was gone. Again, the woman seemed to have forgotten the social dictates of proper introductions. With the unerring sense of the firebrand, she had spied newcomers of whom she evidently wished to make an inspection and had disappeared into the crowd of the drawing room.

And a crowd it was. In a way, Dodo was delighted to be seated in the crush rather than having to force her way through it. But that did not mean she was welcome at the table...

As no one else seemed eager to provide their names, Dodo turned nervously to her new companions and attempted a pleasant expression as her pulse beat a frantic tattoo under her ribs. "Miss... Miss Loughty. Delighted to make your acquaintance."

The lady she knew. Everyone knew Lady Amelia Zouch—everyone. Charming, beautiful, and her brother was a duke, of course. That was someone to know.

Not a vicar's daughter from the middle of nowhere who has come to Bath to seek her fortune, Dodo thought wryly as she accepted the dealt cards with a meek inclination of her head.

Well, that wouldn't matter. All she had to do was win.

"It's a penny entry," said the hawkish, thin man to her left with a leer that was perhaps supposed to be a smile. "I can stand you for it, Miss Loughty. Always delighted to have a lady owe me a favor."

If the glare Lady Amelia was giving him was any indication, it was a dangerous thing indeed to be indebted to the man who had not yet had the manners to introduce himself.

Dodo shifted in her seat, her light-cream gown suddenly too hot, too tight. And a penny was a penny. She had come here to earn money, not to lay it down on a table with the risk of losing it.

She glanced at her hand.

"I will pay my own penny, Mr. ...?"

"Mr. Packham," said the man as he crinkled his sharp nose, clearly ruffled by the fact that she was unwilling to make herself an easy target. "Fine. Well. It's your money."

It was indeed her money, and now Dodo had seen the cards she had been dealt, she was perfectly happy to risk it.

Risk it. It was hardly a risk. Almost a certainty. The odds were she would sweep the—

"It is your move, Miss Loughty," said the quiet gentleman to her left.

Dodo glanced at him. He did not appear to be interested in her, which was a great comfort. She had so few connections as it was—it would be difficult, as she moved about Bath society, to discover which gentlemen were appropriate to be speaking with and who should be avoided at all costs.

She silently placed Mr. Packham in the latter group as she put down a sixpence, raising the stakes for all at the table.

If only I had friends. Or if Ellis were—were here.

It was a pathetic thought, and one Dodo attempted to push aside swiftly. Her brother was gone—he was dead. And that left her, the only person who could attempt to solve this problem.

The room was growing more raucous as the game of whist continued. Someone had opened a bottle of brandy, for some of the gentlemen passing their table were holding large glasses of the stuff. The room buzzed with excitement as a table whooped with laughter at someone's expense.

The trouble was, though her deep-seated desire for connection was a pathetic thought, it was also a true one. Dodo had never been one for a large acquaintance, and after the year she'd had…

Well. Suffice to say, the fact that she had managed to find lodgings at all in Bath, and respectable and cheap ones at that, was a minor miracle.

All she had to do was win...

Dodo looked at the cards in her hand. So, hearts were trumps, and a series of tricks had been played by Lady Amelia which had set them up well. They were playing Long Whist rather than three rubbers, which could keep them trapped at the table forever. The cards left remaining in hands were two of clubs, three of clubs, nine of clubs, eight of spades...

It did not take her long. Numbers never did. They behaved in a way so unlike people: orderly, controlled, and always the same each time. It was a relief to lose herself in the probabilities and start stacking up the potential winning routes.

Mr. Packham cleared his throat nastily. "Is this a forfeit, Miss Loughty?"

"Certainly not," Dodo said, a small smile creeping over her lips. It was always pleasant to win, but the pile of silver before her was going to make the game ever so sweet. "I believe my partner and I have the honors, and therefore the game."

She placed her cards carefully before her.

Genteel applause. Dodo blinked. They had gained an audience— one she had not noticed, and which could certainly have put off a lesser player from their counting and calculations.

As it was, her cheeks pinked and she turned swiftly to look at the pile of coins on the table. At least four shillings. Well, it wasn't outstanding prize money, but—

"Well played, Miss Loughty," said Lady Amelia with a stiff look. "Shall we split our winnings?"

Dodo's smile faded, but only slightly. With a great effort, she managed to retain her cheery expression as she inclined her head as generously as possible.

Of course. Whist was a pairs game. She had entirely forgotten in the exhilaration of winning. The winnings would therefore be split, leaving her with only—

"Two shillings fourpence," said the man on her right quietly. "A hefty sum, for the risk of a penny."

Dodo did not look at him as she accepted the coins silently from Lady Amelia and placed them swiftly in her reticule. It hung a little heavier from her wrist. Not heavy enough, though.

There was the interest on that loan her parents had taken and the butcher's bill, the wages for their maid were overdue, and then there was that pound they had borrowed from a friend who really needed to be paid back...

The night is still young, she tried to tell herself as she rose awkwardly from the table, hardly able to push her chair back because the crush of spectators meant she would have to hurtle into someone's knees. There were to be plenty of opportunities to play another—

"So you play well." Mr. Packham leered at Dodo. "What else do you do well, Miss Loughty?"

"Miss Loughty? Will you come with me to get a glass of punch?" asked Lady Amelia quietly.

Dodo could not acquiesce swiftly enough. "Yes! Yes, most definitely."

To walk about the room with someone else, to look as though she belonged, to make it clear that she knew someone else, even if it were in the smallest and most insignificant way—

Yes, that would be greatly appreciated.

Lady Amelia rose in her turn, and the two of them pushed awkwardly through the crowd that was watching a poker match on another table, and then they moved past those surrounding a whooping table, who appeared to be crowing over an unfortunate gentleman who had lost an entire pound.

Dodo shivered. That would be awful, indeed.

Biting her lip as she and Lady Amelia approached the punch table, she felt the weight of her reticule again and calculated. She knew how heavy it should feel after a card party, and she wasn't even close to halfway yet. She would have to join another table as swiftly as—

"You were disappointed, weren't you?" asked Lady Amelia, as though they were continuing a conversation.

Dodo blinked. "I-I beg your pardon?"

"Punch?" Lady Amelia gestured with the ladle.

Nodding and hurriedly holding out a glass that she'd taken from the row on the table before them, Dodo watched as one of the toasts of the *ton* poured her a glass.

"Disappointed," repeated Lady Amelia, now helping herself to a glass of punch. "With your winnings, I mean. You were hoping for more."

She fixed her clear gaze on Dodo, whose cheeks burned.

What was a lady of the *ton* supposed to say to that? How was she supposed to answer honestly yet keep her secret? What if her continued silence prompted the already forward Lady Amelia to ask after her chaperone this evening, another topic Dodo hoped desperately to avoid? Would she have to tell her an old aunt was just around the corner, milling about one of the tables?

Hoping that inspiration would strike—though it never did with words—Dodo took a sip of her punch and almost choked.

"Yes, Lord Llyne does make it strong," said Lady Amelia with a wry look. "Come over here, away from the crowds. Then you can tell me whether you're here to swindle the rest of their guests."

Dodo almost considered bolting.

After all, the last thing she needed was to be found out. Well, not found out, exactly. She hadn't cheated. She had never cheated—she had never had to. When one could see how the cards were going to move, there was no requirement to cheat. It was merely a simple case of calculation. Anyone could do that.

Why no one else did was a mystery to her.

But running would only emphasize her guilt, would it not? And this Lady Amelia, part of Bath's society as she was, could hardly imprison her or defame her merely for winning a hand of whist.

Not, Dodo thought bitterly, *that it was even worth much.*

"You need money, I suppose," said Lady Amelia quietly, sipping her punch as though they were discussing the latest bonnet design that had appeared on Milsom Street.

Dodo knew her cheeks must have been crimson, but there was nothing she could do about it. She didn't even trust her voice, and as no words had occurred to her, she did the only thing she could. She nodded.

Lady Amelia mirrored her, nodding in turn as she put her half-empty glass of punch on the tray of a passing footman. "You're not alone, you know. There are plenty of young ladies in Bath, and London, who receive an insufficient allowance from their parents and attempt to find more at card parties."

Forcing a smile she did not feel, Dodo croaked, "Ah."

The pair was forced to take hurried steps back as a trio of laughing gentlemen, smelling strongly of brandy, marched past them with no consideration for personal space. Or toes. The contents of Dodo's glass sloshed dangerously and she quickly put it down on the nearby table, but not before noticing a fresh stain on the only pair of fine gloves she had without holes.

"There is no shame in it," said Lady Amelia airily. "Naturally, I do not have to worry about such things, but I am aware. Here."

Dodo almost did not put her hands out in time. As it was, one of the pennies that her conversation companion suddenly thrust toward her escaped Dodo's hands and fell to the floor.

The other two shillings and thruppence, however, were now inexplicably clasped in Dodo's own hands.

"I have no need of it," Lady Amelia said airily. "Go get yourself whatever ribbons you wanted."

And with that, she sauntered off into the crowd.

The instinct to throw the coins after the woman's condescending head swept through Dodo. Perhaps if she had finished her glass of punch and was more reckless than she typically was, she would have done so.

As it was, her pride got the better of her. She even bent to pick up the fallen coin.

It was easier to slip the coins into her reticule. When Dodo allowed her hand to fall back to her side, her reticule was heavier. Comfortingly heavier. But not enough.

Her pulse was pattering painfully, and she permitted herself five minutes—and no more—to continue standing by the wall considering her next move. The question was, which table would she approach?

Whist, it appeared, would not provide her the opportunity to win sufficient funds—that was clear. Poker, then? Cribbage?

But as Dodo looked out at the plethora of tables, almost all of them now occupied, she noted with a sinking feeling that most were only playing for pennies. A winner may walk off with two or three shillings, if they were lucky, but some of these games lasted for ages. Twenty minutes, perhaps even half an hour.

That would leave her with…

Well, say the average card party lasted until midnight. It was a quarter past eight now, according to a grandfather clock in the corner. So, let's say half past, both for ease of calculations and to take into account the difficulty of being cut into a game. That left her only seven opportunities to play and win money—and that, Dodo knew, was a best-case scenario, only to be achieved if she were accepted into every game.

Seven games, winning, say, three shillings a time, and that was generous—so twenty-one shillings. Not even a guinea.

Picking up her glass again, Dodo swallowed the last of the punch and blinked, the strength of the drink overwhelming her senses for a mere moment as she set the glass back down.

No, she couldn't possibly win enough here. Yet what other choices did she have? There were only so many times she could escape without her parents noticing, only so many card parties hosted in Bath at this point of the Season, and it wasn't as though she was going to be invited to every single—

"Excuse me," said a quiet voice that she somehow recognized. "Forgive me, but I couldn't help but overhear."

Dodo glanced to the left and saw, to her horror, that the gentleman who had been seated on her right at the whist table was standing nearby.

Very nearby. Nearby enough, as he said, to have heard her conversation with Lady Amelia.

Stomach twisting and wondering whether it would simply make the most sense to leave the card party, she attempted to remain calm. "I don't know what you mean, *sir*."

Although she had not intended to put a slight emphasis on the final word, she had, and Dodo could see that it had had an impact.

The man grinned, and a curious dimple formed in one cheek. "Yes, abominably rude of me not to introduce myself. My wife will have my guts for garters. She's a stickler for manners."

And somehow, those words calmed the initial panic washing over Dodo, and not merely because he offered safety for an unchaperoned lady, standing beside a very much married and therefore ineligible gentleman.

Well, if he were a married man, he could not be all bad, could he? Someone had agreed to marry him. It was not precisely the vote of confidence it could have been—some awful men were married, though how, she was not sure—but it certainly calmed her. A little.

"She says my ability to overhear things that are nothing to do with me is another of my worst qualities," said the man cheerfully. "But

Florence never holds it against me, thank God. You're looking to make some money, then?"

Dodo took a step back, wary at the man's words.

Well, nothing good came after thinking something like that, did it?

The man's face fell. "Oh, dear God, not like—Miss Loughty, isn't it? I would never—oh, blast."

The man truly did look mortified. Dodo's shoulders loosened, just a tad, though she still glared at the man with a wariness that he absolutely warranted.

"Look, I've done this all backward," said the man heavily. "I'm John Chance, Marquess of Aylesbury."

Dodo took another step back, almost tripping over her own feet. This was not what she'd intended. Gentlemen introducing themselves to her at card parties, making insinuations—even if it had been accidental...

This was precisely why her parents had not wished her to come to Bath. But what choice did she have?

"You need to make money, right?" said the man—the Marquess of Aylesbury, if he were to be trusted—asked quietly.

And for some reason, one that Dodo could not fathom, she nodded. "Yes."

The marquess grinned. "You sound like my brother. George Chance. He's always looking to win or lose a huge pile, and I have to say that he's not particularly good at the former. Rather better at the latter."

Despite herself, Dodo was intrigued. A brother who was an expert at losing money... Well. That was the sort of man to be around. Particularly if he could lose a huge pile to *her*.

"In fact, I believe that is what he is doing this very evening," said Lord Aylesbury conversationally.

Dodo swallowed. It was up to her to say something, she knew. And she could hardly be blamed for her curiosity. It was the man who had raised the topic, after all. "And... And he is here, is he?"

"Here? At Lord Llyne's?" Lord Aylesbury snorted. "Never fear. You simply can't win or lose enough here for Lindow's tastes."

She tried to smile, her pulse thumping faster. Lindow? A strange sort of nickname.

"No, he's at McBarland's. It's a gaming hell, about four streets over," said the interfering man happily.

Dodo froze.

Well, that was it. There was no possibility, absolutely no possibility, of her going there. The odds were not just astronomical, they were impossible.

A lady like her, go to a gaming hell? Go to "McBarland's," which sounded just as scandalous as she was sure it was. No. Even with the temptation of being able to earn more money. Even if she could win enough to—

No. Absolutely not.

The man's pinched expression was a little too knowing. "Yes, you are correct. Ladies, particularly ladies of the *ton*, are not generally accepted there. Well, I say 'accepted.' They do not typically *wish* to go. What lady would? She'd lose all her money."

And that was when Dodo squared her shoulders and spoke in as icy a tone as possible. "And what, precisely, is the address of this place where ladies aren't supposed to go?"

Chapter Two

GEORGE CHANCE, EARL of Lindow, was going to buy the entirety of Bath.

"But why stop at Bath?" he crowed, grinning as his opponent slunk away from the table with a downcast expression. "If I keep on like this, I could buy London!"

It was a heady thought. For a man who rarely managed a winning streak of more than... well, two, this evening was turning out to be one of the greatest of his life.

"I'm going to buy Milsom Street." George chuckled as he leaned back in the rickety chair that was always his whenever he graced McBarland's with his presence. "At the very least."

Not that he could. The gold that had slipped into his pocket, along with the bad-tempered IOU from Mr. Lister, was probably not quite sufficient to buy even one building on Milsom Street. The place was becoming so damned fashionable.

But still—it was far more than he had won in a long time, and almost as much as he had lost that morning at the races.

George's smile faltered. *Oh, blast.* He had forgotten about that.

It was a crying shame, that was what it was. His horse, Scandal of Lancelot, should have won. Everyone said so. The breeding was impeccable, the feed had been damned expensive, and he'd even paid that jockey, what was his name, a small fortune.

The race should have been easy.

As it was, George had been forced to watch some other brute

speed past to take the winnings. Scandal of Lancelot had arrived at a respectable third—respectable, but not profitable.

It simply wasn't fair, that was all there was to it. He'd have to hope Scandal of Lancelot won again in the future. Tomorrow, if at all possible. There was definitely supposed to be more money in his pocketbook than there was. All he had to do was make a winning bet.

"Ah, well," George said aloud, for the benefit of absolutely no one. "I'm winning now."

Which had come as a great surprise, to tell the truth. Oh, McBarland's was a place where one could technically win a great amount of money. The reason he didn't, George kept telling himself, was merely because of bad luck. And bad luck turned.

Perhaps it didn't in a place like this. After all, it was hardly reputable. The paint was peeling off the walls, wallpaper long gone. The few paintings that were still on the walls were only still present because they had been nailed on—a few of them, directly through the canvas. All that glittered here was brass, not gold, and that was with Ivan the barman ensuring he kept the worst of the rascals out of the place.

There were still plenty of blaggards.

Including me, George thought cheerfully as he stretched out and discovered a discomfortingly sticky patch of the carpet. What had once been carpet, and now appeared to be a very light dusting of fabric.

Though he probably couldn't count himself a true fellow of the rascals and ne'er-do-wells that populated McBarland's on a Monday night. He was, after all, an earl. Even if he didn't quite have the manner and bearing of one.

Or the pockets of one.

"Lindow!" came a cheerful voice.

George looked up and saw Walden. Well, he saw his lordship, Albert Halifax, Viscount Walden. But titles were not the sort of thing one bandied about in a place like McBarland's. Not if you wanted to live long enough to come back.

"Walden!" he cried, gesturing that the man should sit beside him. "I did not think you were in Bath."

"Nor I you," returned Walden. His lopsided grin drew attention to his rather prominent ears. "Last I heard, you were in London, marrying off your brothers."

George snorted. "Well, I had to give them *something* to do."

Two weddings this year—it was almost catching. That was why he had fled—er, had decided to remove himself from London, where this marriage fever seemed to be doing the rounds of the three Chance brothers, and abscond to Bath.

No one got married in Bath.

"You've had a successful night, then?"

George gave his friend a mock grimace. "You can tell?"

"You only have that irritating look on your face when you've had a particularly good run," said Walden dryly. "Poker?"

"Of course poker," said George, waving a hand. "I think I'll have another drink, you know. Now I can actually pay off my tab."

He shot a grin at his companion.

Walden had known him for, what… five years? Perhaps longer, it was hard to say. The man was polite enough, but incredibly, married since last autumn. It had put rather a dampener on their friendship, though George would never be the one to admit to as much.

Not aloud, anyway. Heaven forbid.

"You know," Walden said. "I think you've had enough."

George blinked. "Dear God, you haven't joined a temperance league, have you?"

It would certainly be most unlike his friend, though sometimes the absolute worst did happen to some of the best people…

Walden snorted. "Not likely. And I didn't mean drinks, either. I think you've had enough gambling, at least for this night."

George rolled his eyes as dramatically as he could manage. "You sound like Cothrom."

The oldest Chance brother had a most disobliging habit of wishing his brothers to set aside all worldly and earthly joys. It was something about which George had argued with the man most profusely, but George dared any man to try arguing with the Duke of Cothrom when he had the bit between his teeth and was absolutely certain he was right.

The fact that he was usually right was hardly the point. And it was most irritating of his brother to always pay off his debts, on time, without lectures.

Just looks of disappointment.

George shivered. Yes, he'd been smart to leave that rascal behind in London.

"Your brother is well?"

"My brother is dull," said George with a bark of a laugh. "He wouldn't countenance me playing another hand in all my days, but I never thought you were the sort to take the happiness from a man's life."

A roar rose from a neighboring table—a roar of triumph coupled with a roar of outrage. Then there was the sound of a chair hitting the floor and the pointy end of a knife hitting a table.

Walden shrugged, as though they were taking tea at the Pump Rooms. "You're on a lucky streak, to be sure—but you'll lose it."

George grinned. Something in him knew, just knew, he wasn't going to lose tonight. Not at cards, not in this argument, not in anything. It simply wasn't possible. Luck was on his side, and if there was one thing you could depend on, it was luck.

Sort of.

"I'm confident," he began.

"Famous last words."

"That horse was supposed to win and you know it," George said sharply, pointing a finger at his friend, who was now snorting. "No, it was most unfair. I don't know how they did it, but I was robbed."

"You've got to stop pouring money into those horses," Walden said sternly.

George waved a hand as the fight at the table beside them increased in intensity and noise. A man was pushed to the floor. "It's an investment. It's going to pay off in the hundreds, perhaps the thousands."

"That's as may be," said his friend seriously. "But if you aren't careful, you're going to find yourself…"

Precisely what he was going to find himself, George could not tell. Not because Walden had ceased speaking—quite the opposite. He continued blathering on, something about how no one could win all the time, cut your losses while you're ahead, the usual sort of rubbish.

George could not concentrate. How could he, when the world's most beautiful woman had just stepped into McBarland's?

Beautiful was not even an accurate word. Ethereal. Hair so dark, it was almost black, trimmed with a ribbon of yellow, all lace and delicacy. On another woman, it would have been a trifle, but on her, it appeared to be a coronet of gold.

She was perhaps a princess. No, that was foolish—but she certainly had the bearing of one. A proud mouth, George saw as she turned to look about the room. An elegant figure that was absolutely ruined by being covered by a silk, cream gown that didn't fit well, more's the pity. And a shyness, and a softness, in the eyes that made her the perfect target.

It had to have been a mistake. It just had to have been. Women—particularly not women like that—did not come to places like this.

Not if they wanted to be able to walk out.

Within a heartbeat, she was almost completely surrounded. George wasn't surprised. If he had been closer to the door, he would have leapt up and approached her himself. It would have been impossible not to. There was something… magnetic about her. Something he had never seen in another woman before.

"—obsession—"

He caught the word from Walden and scoffed at it. He wasn't obsessed with the woman he had just spotted. True, he wished to go over to her. Talk to her. Learn her name. Take her hand and—

An unsavory character reached out and attempted to take the woman's hand in his.

George did not even notice himself rise to his feet.

"And where the devil do you think you're going, just as I start to persuade you to stop gambling?" said Walden, his jaw agape. "What are you—my goodness. What is a woman *like that* doing here?"

It was an excellent question, and one George intended to answer.

Not merely because of her beauty. No, though that was a definite attraction, there was something else his focus had alighted on.

She was wearing a most extravagant sapphire necklace.

It twinkled in the mediocre candlelight of the gaming hell and told him all he needed to know. A woman who could risk walking into a place like this with a sapphire necklace that large and excessive? She had money to burn. Money, more importantly, to lose.

"Where are you going?"

George ignored Walden and stepped forward as she pulled away from the unsavory character, her chin dipping down and her shoulders curling forward. It would only take him a few moments to reach her, then introductions could be made, he'd invite her to the table…

And he'd see how deep that reticule on her wrist truly was.

When he reached her, the woman was attempting to extricate herself. "I do not need a tour of the place, I thank you. I just want to—"

"George Chance, at your service," said George smartly, pushing past two men and speaking over a third as he bowed.

When he raised his head, it was to see the woman flushing. Flushing—and smiling. Smiling at him.

A jolt in his stomach told George that he had been right to stand and approach her. Because he could win coin from her, obviously.

There could be no other reason.

"Miss Loughty," she said shyly, dropping into a curtsey.

"But—" began one of the two remaining men circling her like piranhas.

George nudged him firmly out of the way. One lanky man almost tripped over the other, leaving just himself and Miss Loughty. The beautiful Miss Loughty. The beautiful and rich Miss Loughty.

"May I escort you to a table?" he asked smoothly, laying on the Chance charm as thick as he could manage. "Perhaps order you a drink, a glass of sherry, something of that nature?"

For a moment, he thought there was a flicker of mirth in her eyes. It was only there momentarily, and if questioned, George was not sure he could swear to the fact it had been there in the first place.

As he blinked, he saw only a delicate pink flush traveling across Miss Loughty's cheeks and down to her—

He swallowed. *Damnit, man, you're here to win money, not stare at breasts!*

Even if they were a fine pair of—

"I actually hoped to play cards," said Miss Loughty timidly, her pupils dilated as she eyed both the gambling tables and the exit. "I... I don't suppose you play?"

George was enchanted.

It was hardly difficult. Her voice was sweet, melodious, almost musical. And she wished to play cards. Playing cards meant losing money. *Her* money, preferably.

He could not have orchestrated this better himself.

Besides, it would not hurt her to be taught a little lesson about the recklessness of entering a place like McBarland's without a proper chaperone. Or at all. Surely, the woman knew just how dangerous it was to be cavorting about a place like this, particularly without a gentleman by her side?

Not that Miss Loughty could be reasonably accused of cavorting.

Not yet.

George offered his arm. "Please, Miss Loughty. Allow me to teach you."

She took his arm without another word, and the gentle presence of her hand made George's first step somewhat more of a stumble. He soon recovered himself, however, and by the time he had helped her to the seat formerly occupied by Walden, who had disappeared from his table, he was entirely in control of himself again.

As Miss Loughty sat, he was, however, offered a rather splendid view of her bosom. It was straining against her stays, and a slight twist of her shoulders revealed a hint of dark pink nipple.

It was gone the instant he saw it. *Thank God.* George wasn't sure if he'd have been able to contain himself after a second glance.

"You said you would teach me?" Miss Loughty repeated as George hastily helped himself to a seat and crossed his legs. For no reason. "Do I look like a woman who needs to be taught?"

The delicate flush on her cheeks became a darker one, but she did not drop her gaze.

Swallowing his groan and grateful beyond measure that he had taken the precaution of crossing his legs the instant he had sat, George forced himself to take a few calming breaths before attempting to speak.

Dear God, did the woman truly have no idea how she was coming across?

It wasn't possible. Yet she was clearly well bred. As the Chance family was more generous with its titles than many of their peers, third-son George had been an earl from birth. He had mixed in the best circles, been introduced to the most refined ladies, and knew one of breeding when he saw one.

It was something about the eyes. Though she was attempting to look calm and collected, there was a nervousness about her she could not hide.

And yet... yet there was a boldness there, too. She had said something that could have been construed as shameful, and yet she had not backed down.

This was a woman, George decided, who perhaps visited gaming hells like this far more regularly than her mama and papa realized. That suggested that she was not averse to a little romp between the sheets, either. Perhaps that was the reason behind her inexplicable lack of a husband.

Well, he would make it a hattrick. He would charm her, win all her money, then bed her. Everyone would be satisfied.

"Poker," George said aloud. *Yes, that was it. Poker.* He had to concentrate on the game before them.

Which was poker. Wasn't it?

Miss Loughty watched him start to deal the cards. "That's a card game, isn't it?"

George forced down a smile. *Really, this is too easy.* "It is indeed, Miss Loughty. I presume you have never played?"

"Playing poker is not the sort of thing that... that polite young ladies do," she said softly, her eyes wide.

And she thought she was being so rebellious, George thought, stifling a laugh. Dear God, the lengths these ladies would do to catch the attention of a gentleman. Well, she'd done it—come here, and caught his eye. All she would have to do was suffer through a few games, hand over her money—the jewels too, if he was lucky—then he could take her to a quiet corner and—

"Mr. Chance?"

George looked down. His shuffling hands had dropped most of the cards, even though his fingers had continued to move.

Mr. Chance. Of course, he hadn't been so foolish as to announce his title in a place like this. Mr. Chance—how odd.

"Right," he said hastily, gathering them up and preparing the table for a game of poker. "It's quite simple, Miss Loughty. The best hand wins. Ace is higher than a king, yes, even though it is sometimes a one.

Three of a kind is better than a pair, four of a kind better than that—I'm not going too fast for you, am I?"

It had been half a tease, half a serious question. But as Miss Loughty met his eyes, a smile slipped across her lips. Her perfect lips. "You aren't going too fast for me, sir."

A twisting lurch in his stomach—fine, not his stomach, lower than that—made George almost drop the deck again.

Dear God, he would have to focus.

It took another minute to explain the rest of the rules, then George dealt out the cards. Well, now to see how much the woman was prepared to lose. Wager, that was.

"I've had a pretty good evening so far myself," he said smugly, leaning back in his chair with a grin. "Three whole guineas."

Miss Loughty lifted a hand to her breast. "La, sir!"

George blinked. *Dear God, do women really say, "la"?*

But he was instantly distracted by a delicate hand reaching into her reticule and taking out—just a shilling?

"I suppose this is too low to start off the game," Miss Loughty said shyly. "But you understand, it would be foolish of a novice to risk too much, right at the beginning of a game."

"Of course. Of course," George said magnanimously.

After all, what did it matter how low they started? He would soon win all the coin off her in that little reticule of hers.

He had not accounted for beginner's luck.

"Oh, my," said Miss Loughty, her cheeks pink. "I suppose my little king here beats your queen, is that right?"

George's expression was as relaxed as he could make it, though it galled him to push the four shillings across the table toward his beautiful opponent. "Yes. Yes, it is. Well done."

"Beginner's luck, I suppose," Miss Loughty said with a shrug that almost appeared apologetic. "I am grateful for winning, at least once."

That thought perked George up. Yes, it was only right that she won once. Once was fine. Once was enough to give her courage to play again. Perhaps bet more this time, when he would surely—

"Look at that, three jacks and an ace high," said Miss Loughty, almost apologetically. "Goodness, the cards just seem to know what I need, don't they?"

George's smile was, he hoped, not as thin as it felt. "They certainly do."

It was after the third hand that Miss Loughty won that he really started to get suspicious. Yes, there was something like beginner's luck. He did not attempt to understand how it happened, but more often than not, the least experienced at a card table was usually able to take a few coins off the regulars at the start.

At the start, mind. It wasn't supposed to continue on for another two hands. Three hands. Four—now it was starting to get ridiculous.

Two of the three guineas he had won earlier that evening had gone from his pocket into that damned reticule, and they hadn't even been playing an hour. How was that possible?

George glanced up at the calm and refined Miss Loughty. Her breaths even, her voice firm with every announcement of her wins, she appeared to be utterly unconcerned—though admittedly, if he had just won another two guineas, he would have been remarkably unconcerned, too.

Still...

"Another hand?" Miss Loughty said lightly, picking up the deck.

She started shuffling the cards. Then a mite faster. Then so fast, the deck was a blur in her hands.

She met George's eye and grinned.

George glared. "You've been having me on."

"You were the one who offered to teach me how to play cards," Miss Loughty reminded him, placing the cards on the table with a flourish. "At no point did I ask for your help."

"But—But you've played before!"

"So have you," she said evenly, ignoring George's growing outrage. "You did not think there was any problem with an imbalance of experience... when you believed it to tilt in your favor."

George could hardly speak, he was so incensed. He'd been had—and worst of all, he'd been had when he had been most certain that he had been the one doing the having. Or whatever.

This woman—and his blood boiled even to think about it—*this woman has put me down as a mark.* She'd used him. Her feminine wiles, and her beauty, and the way that gown barely covered anything of import—she'd used them to win almost all his money off him.

The money he'd won to balance out his loss earlier at the racetrack.

God damn—

"And now I think I'll take my leave," said Miss Loughty calmly, rising to her feet.

George mirrored her, hardly knowing why. "You can't leave now!"

"Why not?" she asked primly, tucking the last of her winnings into her reticule.

He opened his mouth, closed it again, then spluttered, "B-But my money!"

"I think you will find that it is *my* money now," Miss Loughty pointed out in a quiet voice, though not entirely meeting his eye. "I think that is why they call it gambling, sir. Good evening."

So stricken with shock was he that George could do nothing but watch her go. The elegant woman carefully wove her way through the crowd in McBarland's, ignoring them all, and slipped out of the door before anyone else could accost her.

Which is to their betterment, George thought darkly. *By God, she totally had me!*

Well, he may have been stunned now, but he would rally, he told himself decidedly. He would find her again. Bath was not that large—and next time, he would be certain to ensure that Miss Loughty was the one to lose.

Chapter Three

September 16, 1812

THERE WAS ABSOLUTELY nothing—nothing—that was going to stop Dodo from smiling.

"There," she said quietly to herself in the small room that served as both dining and drawing room.

She had been fortunate to get the lodgings. Well, lodgings. Two rooms in a boarding house for respectable ladies that were relatively small, though *relatively* clean was perhaps not "lodgings," in the traditional sense. But still. Dodo had managed to get them, and last night she had managed to win just over two guineas.

Two guineas!

One pound of her winnings had already been folded carefully into a piece of paper. It wouldn't have been so difficult, irritatingly, if she had been able to place four crowns into the paper and fold it twice around to keep them safe. But her winnings had been in shillings and pence, and it was darned difficult to get them to all stay in place long enough to be folded.

Eventually, she managed it. Dodo would hardly call the result of her efforts particularly beautiful to look at, but it wasn't the outside that mattered. It was the inside.

All she had to do was take it to the post office, and her day's work would be done. *And not too soon, either,* Dodo thought as she yawned, slipping the letter into her reticule. It had been an awful time to arrive home last night without waking her landlady or neighbors, and she had earned a rest.

The post office was not far from her lodgings. She had attempted to find somewhere that was not too central—the prices! Robbery!—but at the same time, not too far off the beaten track.

When a woman had to get herself home alone, it was far more pleasant to do so on respectable streets—even if she had to wear her least lovely day gown to make it quite clear she was hardly a gentlewoman. Her mother would have a fit if she ever found out.

And when Dodo stepped out of Johnson's Buildings without clean gloves to wear and in a dress much less fine than the one she'd worn last night, it was to discover a small market had been set up selling pies, ales, bread, ribbons, gloves—all manner of things.

She looked wistfully as she stood for a moment, watching the day's trade bustle by.

How long had it been since she had treated herself? Really treated herself—bought something that wasn't just pleasant, but extravagant. Unnecessary. Ridiculously overpriced for what it was yet highly enjoyable?

Months. More than months. A year?

Dodo swallowed, the delectable mingled scents of a thousand different things to eat filling her stomach with ideas like hunger and food and *now*.

No, she really had to go to the post office. It was ridiculous to stand here and tempt herself with things that she most certainly could not, would not buy.

Stepping forward, she had almost made it across to the other side of the street but was hampered by the growing crowd around the stalls. Try as she might, Dodo could not push through, and she was hardly willing to force herself through.

"Pastry, miss?"

Dodo turned.

She found herself most inexplicably by a baker's stall. The woman behind the trestle table looked as though she had been working since the early hours, a hint of tiredness around the eyes coupled with a stained apron.

But the pastries...

Just for a moment, Dodo forced herself to close her eyes. Perhaps that would help with the temptation.

When she opened them, it was just as bad. Worse. The pastries looked and smelled exquisite, and it was her bad luck that pastries were her favorite treat.

Well, why not?

The thought rushed through her mind before she could stop herself. *After all,* she argued with herself silently before the waiting stallholder. *You haven't given yourself any sort of reward for tricking that fool out of his money...*

"You can't leave now!"

"Why not?"

"B-But my money!"

"I think you will find that it is *my* money now."

Dodo grinned. She had done well there. She had almost felt sorry for the man—not completely, but enough not to take him for another guinea. And she had an additional pound at home to cover the costs of the next fortnight. Why not treat herself to a pastry? It was hardly going to beggar her.

Not after her success yesterday.

"Just one, then," she conceded.

The stallholder might have been disappointed with her self-control, but she carefully picked up a pastry, wrapped it in a bit of brown paper, and handed it over to her. "A penny."

A penny? "How often does this market—"

"Every Thursday, miss," said the stallholder.

Dodo nodded. That was information worth knowing. A stall with pastries that smelled so fine, and only a penny each? Vital information.

Through the brown paper, which she took as she handed over a penny, she could feel the freshness of the sweet thing. There was no point in waiting to take it home, Dodo reasoned. She wouldn't be able to take it into the post office, by all accounts, so it was far better to eat it now.

Right now.

Slowly, fully aware it was not seemly for a woman to be eating on the street, Dodo lifted the pastry to her mouth.

Oh, the sensations were heavenly. A heady sweetness, the soft flakiness of the pastry, the warmth that neither overpowered nor burned, but instead filled her with a giddy delight...

How long had it been since she had eaten something so delicious?

A long time. Mrs. Bryson did for her, as it were, sending up a bowl of stew almost every evening for Dodo to enjoy. It was another one of the perks of the lodgings she had taken, and she knew how fortunate she was. It was hardly as though there were the means in her two rooms to prepare herself a meal. She hardly knew where she would start around a kitchen, anyway. The Loughtys had always had a cook.

But the rich, hearty stew she consumed every night was nothing to this. This pastry, infused with honey and something else—vanilla, perhaps—crumbled into enchantment on her tongue and filled her with delight.

Dodo closed her eyes, just for a moment. Just so that she could lose herself in the flavors.

Then she opened her eyes.

The stallholder was staring, transfixed. "'Tis... just a pastry."

"Itsnojussa—" Dodo swallowed, heat searing her cheeks at her own rudeness. "It's not just a pastry. It's a delight!"

"Oh. Good," said the stallholder, frowning. "Have a good day then, miss."

She was going to have a good day. She could just feel it. The pound lay heavily in her reticule, all parceled up to be posted, and she had another laid by at home which would see her right in Bath for another two weeks. Two weeks in which she could surely earn a little more—

"I think you will find that it is my money now. I think that is why they call it gambling, sir. Good evening."

Her stomach twisted, the deliciousness of the pastry unable to completely cover the distaste of Mr. Chance's response last evening.

Well, it was hardly my fault, Dodo thought decidedly. She was not going to worry about a gentleman's feelings when she was certainly not going to see him again. She would have to be careful, if she ventured into McBarland's again, but there it was. She had nothing to be ashamed of.

"Thank you," she said to the stallholder, who nodded.

The post office. That was where she should go to next. To get this pound to those who needed it. She would have to explain later what she was doing in Bath and not at her aunt's in Bristol—once she had earned enough to make any objections to her actions meaningless.

Dodo turned around and there was an explosion of pastry.

Well, not precisely an *explosion*, but it wasn't far off. So hasty had she been in making her way to the post office on Broad Street, she hadn't waited to see whether there was anyone directly behind her. When she took a hasty step forward, she therefore thrust herself—and the pastry that had been in her fingers—directly into a gentleman.

The pastry puffed out, spreading little flakes all over herself, the gentleman, and anyone within a foot of them.

"Oh, no!" Dodo cried out with dismay.

Honestly, she would have to get more accustomed to looking where she was going. This wasn't Croscombe, the village where she had been born where there were never more than one hundred people in the place at any point in time.

This was Bath!

"Oh, dear," she said hurriedly, reaching out to try to brush the pastry off the unfortunate man. "Dear me. Oh, no…"

The more she attempted to remove the pastry from the man's woolen jacket, the more it seemed to spread, breaking apart into a million pieces and carefully threading its way into the fabric.

Dodo bit her lip as she looked up at the man's surely irritated face. "I am so sorry, I... Ah."

Ah, indeed.

The man's eyes bulged. It was Mr. Chance of McBarland's. "You!"

"Ah," repeated Dodo, her heart beating frantically. "Well, good day, sir, sorry about the—"

She had taken only one step from him. That was all she could manage—all that surely anyone could manage. It was, after all, most difficult to escape someone when they had a tight grip of your wrist.

"Miss Loughty!" Mr. Chance said sternly.

Try as she might, she couldn't exactly remove her wrist from his grip, no matter how she attempted to twist away. Panic flared, but as Dodo looked around, there did not appear to be a single person on Charlotte Street who was concerned that a young lady was being accosted by a perfect stranger!

Well. Not a stranger. But still!

"What are the odds!" Mr. Chance was saying. "In all of Bath, the chances of seeing each other again—"

It did not take long for Dodo to work out it—though in hindsight, she wondered whether Mr. Chance had intended it as a rhetorical question. "With an estimated population in Bath of just over forty thousand, adding an additional twenty percent for this time of the Season, I would guess—"

"I don't care about—look," said Mr. Chance, speaking over her most rudely. "I want my money back."

That was the moment Dodo was able to wrench her hand from his. It should have been the moment she also disappeared into the crowd, abandoning her pastry behind her.

Perhaps she could... throw it at him? Use it as a distraction? Cover him with sticky honey?

Ridiculous, Dodo thought desperately. *Besides, the odds of that working are—*

"You should have told me you were a good card player."

And it was that statement that gained her attention. Dodo straightened up, glared at the man who was so presumptuous as to speak to her in that unfathomable and unforgiveable manner, and lifted her head high.

Well. As high as it could go. The brute was still a good half a head taller than her.

Still—she could hardly help that.

"Go away," Dodo said clearly, then she turned and disappeared into the Bath crowds.

That had been her intention. Apparently, however, it was far more difficult to disappear into crowds than she'd thought, even though she did her best to duck and weave through the hordes of people who were out on that bright Wednesday.

"You can't escape me that easily," said Mr. Chance darkly, walking alongside her.

Try as she might, Dodo was unable to speed up to a pace he could not also walk. *It comes with having tiny legs*, she thought gloomily. That was the only reason he was still with her. And spouting such nonsense!

"You said you'd never played cards before—"

"I did not," Dodo said, unable to help herself.

She wasn't going to permit the brute to just cast aspersions on her like that!

She stepped behind a market stall selling gloves and slipped down a side street, almost ready to congratulate herself on losing the blaggard, but—

"The point is, you made me think you had no idea what you were doing," pointed out Mr. Chance, as though she owed him something.

Owed him? Her! The cheek!

"That was *your* assumption," she said, cheeks burning both with the embarrassment of having this conversation, and the effort she was having to put in to keep walking at such a pace. "And I—oh!"

Dodo had not intended to call out, but then, what else could she do? The man had grabbed at her again, this time by the arm, and she was unable to free herself from him.

The sense of entrapment, of being caged like a bird, swept over her, clogging her lungs, making it difficult to take in air. The side street they were now standing in was almost empty—there was no one to rescue her, no one to witness the outrage she was currently experiencing.

Try as she might, Dodo could not pull herself away, and his hold of her tightened as she struggled. She cried out again, no words, just panic.

That seemed to do it. Perhaps chastened by her plain fear, Mr. Chance cleared his throat but maintained his glare. "You are a cheat." His eyes darted over her beige dress—quite faded, and nowhere near as refined a dress as the woman from McBarland's she'd pretended to be would have worn, even in the day. The dress afforded Dodo some freedom to walk around without a chaperone in the daylight like a woman of the working class, but now, under the penetrating gaze of Mr. Chance, she had cause to regret wearing it.

Dodo would have lifted her chin and pointed out the statistical likelihood of achieving the hands she had been dealt, let alone the anomalies in his own poor decision-making that had made it easy to predict his next moves…

But she didn't. She merely rubbed at the spot where his hand had so recently been gripping her, feeling the pain in the area subside.

And something in her stomach lurched.

It was most unfair that the man was so good-looking. She had forced herself to ignore that fact last night, at McBarland's, because she had been so focused on playing poker and winning money. Which she had done.

But now as they stood here in the cold light of day, with nothing else to distract her, Dodo could not deny that the man was very... intriguing.

Tall. Taller than her, not that that was saying much. His sky-blue eyes were sharp, determined, with a strength of character within them that one rarely saw in a gentleman that young. And he was young—at least, he could be no older than five and twenty.

His chestnut hair was coiffed in the latest of styles, but he hadn't shaved that morning. At least, not since yesterday. The dark shadow of stubble outlined his jaw in a most inviting way. Inviting her to reach out, to run a hand along his chin and—

Dodo stood back hurriedly and looked away, as though she had not just been staring at a gentleman.

Certainly not.

"You are a good card player, and you had me for a fool," Mr. Chance said quietly.

Swallowing hard, she managed, "I am not a good card player, and you *are* a fool."

"Why, you—"

"I am an *excellent* card player," she said, hoping to goodness her voice would hold.

This was Bath, after all. This was 1812! Men did not go about accosting young ladies in the street and getting away with it. Even unchaperoned ones. No, her imagination was getting away from her. There was no possibility Mr. Chance was going to hurt her, *really* hurt her.

Perhaps a one in a hundred chance, Dodo thought wretchedly, unable to switch off her calculating mind. But those were good odds. In most places, she would take—

"You took me for a pound," said Mr. Chance quietly. "No, more. Two whole guineas."

Dodo swallowed.

She could feel the weight of one of the pounds she had taken from him in her reticule. Not that she was about to admit to that. The half-crazed man may do something ridiculous, like ask for it back.

And there was no chance she was going to part with it. She needed it. Badly.

If only she had decided to do the intelligent thing and gone to the post office first. It would have been so much simpler if she could stand before this Mr. Chance and tell him she had already spent the money. It would not have been a falsehood.

"I-I am sorry, Mr. Chance," Dodo said, feeling far more sorry for herself than the fierce man before her. "You entered a game of hazard, and you lost. That is all there is to it."

She actually managed to dart to the left, but she wasn't swift enough.

Mr. Chance stepped ahead of her, preventing her from moving forward. "What do you care, Miss Loughty? It's only a pound."

Dodo almost laughed in his face.

Only a pound? Oh, only a pound. Only the difference between a meal and starvation. Only the gap between a roof over one's head and suffering out in the gutter. Only the option to live or die.

Honestly, did most gentlemen have this cavalier attitude about money, or was she unfortunate enough to be faced with one of the worst?

Wait… Only a pound?

Dodo swallowed and looked up into the face of the man who was fast becoming one of her least favorite people.

Only a pound? He must think her rich, then, despite the fact that she was out here on the street without a lady's maid, wearing a dress more fashionable women would find a few years out of date. Perhaps he knew little of women's fashion. Yes, he certainly believed that a pound to her was nothing more than an inconvenience, rather than something that was absolutely crucial.

Why would he…?

Ah. The sapphires. Or in truth, the glass-jeweled necklace that she had purchased specifically because they looked so akin to sapphires. The idea that she could actually afford jewels like that—but he wouldn't know, would he? Mr. Chance would merely look at her, see a woman with a great amount of wealth, and baulk at the idea of losing a pound to her.

Which begged the question—

"But you are a gentleman. Probably," Dodo said, forgetting her manners in her surprise. "What difference would a pound make to you?"

Mr. Chance drew himself up. "I am not, in fact, a gentleman."

Well, he did not need to tell her that. The man had made it perfectly clear, thanks to his ill-manners and disgraceful habit of grabbing at her, that he was no gentleman. "Yes, but—"

"I am an earl," said the man haughtily. "The Earl of Lindow."

Dodo's mouth fell open.

It was not the most complimentary expression. The veins on the temple of the man—Mr. Chance, Lord Lindow if he was to be believed, despite the fact that his brother had introduced himself as a marquess—purpled. Perhaps the earl suspected she was shocked to discover he had blue blood in his veins.

But really! She'd known him to be a marquess's brother, but that did not mean he was not a rogue. The man had not acted like an earl, from the moment she had met him.

Perhaps a gentleman. At the very least, gentry.

But a titled man himself?

"You… You are the Earl of Lindow?" Dodo repeated, as though testing the water.

A man in workman's clothes passed them by, and just for a moment, she considered speaking out and asking him for assistance.

But the moment passed just as the Earl of Lindow said, "Of course I am. I know who I am."

"But your brother—Lord Aylesbury—he never said—"

"I should have known old Aylesbury would be at the bottom of this, somehow," the Earl of Lindow said wearily, dragging a hand through his hair. "Our eldest brother shared out the titles—yes, I know it's unusual, but that's the way Cothrom is. And speaking of my good-for-nothing brothers, why would you let a marquess use you like that?"

He kept speaking, but Dodo could not take in a word. Use her? The marquess had *used her* somehow when he had accosted her at Lord Llyne's card party and suggested... suggested she go to McBarland's?

Her mind was spinning, struggling to keep up with the change in the way she must think of the man before her going forward. Lord Lindow. But he was so much better suited to "Mr. Chance."

Yet one moment of clarity remained.

"But then..." Dodo laughed, and it was with such relief that she felt a weight lift from her. "You cannot possibly need it, then!"

The idea of the Earl of Lindow, if that truly was his title, needing a mere pound—well, it was laughable! She knew some second and third sons struggled to make their own fortunes, but a titled gentleman himself? It relieved a great deal of stress from her shoulders. There was no need to feel guilty about relieving the man of two guineas last night. Why, it would be nothing to his accounts!

Yet the earl was staring with a curious expression. "And you do, then? Need it, I mean? The pound?"

Dodo swallowed.

If only that blasted heat did not have to move up her chest and completely cover her neck and face, making it so obvious she wished to hide something.

Because she did need it. Desperately. Though they did not yet know of her presence in Bath, there were people waiting on that pound, the pound weighing down her reticule, and if she wasn't able to help them soon, the guilt would start to rise once more and overwhelm her. She had to get it to them.

But she didn't have to admit to such things. She was Miss Doris Loughty. Her business was her business. And it was none of his. Mr. Chance's. Lord Lindow's.

Oh, Lord...

"Go," Dodo said clearly, in as impressive a voice as she could make it. "Away."

She managed three steps this time, and though the earl kept up with her as she attempted to find her way to the post office, she did not look at him.

There was no need to look at the man. Even if he was handsome.

"You have to tell me how you won," he said firmly.

"Absolutely not," Dodo said, almost as firmly. Just as firmly. As firmly as she could manage while holding up her skirts just a tad to step over a puddle.

If she had hoped her stern tone would force the man away, she was most disappointed. The earl did not touch her again this time, for which she was extremely grateful.

Probably.

"I will dog you everywhere you go," said Lord Lindow lightly, as though he were not threatening a lady whom he barely knew in the street. "Wherever you go, whoever you attempt to scam next, I will be there. I will prevent you from winning. I will be your worst nightmare."

Dodo snorted. *Like the Earl of Lindow would go to the places I intend to go.* "I'd like to see you try."

"Oh, you would, would you?" His voice was light still, but there was a steel to its center that made her shiver as she reached—

Ah. The post office.

"Good day, my lord," Dodo said stiffly, stepping up to the door of the post office and reaching for the handle.

"Good day, Miss Loughty," came the teasing yet unamused voice of the earl from behind her. "And good luck."

Chapter Four

September 20, 1812

"But that's what I'm saying," came the weary voice of Mr. Eaton. "If someone else bets against you—"

"I think it's criminal," said George haughtily. "Against nature. I can't have lost—again!"

But lost he had. And the trouble was, Scandal of Lancelot had been absolutely outstanding. Until the very last corner, George had been convinced the horse he had bought and trained and for which he was paying a small fortune for its upkeep was going to finally return the investment he'd made.

Until…

Mr. Eaton, the bookkeeper with whom George was spending more time than anyone at the moment, sighed heavily, scratching silver-and-brown side whiskers on a pockmarked cheek. "Mayhap it's time to give it up, m'lord. Mayhap—"

"I have a winning horse there," George pointed out, picking up his ale and giving it a swig. Too violently, as it turned out. He was forced to wipe the froth from around his lips before he continued. "And you know it—that horse is perfect!"

They had agreed to meet at the King's Head. It was where so many went after the races, and George had hoped to treat the place to a drink once he had cashed in his winnings.

The winnings that, as yet, had not appeared.

"If someone else bets against you, and are more right about how the race runs, y'lose y'money," said Mr. Eaton patiently, as though they had not had this conversation several times over the last few weeks. "You know that, m'lord."

"Yes, yes, but the question is, how are they doing it?" asked George, leaning back in his chair and frowning. "I always thought I had a pretty good eye for horseflesh. I thought I'd be onto the winners."

"Someone's there afore ye," Mr. Eaton said mysteriously.

George shot him a look. "And you know who he is."

"Now then, m'lord, you know I couldn't—"

"No... No, I suppose not." Infuriating as it was, George had to admit the man was right. He had to keep the details of his winners a secret. After all, he wouldn't like Mr. Eaton telling everyone when he, George Chance, Earl of Lindow, started winning a fortune on the horses. Which was sure to come soon, wasn't it? *Wasn't it?*

Mr. Eaton examined him with a wry expression. "Never thought I'd see an earl here."

It was an old-fashioned place, but that was how George liked it. Dark timber beams, a hatch where drinks were served, and plenty of tables and chairs jammed it with little space between them. Raucous laughter from almost every side and—George's eyes gleamed to see—cards in every hand.

Well. If he couldn't make a killing on the races, perhaps it was time Lady Luck decided to reward him in the deck.

"Y'horse is good," said Mr. Eaton, rising from his seat and bowing his head. "It's your wagering that needs some work. M'lord."

George's mouth fell open at the effrontery—and likely as not, the truth—from the man, but he was prevented from saying anything by the bookkeeper's rapid disappearance.

It wasn't as though he had a particularly good retort. The man was right. George's confidence at the races was not borne out by any winning streak and it was starting to become obvious, he had worse and worse luck.

Even more than that, his other project hadn't been coming up trumps, either...

Taking another swig from the ale, George glanced about the King's Head. He didn't expect her here. Miss Loughty. This was a working man's pub. The only ladies here, well... were not ladies. They were *women*. Women of a different class, all serving the cheerful men their pies and ale.

But he had tried two other gaming hells the last few nights. She wouldn't return to McBarland's, George was almost certain, though he had slipped a shilling to the doorman and asked for news if a beautiful woman turned up.

After three notes, all of which described women nothing like Miss Loughty, George had been forced to return to McBarland's and attempt to explain what he meant by "beautiful."

"You know, utterly divine," George had said to the open-mouthed, slack-jawed doorman. "Hair like... like shimmering starlight. And eyes like—and a way of moving, you must have seen her. Miss Loughty. You don't remember her?"

It appeared few did. Despite asking around the Crescent, dropping into his club, and speaking to a few acquaintances who were staying in Abbey Green, no one had heard of Miss Loughty. George had gone to the Pump Rooms and seen no signature of a Miss Loughty in the book. He'd even spoken to Mr. Parsons, the announcer at the Assembly Rooms. The man had never heard of any Loughty, let alone a miss who appeared to be wandering the streets of Bath alone. Where was her chaperone? Her lady's maid? Not that he imagined either type of person permitting a trip to the likes of McBarland's. But she'd been alone even on the street the next day. Most unusual.

George bit his lip. Other than the two encounters he'd had with her, and the assurances from Walden that he had also seen her, even if the viscount had never lain eyes on her before or since, it was almost possible to believe George had dreamt her up. She certainly had been beautiful. And she'd most definitely beaten him at his own game of cards, which was unfathomable, and—

Heads turned. There was a growing silence by the door as a figure appeared. George's stomach jolted.

There she was.

Miss Loughty. There was no mistaking that figure, even from a distance. Third time's the charm, then? This was the third place he'd tried. Though admittedly, George had only come to the King's Head to commiserate about his terrible losses at the races.

Damnation. If this went on much longer, he was going to have to do the unthinkable and write to his oldest brother, the Duke of Cothrom, and... ask for money.

George shivered. *God forbid.*

"Lindow!"

He blinked. It appeared Miss Loughty was not the only person who had entered the King's Head.

"Aylesbury," George said with a grin. "Come to cure me of my wicked ways?"

His elder brother, the second Chance in the family and by far the tallest, clapped him on the shoulder before dropping into a seat beside him. "You think there's any hope of that?"

"Not in the slightest."

"I won't waste my time, then," John Chance, the Marquess of Aylesbury, said cheerfully. "What rot are you drinking?"

"Something far above your palate, you philistine," George shot back, easing into the rapid banter that epitomized their relationship.

Well, you could always rely on old Aylesbury to speak nonsense. But what was he doing here? The brute was married. George had come to Bath to get away from all his wedding talk. And Aylesbury had had the audacity to follow him.

"Shouldn't you be with your wife?"

His brother's eyes gleamed. "Very soon I will be *with* my wife."

George made a face. "Have a heart. I will need to eat something soon and the last thing I need is the thought of you... "

He had been about to say something cutting, he really had been. The thing was, his attention meandered across the room and caught sight of Miss Loughty again.

She was lovely. And wearing the same necklace she'd been wearing at McBarland's. And she was here—which was odd.

"You're staring at a woman, aren't you?"

George swallowed. "No."

His eyes watched Miss Loughty as she carefully picked her way through the mess of tables, chairs, and legs that stood in her path between the door and the hatch. Even in the dark gloom of the evening, he could not help but mistake her.

The elegance, the balance, the refinement. This was a woman, despite her brazen visits to seedy places and walks unaccompanied and her seeming inaction in the politest quarters of Bath, who had been raised well.

So what was she doing in a place like this?

"... join... willing to... "

Her words drifted across the raucous noise of the pub. George could not quite make them out—she was just far enough away from him to make it impossible to know precisely what she was saying.

What she was doing was obvious. Tucking a wayward strand of black hair behind her ear, it appeared that Miss Loughty was trying to...

Join tables.

"—heard about the latest gambling debts—you really ought to be careful, old man. Cothrom stopped the financial floodgates for me. It's only a matter of time before he does so for you—"

Aylesbury was talking about something or other. George could not tell. There was something far more interesting happening than a little money worries from his spendthrift brother.

He shifted in his seat, fascinated. It appeared she was not welcome at any table she attempted to join, which was strange in and of itself. He would have presumed that a woman like that—who appeared to be an easy mark—would have been welcomed.

Hell, it had been what he'd done, at McBarland's. Taken her for a mark and attempted to take all she had.

But it appeared Miss Loughty had been here before—or the inhabitants of the King's Head had been warned. No matter which table she approached, there were shaking heads to welcome her.

George watched, rivetted. The expression on Miss Loughty's face was spectacular.

Not just because she was beautiful. That she was beautiful was impossible to deny—that doorman didn't know what he was about!—but it wasn't that. It was the way her expression shifted slowly over time with each table from which she was dismissed.

At first it was confusion. A genteel furrow of her brows brought together in perplexity as she attempted to understand why she was being rejected.

Then it was frustration. At one table, George watched as Miss Loughty attempted to talk down the most vocal of the people there but found herself outgunned.

"—can't allow—"

"Not again…"

"Four shillings last time…"

She was closer now and George could hear some more of the conversation. When she reached the next table, there was no conversation. Just shaking of heads and waving of hands for her to depart.

The expression on Miss Loughty's face was different now. Flaring nostrils, her lip curling. She was angry. She was—

A sudden sharp, agonizing pain poured through George's shin.

"God in his Heaven!" he blurted out, drawing his leg closer as he grabbed at his shin, rubbing it furiously. "What was that for?"

Aylesbury was smiling in an irritating, self-satisfied manner. "Getting your attention."

"You couldn't have said my name?"

"You think I haven't already been trying that?" Unfortunately, Aylesbury had plainly noticed his interest in a certain young woman, for he glanced at Miss Loughty, his head turning quickly twice in succession. He clamped his lips together before speaking again. "You've bedded her, I presume."

Much against his will, and most unlike him, heat suffused across George's face. "N-No. No."

Why was it so odd to admit to such a thing?

Aylesbury raised an eyebrow. "Then I don't see the point in you pining after her from a distance. What, she rejected you, Lindow?"

"She stole from me!" snapped George, righteous fury pouring through his veins.

It was mostly true. Miss Loughty had certainly had a system far more impressive than anything he had managed, and what was that, if not theft?

His brother, it appeared, did not agree. He was rolling his eyes. "She beat you in cards. That's not the same thing."

George frowned. "You heard?"

"Who do you think paid your tab at the end of that night?" Aylesbury sighed heavily. "God, I complained that Cothrom was always whining about our bad habits and now I've become like him."

"You got married."

"It's not the same thing," his brother shot back, though there was still a grin on his face. "Well. Not quite. Florence keeps me... honest."

George snorted without looking away from Miss Loughty.

Honest. One of the things he'd always liked about Aylesbury was that they could drink, and gamble, and laugh together. Two rascals, two rakes of the *ton*, together. Dishonest, together.

All that had changed. And now the only brother he had left was—

He wasn't even a brother. Pernrith. He didn't count.

Forcing down the anger that always rose whenever he thought of the Viscount Pernrith, George picked up his tankard and was most disappointed to discover someone had drunk it.

Aylesbury smacked his lips. "Rather good ale, I'd say, Lindow."

George lunged forward with a friendly cuff about the face, but his brother leaned back just in time. "That was *my* drink, you—"

"But as, I suspect, I will be paying off this tab in a few days, I think you will find that it is *my* drink," said Aylesbury with a knowing grin.

A heaving in his chest made George grimace, even though his brother's words were not completely untrue. *I can't exactly argue with that.* "Go back to your wife."

"That I shall, for I think I'll get a far warmer welcome," said Aylesbury, rising and stretching out his arms before fixing his brother with a serious look. "Leave Miss Loughty alone, Lindow. It's not worth the risk."

He was gone before George could ask precisely what he meant by that, but he hardly noticed. His gaze was fixed on Miss Loughty.

She was standing by the hatch now, having a debate with the barkeep. That was never going to go down well. George had not been in Bath long before he'd discovered that the King's Head owner had a short fuse and little interest in being debated.

Well, he hadn't found her at McBarland's. He hadn't spotted her at Sydney Gardens, or the Pump Room, or the Assembly Rooms. She hadn't attended any of the card parties or dinners at which he'd forced himself to put in an appearance.

Yet here she was.

A slow smile crept across George's face. Finally, Miss Loughty would get her comeuppance.

Even better, he was seated just out of her line of sight. Thanks to the dim corner, George was almost certain that he would be able to sit here all evening and watch her, if Miss Loughty decided to stay in the King's Head. At no point would he have to—

Miss Loughty turned and looked right at him.

All breath left his body. George wasn't sure how he was still conscious, for his lungs were empty and his mind was screaming—

But it wasn't screaming for air. It was crying out at the sudden rush of something he could not understand, pouring through his body now that Miss Loughty was looking at him.

And what a look.

George shifted uncomfortably in his seat, unable to prevent his body from responding. From giving a very physical response.

Surely, she could feel this too. Surely, the connection they shared, even though he did not entirely understand it, would bring them to an understanding. He would ensure there would be no child, and he could relish touching that skin, feeling under those skirts—

Miss Loughty stomped over to him, slammed her hands on the table, and glared. "This is all your fault!"

George blinked. *Well, I wouldn't have put it quite like that.*

Then his mind caught up with him. She wasn't talking about the fact that they seemed drawn to each other, no matter what they attempted to do. He had a horrible feeling that he was perhaps alone in that quarter.

No, she meant—

His slow smile became a wicked one. So, the hints he had laid were starting to pay off, were they? "What, no one will play with you? I can't see how that's any of my concern—"

"'I will dog you everywhere you go,' you said. 'Wherever you go, whomever you attempt to scam next, I will be there. I will prevent you from winning. I will be your worst nightmare,'" Miss Loughty recited bitterly, pulling out a chair and dropping into it without requesting to join him. "This is all your fault!"

"Well," George said humbly, shrugging his shoulders. "I didn't do all the work. I had help."

It had not been difficult. It was amazing what people would do for money—or at least, the promise of money. He really would have to write to Cothrom, worse luck. He couldn't keep Scandal of Lancelot going for much longer without a win, and the coin he'd promised to people to refuse to play with a woman matching the description of Miss Loughty, should they encounter her—

"Look, I just wanted you to stop cheating," said George quietly, dropping his voice so no one could hear them. It would never do for the word "cheating" to be heard in the King's Head. "Like you cheated me."

"I was *not* cheating," Miss Loughty hissed back, evidently aware of the danger of their conversation.

And it *was* dangerous. In fact, it gave George a thrill just to partake in it.

Who was this woman? No one had heard of her. She was never seen with a chaperone but was not a widow. He had never encountered her in London, not as far as he could recall—and wouldn't a woman of her breeding and elegance have been presented in town?

There was a possibility, he supposed, they had met in the past. Though not that he recalled. Surely, he would have remembered. *A woman like this…*

"I have never cheated in my life—I have never needed to," Miss Loughty was murmuring, her dark-brown eyes holding him fast against his seat. "You just cannot accept that you were beaten by a woman."

"I don't have to, as I was not beaten by you," George pointed out, leaning back.

He had done so in an attempt to demonstrate just how unaffected he was by this debate, but the trouble was, it gave him a better view of the woman who was fast becoming…

George swallowed.

There wasn't a word for it. Miss Loughty was hardly his enemy. He was an earl, for Christ's sake. He was hardly going to lose his reputation, or his fortune—what fortune there was left—on a mere miss.

But Miss Loughty was the woman least like a "mere miss" he had ever encountered.

Fierce, and yet soft. Gentle, and yet powerful.

There was a mastery in her he just could not understand. And she had cheated, he was sure. George may not have won every time, but he had won enough times to know when he was being cheated.

Ladies did not march into McBarland's and win four hands of poker off him.

They just didn't.

"You have to stop this," she said.

He blinked. "Stop what?"

"This!" Miss Loughty gestured about the place.

Lifting an eyebrow, George said, "I have never presumed to prevent people from entering the King's Head, Miss Loughty, if that's what you—"

"You know precisely that it's not what I meant." She snorted.

A flicker of excitement dashed through George. When she made that motion, her whole body quivered.

By God, arguing with her was far more stimulating than flattering anyone else.

"I need to play cards in Bath," Miss Loughty said slowly, her cheeks pinking as though she were admitting something dire. "And you need to stop... stop whatever it is you've done."

"Fine," said George, leaning forward. The idea was a rash one, and perhaps one he would regret—but it had struck him so perfectly, at just the right time, it felt impossible to ignore. "Teach me."

Miss Loughty blinked, leaning away as though his enthusiasm

were contagious. "Teach you?"

Forcing down all hedonistic thoughts about what *he* would like to teach this woman, George nodded. "Teach me—how you beat me. How you played cards and won again, and again, and again. If you truly did not cheat."

There, he had her now. He could see the indecision on her face, the uncertainty of his offer. And then a slow dawning melted over him—why she was so uncertain.

Miss Loughty... had not cheated.

George stared, but there could be no mistaking it. She was truly considering his offer—something she would not do if she had actually cheated.

By God. So she won by skill?

Now he truly had to know.

Though it was in his nature to press his point, George somehow knew that the best thing to do in this moment was to stay quiet. Shifting in her chair, her mouth in a frown, it was evident Miss Loughty was thinking, seemingly weighing up the advantages and disadvantages of acquiescing to his request.

It appeared to be a close call.

How he knew that, George could not have articulated. There were not words for this sort of interaction. Here they were, an earl and a refined miss, seated in one of Bath's less reputable pubs, concocting a plan to...

To what?

His mouth was dry. His heart was hammering. And still he said nothing.

"Not... Not all my knowledge," Miss Loughty said finally, her voice hesitant. "I would hate to give you the tools to beat me."

He didn't want to beat her. He wanted to soundly destroy her. Place her on the card table, lift up her skirts, and—

"Fine," he said hastily aloud, attempting to clear the vision of perfection from his mind. *Concentrate on the cards, man!* "We have a deal."

He offered out his hand.

For a moment, George did not think she would take it. It was a lady's prerogative to offer her hand first, but this was business. Miss Loughty stared at his hand, plainly unsure whether she would. Slowly, inch by inch, she leaned over and took it.

It was all he could do not to groan aloud. Neither of them was wearing gloves, something outrageous by the *ton*'s standard but not entirely unexpected here in a place like the King's Head.

And that meant it was skin on skin, his fingers slipping past her own, her palm soft against his, her pulse throbbing against his thumb—or was that his own? His pulse was certainly racing, making it impossible to do anything but feel the heady sensations between them.

Then Miss Loughty pulled away. The moment faded.

"But not here," she said sternly, returning her hand to her lap as though she'd been burned. "Anyone could see us here, and... Well. I'm already regretting agreeing to teach you. I'd hate for the whole of Bath to learn."

Well, that played right into his hand.

George grinned. "I know just the place."

Chapter Five

September 21, 1812

SHE HAD BEEN a fool to agree to this.

Dodo knew it. She'd returned to her lodgings yesterday and thrown herself on the bed, attempting to concoct five good reasons how she could escape the agreement.

"Fine. We have a deal."

Anything she thought of was discounted. It just wasn't possible. The Earl of Lindow had turned the gambling folk in Bath against her, preventing her from sending money home, and without it…

It just didn't bear thinking about.

The stupid man is making things impossible, Dodo thought viciously as she walked up Charlotte Street. All she had to do was teach the little saucebox a few of the basics—Lord knows, he didn't seem to have a handle on any of them—and she could be on her way, back to the card tables.

Back where earls did not wander about sabotaging ladies and forcing agreements on them.

Five, seven, nine…

Dodo was calmed by the gentle repetition of the odd numbers of the houses on this side of the street. No matter what happened with people, she would always have numbers. Reliable, unchanging, steadfast—

Fifteen.

She looked up at the tall building which bore the address Mr. Chance—Lord Lindow, she truly must remember to call him that—had given her.

And swallowed.

It was a large building. Grand. Pouring with wealth. Stuccos all over the place. Large, mullioned windows lined with lead, elegant curtains just visible through each one. The paint was a crisp white, the geraniums in each planter on the windowsills were blossoming, and it was altogether magnificent.

Her brother, Ellis, would have been horrified. His dislike of nobility had always been a source of mirth for her parents, but she had never understood it. Never understood so much of him, and now she would never have that chance.

Dodo swallowed again. *What on earth did an earl want with her knowledge?* The man obviously had money to burn. A place like this would cost a fortune to run.

But there was nothing else for it.

The large, brass knocker made a satisfying noise, and when it was opened, a younger footman stepped back, revealing the severe expression of an elderly man wearing a dark-green livery.

"Deliveries," he intoned, "are made around the back."

Dodo bristled. She actually felt the hair on the back of her neck stand up. "I am not here to make a delivery."

"Charitable requests," the butler said in the same dull tone, "are made around the back."

"But I—"

"Maids seeking work are to seek work around—"

"Around the back," she said darkly. "But—"

He went to shut the door, but Dodo had the presence of mind to stick her foot in the gap. It hurt like hell, but it meant she could continue to glare at the servant.

"I am not here on behalf of a charitable request, nor am I a maid seeking work," she said stiffly, though she was painfully aware no other lady her age of the genteel class would have shown at the door without a chaperone. "I am Miss Doris Loughty, and I have an appointment. The Earl of Lindow wants me. Is expecting me!"

Heat poured through her cheeks at the idiotic words that had escaped through her lips.

The corpulent butler raised a bushy eyebrow. "My word. Miss Loughty, yes. You had better come in."

Stepping into the Earl of Lindow's world was far more overwhelming than Dodo had predicted. Oh, she had seen wealth. She had once been invited to a Christmas ball at the home of a viscount.

A very poor viscount. But his father, an earl, had been rich.

Nothing she had seen before compared to this. The sweeping staircase in the hallway was matched only by the sweeping ceiling above her. Dodo turned on her heels, attempting to take it all in. It was the golden mean, of course, the perfect balance between height and depth, giving a pleasing sense to the eye—

"This way, miss," said the butler quietly.

Dodo tripped along in the wake of the servant, trying not to stare at the great urns on plinths, marble statues of Greek and Roman gods, and the plethora of china about the place.

What could a man who lived here want with a few shillings?

When she was shown into a room, Dodo saw immediately that it must have been a smoking room. It was comparatively small, perhaps half the size of the hall, and set out in dark leather and wood tones.

It was also covered in gold.

A gold clock on the mantlepiece, a gold candelabra hanging from the ceiling, gold-gilt frames…

Before she could take in any more of the splendor, footfalls echoed on the marble floor behind her. Dodo spun around.

There he stood.

"Ready to lose?" asked the Earl of Lindow with a grin.

It wasn't her fault her stomach lurched so wildly. It wasn't her fault, either, that her whole body warmed a few degrees merely at the sight of him. It *was* her fault, Dodo would have to admit, that she allowed a coquettish smile to spread across her lips as she said words she had never even countenanced before.

"Ready to learn?" she countered.

Her cheeks pinked immediately—as she should have known they would. She was also suddenly painfully aware she was in a man's home without a chaperone—and that he'd yet to ask why she'd failed to ever produce one. One whisper from him in the wrong ear and her reputation as a lady would be… In any case. Her reputation was less important than her family's current need.

What do I think I'm doing, flirting with this man?

Flirting with any man would have been bad enough, but this was a gentleman. A gentleman who had managed to extort an agreement from her that Dodo was certain she would regret in time.

Worse. He was an earl.

It was hard to believe she was doing this. Though Dodo had considered sending a short, polite-but-curt note to the earl's residence early that morning, she hadn't been able to.

They'd shaken hands.

Once an agreement like that had been made, it was difficult to escape. Even if she'd wanted to.

Which she didn't. Obviously.

The Earl of Lindow was grinning. "My, you look pleasant when you flush."

Which of course made her flush all the more. *Damn these cheeks!*

Dodo cleared her throat noisily, as though that would force the burning sensation to dissipate. "Right, well, let's get started. I haven't got all day."

"A hectic schedule of cheating men out of their money on the cards for you, is there?" quipped Lord Lindow as he stepped into the room.

It took all her effort not to step back. "N-No. No, definitely not!"

But it appeared the man was not serious. In fact, Dodo could not recall him being serious, except when accusing her of cheating. *What rot!*

"I thought I'd provide a table for our lesson." The earl gestured to the corner of the room.

Dodo followed his arm and nodded appreciatively. Yes, that was convenient. The small card table was large enough for two to play, with a pair of what appeared to be Chippendale chairs beside it.

Her nod became a slight frown. Someone had been a mite foolish. Instead of placing the chairs on opposite sides of the table, someone had placed the second at right angles to the first.

Well, that would never do. Heavens, they would be so close together, their knees would be touching!

The very thought...

"Almost a perfect setup," Dodo said quietly, stepping over the table.

The wood was warm under her hand, the carving exquisite, but as she moved to pull it out from under the card table so she could drag it around the table, a hand closed over hers.

"No, Miss Loughty," came a quiet voice that somehow thrummed through her entire body. "I think not."

Dodo dropped the chair as though she had been burned. Her fingers certainly felt that way.

It was inexplicable, this power—no, this attempt at power that the Earl of Lindow had over her. Any other man would have been glared at and realized his actions were far beyond what was expected from a gentleman.

Any other man would have refused to let her meet him at his home without a chaperone present.

But as Dodo turned to protest, her voice faltered. The Earl of Lindow was so close to her, mere inches away, and his heady presence somehow halted her tongue.

It was most infuriating!

And pleasurable.

Yes, and—

No! Dodo forced the thought away as best she could, but for some reason, it had managed to lodge itself into her mind, repeating over and over again as she looked up into the stormy eyes of the Earl of Lindow.

Pleasurable? She certainly wasn't here for anything like... like that.

"I need to move the chair—"

"And I need to stop you," said Lord Lindow pleasantly. "I am sure you can understand, Miss Loughty, that if I am truly to learn from you—if, indeed, you have not been cheating—then I need to be close. Close to you. To see the cards."

Dodo swallowed. The worst of it was, she could almost see his point. If she had been forced to teach a lady, that was precisely what she would have done. Placed the chairs close by and instructed the woman to pay careful attention to her teacher's hands.

The thought of the Earl of Lindow paying close attention to her hands...

The warmth was expected—she knew that about herself now. What Dodo had not expected was the liquid fire that surged through her body and settled between her thighs. A hot, hungry sort of fire that burned so brightly, it needed more fuel to keep burning.

And it wanted more. *She* wanted more.

Dodo took a hasty step back. If that was what she felt merely *thinking* about Lord Lindow sitting so close to her, she certainly could not permit—

"You did agree to teach me," the gentleman who was having such an effect on her pointed out, sitting and leaning back, his long legs poking out the other side of the card table. "Are you about to renege on that agreement?"

It was a tempting thought.

But not for long. Dodo could not go to London. The Loughty name was better known there, Ellis having spent time there. No one could know the ruin that had befallen them, the lengths she was prepared to go to earn money.

Not that far. At least not yet.

And the Earl of Lindow had been as bad as his word. He had made it almost impossible for her to win a single penny in Bath, and she was uncertain if she could find such cheap lodgings in somewhere like Brighton or York.

She needed to be where the *ton* was. That limited her options. And thanks to Lord Lindow, her income ability had also been limited.

Just a few lessons, Dodo told herself silently as she slowly lowered herself into the chair at right angles to her—for want of a better word—student.

One lesson. Maybe one more. That was all. Then she could go back to the gaming hells and elegant card parties of the *ton* and attempt to earn at least a pound a week. In peace.

She reached out for the deck of cards.

"Let me," said the earl softly, reaching out in turn.

Dodo did not have time to pull back and her arm brushed up against his sleeve.

It should not have had any impact. Lord knew, she brushed up against enough people in the packed streets of Bath without giving it another thought.

But those faceless strangers were not this handsome earl who appeared determined to... *to ruin her.*

There. Dodo let out a long breath as she finally accepted the thought that she had pushed aside for so long.

She was no fool. Oh, technically, she was an innocent, but she knew enough about the theory to guess at what the Earl of Lindow really wanted.

"Card lessons"? No, he wished for something far more intimate, something she could not, would not give him. He thought to take advantage of her in the absence of a chaperone—that had to be why he'd never questioned her lack of one. But as long as she kept their focus on the cards, Dodo told herself resolutely, then there was absolutely no possibility of that happening.

None whatsoever.

The Earl of Lindow dropped the deck of cards in her hands. "There you go, Miss Loughty."

Dodo cleared her throat. What she needed was some inane, dull conversation. That wouldn't be hard, would it? Gentlemen loved hearing their possessions being praised—that was an easy topic. It would perhaps be foolish to start on the earl's person, so—

"What an interesting painting," she said in as monotonous a voice as she could.

Lord Lindow glanced over his shoulder, giving her momentary relief from his intense gaze. "What? Oh, yes. Scandal of Lancelot. It's mine, you know."

Dodo nodded as she started dealing out the cards. *All of them, to start with. Demonstrate the complexity of suits, the probability of colors—*

"I mean the horse itself, not the painting," clarified her companion. "I race them. Bet on them too, though not with much luck at the moment, I'm afraid. It's a shame Scandal of Lancelot isn't doing too well. My jockey tells me the beast has a weak left flank, though I don't believe it."

She nodded again as she turned the final card. There. The whole deck was visible now on the elegant card table. It really was beautiful. The green baize—

Then something nudged at her mind.

"Left flank, did you say?" Dodo said suddenly.

Lord Lindow nodded. "It's a real shame, but I'm determined to improve it. Such things can be done, of course. The left flank won't be a weakness for long."

Dodo nodded as she filed that information away for later. One never knew. It could be useful.

"So," she said aloud. "Cards."

"Cards?" asked Lord Lindow, blinking.

She almost laughed. "Yes, cards. You... You wanted me to teach you."

"I *did* want you to teach me," the earl said softly, placing his hands on the green baize of the card table. Far too close to her own. "Then, perhaps, *I* could teach *you*."

Try as she might, Dodo could not control her rushing blood, nor prevent her cheeks from darkening with color. She could, however, control her tongue. "I doubt there is anything you could teach me that would interest me, my lord."

The man's jaw dropped.

"Looking at the cards, then," Dodo said hastily, taking advantage of his sudden silence. "With fifty-two cards in the deck, two colors and four suits, there is around a two percent chance of any specific card coming up. When you break that down to color probability, that is one in four, which can also be expressed as—"

The earl interrupted, screwing up his nose. "That sounds like mathematics."

A flare of irritation settled in Dodo's chest. Naturally, it sounded like mathematics. It *was* mathematics—did the fool truly have no idea what he was talking about?

"Yes, well done," she said, attempting to keep the sarcasm from her tone. "So, when it comes to the game of poker, there are eight variables immediately reduced. The five cards on the table, and the three in your hand—at least if playing by the—"

"Aren't you going to teach me how you did it?"

Dodo's jaw tightened. When she spoke, it was through gritted teeth. "I *am* showing you."

Was the man truly that doltish? Or did he have... another agenda?

She was no complete fool. It had been bold of her to come to the Earl of Lindow's home without a chaperone, to be in this city at all on her own. If her mother had been well enough to leave Croscombe, perhaps she could have come with her instead of Dodo lying to her about visiting an aunt, and Dodo could have snuck away on her own only in the evenings to gamble. Though if her mother had been well enough to leave Croscombe, Dodo would not have been in Bath in the first place.

As it was, so long as no one else discovered she was here, she was almost certain the Earl of Lindow would not actually ruin her. Not that it mattered—she was hardly going to make a match now, with her family's fortune so dire. The trouble was, with each passing moment she sat with him, she was becoming less certain about that fact.

She would estimate at least a one-in-three possibility that the man would attempt to kiss her before she left the room.

The concern was that... Well. That she wouldn't care.

Lord Lindow leaned closer. "I just want to know how you won."

"I'm showing you," Dodo said stubbornly. "The mathematics are crucial to understand before—"

"No, you're going to have to show me through practice, not this numbers and counting rubbish," said the man, waving an airy hand.

Though she perhaps should not have said it, Dodo could not help herself. "Tell me, how much, precisely, have you lost at the races?"

He jerked his head back and his startled expression told her everything. "Why does that concern us now?"

Dodo had enjoyed the races at York, which she had visited once while truly spending some time with her unmarried aunt. Oh, the horses themselves could be taken or left, but the mathematics were fascinating. Every tiny detail changing the odds, sometimes five or six times in a minute. The calculations being made in the minds of the bookkeepers, faster than she had ever done herself.

At that time, of course. She'd improved since then.

"The theory of mathematics is crucial to poker," Dodo said, avoiding his question. "And horseracing. They are much the same."

Lord Lindow snorted. "Nonsense."

"You think it nonsense? How did I beat you, then?"

Perhaps she should not have been so confrontational, but it was irritating beyond belief, having this man sit there and tell her she had merely lucked her way into wins. Or cheated.

The very idea!

"I don't know, not yet," said the earl slowly. "But I have never encountered a situation in which the theory was more important than the practice."

Dodo leaned forward, unable to help herself. "That's nonsense! The numbers prove the mathematics, the probability of which card is likely to come up next—it's absolutely vital! Without the theory—"

"Theory?" murmured Lord Lindow, a spark of something wild in his eyes. "Theory is knowing what is written in a book, that is all. But you can't go through life with mere theory. You've got to—got to know life. Feel it. Experience it."

Dodo swallowed.

Though it was a technical impossibility, she was almost certain the walls of the smoking room had started to creep inward. It certainly felt like a much smaller space, and that could not have anything to do with the fact that George Chance—the Earl of Lindow—was somehow closer.

How could he be that close? And how could the mere difference between twelve inches apart and three inches apart have such a specific effect on her?

Exponential.

Warming her. Making that liquid fire that had flared between her legs flicker back into existence.

Dodo wetted her lips before she replied and heard a strange sort of noise. A noise that could not have come from the earl. Almost... a groan.

She wetted them again. *There it was again. Most odd.* "You are wrong."

"'Wrong'?" His voice was nothing more than a growl now, and its timbre resonated along Dodo's spine. "Well, let me show you."

And before she could do anything to stop him, the Earl of Lindow was kissing her.

"Kissing" was an inadequate word. If Dodo were to guess, he was putting at least fifty percent more pressure on her lips than was strictly necessary, and there was a swiftness of his movement and a dark need in his breathing that was at least a third more than required.

It didn't matter. The numbers poured from her mind, leaving nothing more but the excitement of his passion, and Dodo clung to him. How her hands had reached his shoulders, she did not know. She did not need to know.

Because the Earl of Lindow was in control. His ardor tilted her head and when Dodo gasped, he took advantage of the sudden gap and teased his tongue along the slit of her lips.

Dodo could not help it. Her instincts told him that she wanted more, and her tongue reached out to shyly touch his own.

The sudden guttural groan from Lord Lindow told her in no uncertain terms that it was one-hundred-percent effective.

As his tongue teased into her mouth and started to plumb its depths, Dodo shivered with the intensity sweeping through her body. Oh, she'd never known sensations like this. That a man, an idiot like the Earl of Lindow, could have such an effect on her!

It was maddening. It was—improbable, certainly. Less than a one-in-four chance? Perhaps less.

The exact numbers would have to be worked out later, when her whole body wasn't quivering, and her hands weren't tangled in his hair, and—

The kiss ended as swiftly as it had begun.

Dodo was panting, the room spinning. George—she could hardly think of him as Lord Lindow after such an encounter, though she knew she ought to—appeared to be equally breathless.

When he spoke, it was in a growl. "There. I would bet you a great sum of money, Miss Loughty, that the practical is far better than the theory."

Though unsure if her legs would collapse underneath her, Dodo managed to stand. The cards on the table cascaded onto the floor, scattering hearts as they went.

I can't stay here. Not after—

"I have never," Dodo said quietly, in as calm and as measured a voice as she could manage, "never been so insulted."

And though Lord Lindow should have been chastised, should have flushed, should have immediately apologized for the liberty he had taken...

He did no such thing. In fact, a slow, wicked smile crept across the man's face, making him even more handsome—if possible—than he had been before. And it simply should not have been possible.

"Really?" he said lightly. "And do you *feel* insulted?"

The sensation of his lips still burned on Dodo's own, but she could not lie. She could not admit that the kiss, swift as it had been, harsh as it had been, potent as it had been, was the most intense and delightful experience of her entire life.

"I-I—"

The door opened and Dodo spun around, somehow certain that whoever it was would be able to tell what had occurred, just by looking at her.

The butler who had shown her into the place raised a prominent eyebrow, but said only, "Your brother is here, my lord."

There was an emphatic groan behind her. "Tell him to go to the devil!"

"I have already communicated to the marquess that you are busy, my lord," said the butler without turning a hair. "I am afraid he is quite insistent. Something about news."

Dodo hurriedly stepped forward. "I will go. There's no need for me to—"

"There is every need for you to stay," said Lord Lindow calmly, but with a certainty deep within his voice that made her halt.

How did he do that? Have that effect on her?

She flushed as she met his eyes.

"You stay here," the earl said steadily. "I'll speak with my brother, then we will return to my lesson."

Try as she might, Dodo could not bring herself to disagree. Leaving this man's presence… it was a punishment all of its own. She did not want to leave him. And she could not understand why.

Still. He can't have it all his own way.

"Fine. I will remain here and wait for you to return," Dodo said, holding her head high. "Then we shall get back to the theory. Of cards."

She would absolutely stick to that.

Chapter Six

September 26, 1812

GEORGE SIGHED, AND once again attempted to focus on the conversation going on around him.

"And Doctor says we're far enough along that we can tell the family," William Chance, Duke of Cothrom, and the oldest of the brothers was saying with a proud grin utterly at odds with his usually serious face. "I can't believe it. Almost on the first try, too!"

"William!" Alice Chance, the Duchess of Cothrom, cried. Her chestnut hair had slipped from its pins in her outrage, but she was still smiling.

"Oh, they don't mind, Alice."

"Perhaps not," said his wife with pink cheeks. "But I still don't think it's appropriate to tell them!"

"C-Congratulations," said the Marchioness of Aylesbury hurriedly. "A b-baby! A new Chance in the f-family, how w-wonderful."

George nodded along, hoping he would not be required to input anything at this time.

He had certainly not been surprised when Aylesbury had mentioned it, days ago, most irritatingly interrupting his time with Miss Loughty.

His kissing with Miss Loughty.

Being informed that the oldest Chance brother was going to be a father was indeed good news. But it was not any better than kissing a beautiful woman senseless, which was what George had hoped to return to doing after his brother had departed.

It had been most exasperating to find Miss Loughty prim and proper on his return... and the empty chair markedly on the other side of the card table.

"Any names?"

"No names as such," said Alice prettily as a footman stepped forward to replenish the table's potatoes. "There are some family names to be considered—"

"On your s-side as w-well, I p-presume," said the new Marchioness of Aylesbury said. Florence was a pretty enough woman, with her naturally curling hair in tendrils around her ears and a smile that was always hesitant, George thought, but shy. Very shy. "A-Alice, maybe?"

"If it's a girl," said Cothrom with a laugh, "I can think of no better name!"

Gentle laughter rang out around the table.

George took another sip of wine. He had nothing against family lunches, per se. It had been Cothrom's idea to start with. An opportunity for them to become more of a family.

He forced himself not to snort. *More of a family?* William, John, and George had always gone about the world supporting each other. They were already a family. And as for the fourth Chance brother... *if you could call him that...*

"—in the country, they must be born at Stanphrey Lacey," the Marquess of Aylesbury was saying.

"I think that would be best," said Frederick Chance, Viscount Pernrith, quietly. His hands were folded neatly, as they always were, and his jacket matched his waistcoat, his dark eyes ponderous yet guarded.

George shot him a glare but did not say anything.

This was hardly the place. Cothrom had opened up Stanphrey Hall in Bath just on the outskirts of the Crescent and the dining room was filled with late summer light. The linen tablecloth was covered with a plethora of platters, and it could have been a very pleasant lunch.

If it weren't for him.

Frederick Chance, Viscount Pernrith. It burned right into George's soul that the man even bore the name Chance in the first place, let alone had been given a family title.

Their father's bastard. At luncheon with them.

What did it matter if Cothrom had invited him? Surely, the brute knew better than to—

"George Chance, you aren't listening to a word I'm saying, are you?"

George swallowed. He hadn't been, as a matter of fact. Not that he wanted to be caught out in such inattention—particularly with Pernrith staring politely from the other side of the table.

Blaggard.

"I beg your pardon?" he said aloud, as politely as he could manage.

"I was saying, I heard about Scandal of Lancelot's loss yesterday," said Aylesbury again with a wry smile. "Most unexpected."

As though he needed another reason for his bad temper. "Someone is betting against me, the rogues—I lost almost a hundred pounds!"

Cothrom groaned.

"Not that I cannot handle such a small, insignificant loss," George added hastily.

It was not quite a lie. But his brother didn't need to know that.

Pernrith leaned back in his chair and sipped at his wine before saying quietly, "And is it true that you are courting a Miss Loughty?"

George frowned bitterly at the man. "What business is it of—"

"Courting a woman?" said Alice mildly.

"Miss Loughty?" said Cothrom, eyes wide. "I've never heard of her! Who is—"

"I am not courting Miss Loughty—I'm not courting anyone," said

George hastily. *Blast it all to hell, what right did Pernrith have to say such things?*

Now he came to think about it, how did the man even know he had been seeing Miss Loughty in the first place? Not that he was—he wouldn't have called it courting. Not really. Would he?

"The whole of Bath is agog with it," the blaggard Pernrith was saying. "He's been asking after her, ensuring she is not welcome in certain gaming hells—"

"Lindow!"

"What?" George said defensively at Cothrom's explosion. He could not by now still be the only one who had noticed Miss Loughty's lack of a chaperone. If rumors were swirling about, even if a result of his own actions, he should not suffer, but the lady herself... "You think it appropriate for a young woman to be attending places like McBarland's?"

"Such places shouldn't be mentioned in front of certain people," Cothrom said tightly, gesturing with a nod of his head at the two ladies present.

George rolled his eyes. Cothrom always wanted to wrap those he loved in cotton wool—it was the most frustrating and most endearing of his habits. Even if it did make him want to constantly bicker with the man.

"She's nothing but a card sharp," he tried to say as nonchalantly as possible. "And I may... I may have lost a few pounds to her. A few pounds *only*—"

The rest of his words were drowned out by the laughter of the whole room. Even his two sisters-in-law joined in.

"A woman, and you lost?" Alice said lightly. "I must say, it is pleasant to see you taken down a peg or two."

"I've not been taken—"

"D-Does she know her h-horses?" asked Florence eagerly with a shy smile. "It w-would be n-nice to have another p-person about the p-place who—"

"Miss Loughty is not going to be *about the place*," George said hotly, hating how swiftly they got under his skin. Surely, families were not supposed to be like this? They were supposed to be... He didn't know. Quiet. Supportive. Ignoring of one's defects!

Aylesbury was grinning. "You like her, don't you?"

George opened his mouth, had nothing to say, then closed it again.

"I have never, never been so insulted."

"Really? And do you feel *insulted?"*

Liked her? By God, he more than liked her. If she'd let him, he would have taken Miss Loughty in his arms and shown her precisely what a man could do in practice, far more than with theory. If uninterrupted for long enough, perhaps his fingers could have proven his point just as firmly—and pleasurably—as his mouth had.

George swallowed. Not that thinking such things was a good idea, here or elsewhere.

When he looked up, Pernrith—*Pernrith!*—was smiling. "I think you are a little smitten, brother."

Enough of this. He didn't have to sit here and take this—this slander. This presumption of his affection for—

Not that he felt anything like...

Damnit.

George rose suddenly from his seat, so swiftly, it almost fell to the floor. "I'm leaving."

"Give Miss Loughty our best wishes," said Alice with a teasing grin that was most unfair of her.

Her husband chuckled. "Yes, and invite her to next month's luncheon. We'll be back in Bath, won't we?"

"We wouldn't miss seeing Miss Loughty for the world," said the duchess, with the seriousness of a saint.

George scowled as he marched past his chuckling brothers and the two wives who had so recently joined the family. What did they know? How dare they mock him for something that was absolutely, most definitely—

And Pernrith, too!

He was in half a mind to slam the front door behind him, except Cothrom's butler managed to close it. Instead, George was forced to stand on the doorstep heaving with irritation, every movement pouring his frustration out into the air.

He needed to clear his head.

There was only one place to go in Bath to really clear one's head. There was nowhere like Hyde Park, a place he frequented whenever in London, for losing yourself in when one was truly irritated. Which happened whenever he lost money.

So, relatively frequently.

But in Bath there was no Hyde Park. There was, however, Sydney Gardens, and it was to this quiet and calm part of the city that George stomped.

When he pushed open the gate and heard the birdsong, saw the last of the summer flowers and breathed in the cleaner air, George could feel his shoulders starting to unlock.

Yes, he could calm himself here. There would be nothing at Sydney Gardens to distract him. Nothing at all. He could sit here on a bench for twenty minutes or so, maybe even half an hour. He couldn't stay too long, of course. He'd have to go to the stables at some point this afternoon and talk to his jockey, try to understand what on earth was going on with Scandal of Lancelot. And then he—

George almost fell over his own foot.

It wasn't his fault. It was the most natural reaction to seeing Miss Doris Loughty, again alone, walking toward him farther up the path.

A thundering lurch in his stomach had been what had dislodged his foot, and it appeared he was not the only one affected. The instant his eyes met hers, Miss Loughty flushed a dark crimson that was visible for at least twenty feet away.

And she halted.

George did not. This had been going on long enough. He needed to clear Miss Loughty from his mind, and his conscience, and that meant an awkward conversation that he hoped would clear the whole thing up.

And if it didn't... Well. He had already been losing at cards before he'd met her. It wouldn't be a huge change, he supposed.

Then she did something he could never have predicted.

She turned away.

"Miss Loughty!" George had not intended to call her name, but he did so as he strode toward her retreating back.

The idea of not speaking to her was just as impossible as speaking to her—but now that he was faced with the choice, he knew which he would rather have.

Pushing past a couple who stared after him and ignoring the gravel he was kicking up in his haste, George almost reached out.

Almost.

As though she could feel his intentions that had been swiftly quashed, Miss Loughty turned around. "Don't—"

"I didn't," said George hastily, lifting his hands in surrender.

They had both stopped. How, he wasn't sure. Why was it that whenever he was around Miss Loughty, he couldn't think straight?

And he couldn't keep thinking of her as Miss Loughty, for a start. That staid, restrictive, formal name? For a woman who boldly walked in a park in the daylight on her own? No longer.

"What is your name, Miss Loughty?" George said into the silence.

Miss Loughty blinked, her dark eyebrows pinching together and her color pinking. It went nicely with the sky-blue muslin gown she was wearing, mending around the hemline notwithstanding, but George attempted not to notice that. He also attempted not to notice how wonderfully she filled said gown, or remind himself how they were standing alone in Sydney Gardens.

Completely alone...

"My name," she said stiffly, "is Miss Loughty."

"Yes, I know that—I actually meant your Christian name," said George softly, wondering why on earth his hands were still up. He dropped them to his sides. "My name's George."

She stared up with bemused eyes. "You expect me to call you that?"

He hadn't, not really. He'd merely been curious. But now he did.

Oh, to hear his own name curling around those luscious lips…

As though she could hear his thoughts shouted from the rooftops of the Pump Rooms, Miss Loughty flushed. "I don't—It isn't a good idea to—We aren't… Well. Are we?"

Are we?

George swallowed.

He wasn't sure what they were, if that was what she was asking. There had been no rhyme and little reason for their encounters to date, and now with his brother's words ringing in his ears, he wasn't sure what he was supposed to do next.

"I think you are a little smitten, brother."

"Doris."

George blinked. "I beg your pardon?"

He'd heard the two syllables, but they did not seem to make any sense. Doris? It was such a simple, refined, but unspectacular name.

Certainly not a name to be held by a woman like this…

Miss Loughty smiled, and the sun came out and warmed him, and George was tingling all over and he barely heard what she said next.

"It's a family name, not one I particularly like, to tell the truth. My family calls me 'Dodo.'"

Dodo.

George's smile was genial, and try as he might, he could not inject it with the typical mischievousness that kept refined ladies like this at arm's length. "A rare bird, indeed."

She blushed, furiously not looking at him, from what he could see.

But it didn't matter. Stupid Cothrom and stupid Aylesbury's words were echoing once more in his mind, causing the conscience George hardly knew he had to raise its sleepy head again.

"And is it true that you are courting a Miss Loughty?"

But she hadn't waited for him in the smoking room, had she? Not to do more than teach cards—a lesson he still hadn't grasped, so distracted he'd been by the sight of her. She—Miss Loughty, Dodo, she had obviously been offended.

"Look," George said quietly. "I am sorry. I shouldn't have kissed you."

Dodo took a step back. "You... You shouldn't have?"

It sounded almost like a question, as though she were asking him. Which did not make sense. She had been the one, after all, to point out the inexcusable liberty he had taken.

"I have never, never been so insulted."

Surely, she is absolutely clear on what should or should not have happened between us, George thought feverishly. And what did people do with their hands? Here his were, just hanging about his sides, like idiots! Where should they have been?

He placed his hands on his hips, then immediately allowed them to drop to his sides again as a bird swooped past them, chirping merrily.

No, that isn't it. How could I have forgotten how hands work?

"I may as well tell you," George said wretchedly. "Apparently, the whole of Bath... Well. They think we're courting."

He saw the surprise in Dodo's eyes, and she took a hasty step back. "But we're not!"

"I know that," he said.

"But—But they can't think that!"

"I've certainly placed us in a rather difficult situation," admitted George, his stomach twisting horribly. After so many years bedding women, he had never managed to find himself in this sort of situation.

Compromised.

It was a horrible word. He'd never truly given it much thought. He had never had to. Discretion had always been a core part of his seduction, and on the rare occasion that old Cothrom had gotten wind of one of his conquests, the eldest Chance brother had been able to swiftly make amends with the father, if there was a father, and ensure him nothing had happened. There'd been no consequences for George, anyway.

And now here he was, giving rise to gossip merely because this woman had beaten him at cards!

George's gaze swept over Dodo Loughty and his stomach lurched again.

Well. Maybe not precisely because of that. She was... different. Somehow. Unlike his previous conquests. He couldn't explain it. But he didn't have to. He could feel it, sense it in his very bones.

She was different.

"Well, you'll just have to change the gossip!" Dodo said, her cheeks pink as she dropped her eyes. A couple walked past them, staring curiously as they continued along the path. Only when they were out of earshot did Dodo take a step forward. "You have to stop this!" she hissed.

It was a welcome step forward. George had been debating whether or not to step closer to her for some time, and now that she had done so, he could feel the very tangible difference.

Something tingling along his arms. Pins and needles on his skin.

Dear God, if she could have this effect on him merely by being close to him...

"George Chance!" Dodo hissed, pulling him off the path and around the cover of a large oak tree. "This has to stop—stop it! You need to, I don't know, change their minds! Tell the *ton*—"

George chuckled, spirits soaring at the sudden intimacy the tree afforded. *Now, this is more like it.* "You must be joking!"

"I never jest," she said sharply.

And she didn't. Now he came to think about it, George could not recall a single moment in their brief acquaintance when Dodo—when

Miss Loughty, he must remember to call her that, mustn't he?—had jested.

Still. She couldn't seriously think he could change the *ton*'s mind, did she?

Her eyes darted from side to side as she wrung her hands. "I am not *unaware* how things look. That I am here, in Bath, without a chaperone, will not help matters should it become more widely known."

George felt his eyes fluttering rapidly. He had guessed she had snuck out frequently from under some old spinster's watch, but to be in this city, alone, entirely alone...

Dodo was truly unlike any woman he had ever known.

"Where have you been staying?" he asked. The thought of this vulnerable woman where any sordid sort might come across her...

"A lady's boarding house." She did not look at him as she gave him an address.

He had never thought to look for her in that area of town. What was she doing, hiding among the rabble to make her lack of chaperone less apparent to those in Society who might remark on it?

"The world will think what the world wants to think," he said sternly. "It's not up to me to—"

"Does that mean there's an outside chance you'll have to marry me?"

George halted midsentence, his mouth hanging open as he stared.

Marry her?

The thought hadn't even occurred to him. Why would it? As his stomach jolted painfully and his pulse skipped a beat, George attempted to collect himself and remind himself that such a thing was most unlikely.

Most... Most unlikely. Wasn't it?

"No," he said.

He regretted the resolve of his reply immediately—but not nearly so much as he deplored the relief which immediately swept over

Dodo's face.

"Good," she said heartily, her tense shoulders now relaxed.

George shifted on his feet, grateful the two of them were hidden from the other walkers in Sydney Gardens. "What do you mean, good?"

"Well, good," Dodo repeated, not quite meeting his eye.

"Would it be so bad?"

What had possessed him to say such a thing, he was not sure. The words had been out before he could stop them, unfortunately, and even more unfortunately, they'd prompted Dodo to meet his gaze.

Steadily. Calmly. Without any of the murmuring or cooing that ladies typically offered when fluttering their eyelashes. George had hardly to work at seducing ladies back in London—he was the Earl of Lindow! He was handsome, of a sort, and ladies rather welcomed his embraces.

But Dodo Loughty? "The odds of a successful union aren't good," she said quietly. "Good day, my lord."

She had turned and almost reached the path again before George caught up with her—but he was determined, this time.

This woman, this inexplicable, impossible woman, was going to carry out her side of their bargain, even if the *ton* took this to mean they were courting. Let Society get the wrong end of the stick. If they wanted to bet on the wrong horse, that was fine by him.

He was onto a certainty.

"You still haven't taught me anything, Dodo," George pointed out.

She halted. "You... You can't call me that."

"I'll call you what I like," he said impulsively, hunger for her roaring through his ears and making it impossible to think. "And I'll pay you."

For some reason, that caught her attention.

Dodo opened her mouth, hesitated, then said quietly, "You will?"

George swallowed.

Well, it wasn't as though he had never paid for a woman before. Money had changed hands in the past, though arguably for a very different type of lesson. Strangely, he expected it to be no less agreeable.

But there was something strange about offering money to Dodo Loughty. It shifted the terms of their... their relationship, for want of a better word, from two equals to that of customer and tradesperson.

There was something distasteful about it. Yet the thought of her walking away now, never to return into his life—George could not countenance it.

If coin was the only way to force this woman to spend more time in his presence... Well. So be it. As long as his brothers never found out.

"To be sure—as long as Scandal of Lancelet doesn't lean to the left as he always does, I will pay you for lessons," he said aloud. "Card lessons," he added hastily.

If the slight pink flowing down to her neck was any indication, the merest hint of ill repute in his words had been enough to shock the young lady.

But not to startle her. George watched her, desire building, as she considered his words.

By God, she was incredible.

"Let's negotiate terms," she said quietly.

The thrill that such words gave him was most inappropriate. George knew that. But then, none of their interactions in the past had been entirely appropriate, now he came to think about it. Why would he expect that to change now?

Glancing about to make sure their conversation—their negotiations—were not about to be overheard, George turned back to Dodo. "What did you have in mind?"

"Well... Well, I cannot have you monopolizing my time," she said softly, a light lilt to her voice. "That would be impossible."

"Impossible," George repeated, slightly dazed.

Did she have any idea what effect she was having on him? No, no, he needed to get a grip on himself. He couldn't go around thinking these sorts of things about a woman like Miss Dodo Loughty! When he married—

George caught himself just in time. *Marriage? What on earth was he thinking about that for?*

"—so no more than two hours a day, I think, for lessons," Dodo was continuing, seemingly unaware that the Earl of Lindow had become momentarily lost in his own thoughts. "At a crown an hour—"

"A crown an hour?"

She looked up, eyebrow raised. "You think the cost too weighty for you, my lord?"

George swallowed. He wasn't sure right now what price he could put on Dodo Loughty's company. Far more than a crown an hour. But still. It felt ridiculous to be paying such a cost merely for the woman to talk mathematics at him.

Even if she did so in such a seductive way.

He relented. "Two hours a day, a crown an hour."

"Which makes fourteen a week," Dodo said smartly. "And I would like a week's payment. That's three pounds, two crowns. Now. In advance."

It was George's turn to raise an eyebrow. "Now?"

He wasn't sure anymore if he could say *no* to this woman. It was a most strange position to be in, and not one he knew how to navigate. He knew cards, dice, and horses. He knew how to please a woman, and how to fence. That was all he had been expected to do, as a gentleman.

Not negotiate terms with a woman whose mind was obviously running forty miles an hour faster than his own.

"Fine," George said, exhaling slowly and wondering whether he could borrow a few pounds off Aylesbury. Just for a week or so. "We have an agreement—a proper one, this time."

He offered out his hand.

He had been wild to do so the first time, and he hadn't been sure then whether Dodo would take it. This time, however, she did. Most unfortunately, she was wearing gloves.

"And no kissing," Dodo hissed, leaning toward him to confirm no one else could hear.

George grinned. "No promises."

Chapter Seven

September 29, 1812

Dodo stifled a laugh. It was something she was having to get very good at, spending all this time with George.

With Lord Lindow. Bother. She really would have to watch that.

The thing was, the man gave her so many causes for laughing, but in this particular scenario, she definitely did not wish him to spot the mistake he was making.

And—

Had made.

"You know, I think I'm starting to get the hang of this," said George with a self-satisfied grin, leaning back in his chair and peering at her over his cards. "Don't you think?"

Dodo did not even need to glance at the cards on the table. She had already memorized them, and those in her hand, and calculated the likelihood of what George was clutching. Two kings, almost certainly, by that gratified grin. Perhaps a jack of the same suit?

Whatever it was, it couldn't beat what she held. And he would know that—if he had bothered to consider just how many hearts were on the table.

That's the trouble with men, Dodo thought languidly as she picked up her final card and looked at it with a calm, unmoving expression. They were so swift to believe they had understood the full lie of the land, without any actual proof they had done so. Three lessons, and the man believed he could beat her at cards.

Ridiculous.

Holding the full spread of her cards in her right hand, Dodo reached out to pick up her glass of lemonade with the other. The sparkling sourness with a hint of sweet was remarkably refreshing on this cold, gray day.

Autumn was coming in. And that meant winter. And that meant greater bills, and doctor's costs, and she had already spent money on new gloves, thinking she'd call too much attention to herself if she kept not wearing them, at least outside of these lessons, as she was not eager to ruin another pair—

"Are you going to bet anything?" came George's questioning voice.

Dodo kept her expression steady as she placed the almost-empty lemonade glass onto the card table. "Do you think I should?"

"You'd have to be prepared to lose it," the Earl of Lindow said proudly.

Once again, Dodo stifled a laugh. She really was getting better at it. With every mistake her opponent made, she was having to.

The smoking room had a fire lit for the first time, the flames throwing shimmering light over the gold-gilt frames that lined the place. It made the room feel… not cozy—it was far too large for that. Far larger than the drawing room at home, Dodo mused as she threw down another shilling.

She could have bet higher, of course. As she was guaranteed to win, it would have been pleasant to goad the confident George out of a full crown. But she couldn't push her luck. He would certainly suspect—

"I raise you a crown!" said George, a lock of hair falling over his eyes in his eagerness to lean forward and throw down the coin.

Dodo kept her face still. Well, it wasn't as though the man didn't have enough crowns, was it? The Chances were, she had discovered by careful inquiries about Johnson's Buildings, one of the richest families in England, all four of them, and all four with a title of his own in a most unusual way of a family sharing its inheritance. Though confusingly, some people seemed to be under the impression that one brother was perhaps not of the noblest of origins. Most odd.

"I will see that crown," she said quietly, placing out the crown on the table.

The little pile of silver and a few coppers looked remarkably inviting. The instinct to lean over and help herself, as she knew she would be doing in just a few moments, was strong. Dodo managed to hold herself back. There was still a chance she could earn a few more pennies from the man.

And teach him. Obviously. What better lesson was there than to lose?

"Anything else?" Dodo asked innocently.

Or perhaps not innocently enough. George's face stiffened, and he glanced hurriedly at the cards in his hand and the cards on the table, his smug expression gone.

"Oh, good heavens," he said heavily. "I've lost, haven't I?"

"I don't know what you—"

"You know precisely what I mean, Dodo," George said with an accusing look accompanied by a smile. "You've won."

Dodo's pulse skipped a beat.

Which was ridiculous. There was no reason it should do such a thing each and every time the man said her name. It was just a pet name, after all. Technically, there was no reason why anyone she considered an intimate acquaintance couldn't use it.

Except they didn't. Just her parents. To hear him use it was to feel most strange.

It was impossible not to laugh as George stared crestfallen at the card table, utterly convinced she had somehow beaten him.

She had, but he wasn't to know that.

"What makes you think that I have won?" she asked as sweetly as she could manage.

"You've asked me to bet more money," George said darkly. "That is never a good sign, but with all the cards dealt, there can only be one reason. You've got a straight."

Dodo inclined her head graciously and placed down her cards, face up, on the table. A straight, ace high.

George groaned, his handsome features in no way impeded by the twist in his countenance. "Good Lord, what?"

"You should have paid closer attention to the cards on the table," Dodo said severely, trying not to hasten in pulling the coins toward her but very conscious they belonged in her reticule, not on the table between them. "Three hearts, a ten, and a queen? You should have expected—"

"How could I have?" There could have been a petulance in his voice, but there wasn't. George was laughing, his shoulders loose and his eyes bright as he looked at her.

Dodo swallowed. And he did do a great amount of looking at her, didn't he?

Which was to be expected. She was teaching him, she attempted to remind herself. There was no point in continuing the lessons if the man refused to look at her.

But there was looking and... and *looking*. She couldn't distinguish the difference with words; it was too difficult. But there was most definitely a way of looking at a lady, and a way of undressing said lady with one's eyes, and George Chance, Earl of Lindow, was often doing the latter.

Try as she might, she could not help but look into those sky-blue passionate eyes. Eyes that seemed to bear down into her very soul. Eyes that said just as much as his mouth could: words like *desire* and *sensual* and—

Dodo gasped.

Her fingers, pulling her winnings together, had brushed past the hands of another. George.

"And just what do you think you're doing?" she managed to say.

"I think it's unfair that you won, and with superior skill to boot," teased George, his eyes now dancing with mischief. "I think I'll take back that crown, and—"

"You'll do absolutely nothing of the sort," Dodo said firmly, attempting to extricate her fingers from his own.

The trouble was, the more she struggled to release them, the more entangled their fingers somehow became. There was no logic to it, nor to the lurching in her stomach as George's fingers managed to curl around her own.

"Dodo—"

Dodo pulled her hands away from the table, abandoning the coins. Her lungs was ragged and she was certain her cheeks were pink. They were certainly burning.

It wasn't supposed to be like this. What had she said, when they'd made their agreement?

"And no kissing."

"No promises."

She had presumed he'd been jesting. The man was a tease of the highest order—she did not need to know anything from the *ton*'s gossip to be certain of that. This was a man who had undoubtedly bedded more than his fair share of women, and she was certainly not going to be added to that list.

Not that she was in a position to protest too much about her reputation, considering her trip, unaccompanied, to Bath.

The point was—*the point is*, Dodo thought as she caught his gaze and saw fire in his eyes, *that it is not supposed to be like this*. This was supposed to be a formal teaching experience, and a way for her to earn coin.

"Remove your hands from my winnings," Dodo said sharply, using the severest tone she could.

George did not move an inch. "I don't appreciate being ordered about, Dodo."

"Then learn to lose with grace," she shot back.

A flicker of joy curled around her to see the irritation in him. She shouldn't have felt so satisfied at seeing that, should she have? No, that was most irregular.

Still. It hadn't stopped her from feeling it.

And then George removed his hands from the coins, leaned back in his chair, and sighed heavily. His eyes did not leave her as Dodo scraped the last of the coins into her reticule, which was now a pleasing weight.

"You're a very unusual woman."

Try as she might, Dodo could not prevent her cheeks from burning. She attempted some slow, calming breaths. When she lifted her head to meet George's expression, she could see that it had made little to no difference.

"No, I'm not," she said quietly. She found she could not give in to his assertion, even if she was aware of no other unwed lady of her class who would travel to Bath alone to gamble. "Now, another game? We could try—"

"Yes, you are unusual. You are unusual if I say you are," said the Earl of Lindow. There was no malice in his voice, no censure, but a finality that made it clear that now he had come to an opinion, that was the truth. "You're clever."

Dodo snorted as she picked up the cards and started to shuffle them. "What, you don't think women are clever?"

It was not the most impressive retort, but she could think of nothing else to counter with. That was one of the most difficult things about teaching this man to play cards—properly play cards. He simply... Well.

He is very handsome.

Dodo swallowed, the cards almost spilling from her hands. Fine, he was handsome. She had attempted to deny it for days, but there was no getting around it. The man was so handsome, he was actually delectable. And when he leaned back like that, all broad shoulders and nonchalant gaze, the sheer comfort he obviously felt within his body...

Clearing her throat, Dodo told herself she had absolutely no interest in earls, handsome or otherwise. That was not why she had come to Bath. That was not—

"Women? Clever?" George sounded confused. "You know, I have never thought about it. I certainly haven't encountered any. Not... Not like you."

It was the hesitation that did it. Dodo was fairly certain she could keep her head around a man like the Earl of Lindow, even if he was impossibly charming and irritatingly handsome.

But that hesitation, that flicker of certainty in his voice, the way it thrilled her without him seeming to even know...

It's a good thing I have absolutely no intention of being caught in this man's charm, Dodo thought sharply.

"They've probably all been keeping their cleverness a secret," Dodo said airily aloud, dealing out another hand of poker. "It is so much easier to get around men that way, you know."

George stared blankly, then chuckled. "Goodness, I suppose that's true. Lord, I'd hate to think I've been taken in that many times, but—"

"I wouldn't be surprised," she said, hoping she could navigate the conversation back onto neutral ground. "Now, consider in this hand—"

"Does that mean you're keeping your greater heights of intellect from me?" asked George quietly, leaning forward and reaching out.

For a moment, Dodo thought he was reaching out for her hand. Which would have been preposterous—what on earth would he wish to do something like that for?

At the same time, she heartily wished he would. His fingers against hers had felt... felt good.

So just as she was about to accept that George could, perhaps, take her hand—

He picked up his cards. "You must be."

Dodo blinked. "Wh-What?"

"Keeping your intellect from me—you keep winning. There can be no other explanation," George said lightly. "I mean, it's not as though this is your source of income, is it? A lady like you."

A lady like her.

She had been careful, throughout the lessons she had given previously, to keep as much about herself to herself as she could. Though she had faith thus far in his ability to quieten the rumors about the two of them, since he wanted these lessons to continue, when it came down to it, this was not a man to be trusted. She could see it in the casual way he lost money, the way he spoke about his friends, the way he bet on horses. That reminded her, she needed to talk to Mr. Gillingham about the next race.

George was not a serious man. Not a man who could be burdened with serious troubles.

So even if she had been desperate to tell someone, anyone, George Chance was not the one.

Not the one to tell, Dodo corrected herself hastily. *Right.*

"Everyone has a hobby," she said, ignoring the cards on the table. "I mean, you do, and you're an earl."

George raised a quizzical eyebrow. "I do?"

Dodo's stomach most disobligingly decided in that moment to lurch. *Most unfair.* "You own race horses."

She had not intended her words to be wild and radical, but one would not have known that from the reaction that George gave.

His snort echoed around the smoking room, and he threw down his cards in seeming disgust—yet his eyes danced with delight.

"My dear Dodo, horses are not a hobby. They are a vocation!" And just like that, all the false outrage, all the teasing—it all faded away. George was eager now, earnest, leaning forward with excitement, not in an attempt to woo her.

Not, Dodo thought hastily, *that he has been doing that in the first place. Obviously. Kissing is not the same as wooing. Wooing is not the same as courting. Courting is not an offer of—*

"—Scandal of Lancelot will certainly make a move in the next race, I am sure," George was saying. "I thought it would be Honor of Guinevere who would make the difference, but as it turns out... even the newspapers have guessed wrong. I can't wait for the blaggard who always bets against me to get that wrong!"

Horses in Croscombe, where she had grown up, were for working, not for running around in circles. A horse had to earn its keep, and that meant farm work or carriage work. It was as simple as that.

But George... his passion, it was exuberant, untamed, like himself. It poured from him like froth upon sea waves trickling up the shore.

"I love it," he said simply. "And of course, it makes the gambling all the sweeter when I win."

Dodo smiled, despite herself. "It sounds as though you have a true passion."

"I suppose I do," George said, suddenly awkward, as though realizing he had been ardent. "I suppose everyone has something like that. A hobby, as you said. A passion. And yours is?"

The serious look he gave her, looking her straight in the eye with a slight lift of his chin, was...

She could not understand it. This rake, this rogue—she had heard all the rumors by now. Just the simple mention of the Earl of Lindow was enough for people to pour out the gossip they had heard. The ladies he'd bedded. The duels he'd fought. The money he'd lost.

And yet...

The man of whom Society spoke did not match this sometimes eager, sometimes serious man. A man who appeared to have nothing better to do than learn cards from a penniless woman.

"Your passion, Dodo?" George repeated.

Heat flickered up and across the base of her throat, and no matter what she attempted to force it away, there was nothing she could do.

My passion? Such a word, one which should not have been shared between a gentleman and a lady. It was most improper. *Most... Most dangerous.*

Dangerous? Now where had that thought come from?

"I have always found it easier to keep my love of numbers hidden," Dodo said quietly. "Now, the cards. It's your turn to—"

"You truly do love them, don't you?" George spoke not with condemnation, but with curiosity. "Though there are many who enjoy them, you—you take a *great deal* of pleasure from them, don't you? And... And comfort."

Dodo dropped her hand face-down onto the table and leaned back in her chair for the first time since they had sat down.

Because it was disorienting, to be so swiftly understood. How did he do it? The earl gave the impression of being... Well, not self-centered, but certainly self-focused. A man who was interested in others merely because of what they could do for him.

But the way he spoke, with such perception. It should not have been allowed.

"Dodo?" George said gently.

Dodo swallowed. But then, there could be no harm in sharing a little of what she appreciated from numbers, could there? It was just numbers. Just her thoughts.

"I like numbers," she began stiffly. Her eyes flickered to him, but quite different to what she had expected, George did not speak. Instead, he nodded, spurring her on. "I... They are powerful. Anything can be calculated with them, anything at all. They explain the universe in a way that words just... just can't."

She sounded like a fool. Dodo knew she always sounded like a fool whenever she started to talk about numbers. It was why she did it so rarely.

But George was not laughing. His eyes had not glazed over, he was not nodding off to sleep…

He was waiting for her to continue.

Dodo shifted awkwardly in her seat. *When did this room grow so hot?*

"I mean, think about it—numbers are so dependable," she said softly. "The square root of sixty-four is always eight, when you treble four hundred it is always twelve hundred. The numbers, the patterns, they are always there. You can predict what they will do, manipulate them precisely however you want. They never change."

"'Never change'?" George prompted.

Then the words Dodo had promised herself she would not say spilled from her lips. "They're never going to disappoint you."

The instant she'd ceased speaking, Dodo saw spots in her vision. What had possessed her to say such a thing? Why would she have allowed herself to be so vulnerable?

But before she could think, before her instincts could propel her up and toward the door, George said softly, "'Disappoint'? Who has disappointed you, Dodo?"

Dodo hesitated. This had never been the plan. The plan had been to earn money teaching an earl who appeared to have coin to burn, and even win a few extra shillings off him. Not to start pouring out her heart to him.

Finally, her legs obeyed the frantic and silent begging of her mind.

Dodo shot up. "Is that the time? I should really be—"

"You don't have anywhere to go, Dodo, so don't pretend you do," said George quietly.

He had not risen to go after her, nor made a single movement to stop her from leaving the smoking room of Lindow House. But that did not matter. His words alone were sufficient to halt Dodo in her tracks.

Her whole body was trembling. *Can he see it?*

"Please, Dodo," he said softly.

There was something in his tone. A longing, a need, a desperation she had never heard in it before.

Well. Perhaps once. Just before he had kissed her...

Dodo took another step toward the door. "I... "

What could she say?

She liked him. He was a rascal, an earl without much of a conscience, a man who seemed to dictate the world around him to be precisely how he wanted it with little thought for others.

And he was also gentle, and kind, and in a strange way, honorable.

Dodo's pulse pattered painfully. She liked him far more than she should have. And she should not stay.

"No... " She cleared her throat, willed herself to speak. "No more personal questions. That's an order."

George's smile was wicked, causing something to rush up her spine. "You know, you are the only woman to even consider ordering an earl about."

A smile crept across Dodo's face, unbidden. "And will you obey?"

She had not intended her words to be so provocative. George groaned, covering his face for a moment with his hands. When he finally dropped them, there was a look in his eye that she could not discern—and did not spend too much time examining.

She might actually discover what he was thinking.

"Damnit, Dodo. Yes. Fine. No more personal questions—for now," George said bleakly. "Now come back here, woman, and teach me that trick again. You won't beat me for a third time in a row. Probably."

Chapter Eight

October 1, 1812

McBARLAND'S WAS FULL of smoke and noise by the time George had arrived, but that did not halt his progress. He'd been delayed by a rather dreary conversation with two of his footmen and a maid, all of them attempting to persuade him that Northrup, his butler, was a bad sort. He never gave them time off when needed. He made them work long hours. The maid swore her wages were short but could not, in fact, prove it, and had even balked when George had asked her to do so.

Some people would always seek to drag others down.

Finding a seat on the edges of the room, precisely where he could keep an eye on the door, George was rewarded for his patience.

There she was.

His whole body responded to the sight of Miss Dodo Loughty as she stepped through the door, pelisse tucked around her shoulders and head held high.

Dear God, but she was magnificent.

Dark hair. An elegant neck. Sparkling intelligence in her eyes that could not be falsified—this was a clever woman. A sense of calm and yet of tightly coiled curiosity that could spring forth at any moment. And a way with her… a way that was surely drawing the attention of every red-blooded male in the room.

George swallowed. There wasn't a part of his body that did not respond to Dodo—to Miss Loughty, as he would have to call her here.

And though he was no stranger to the sense of one's body responding with delight to the sight of a pretty woman, there was something different about the way his heart started thumping, the tension in his thighs as he forced himself not to rise, the way his head span.

She was different.

It had been two days. Two days, or three? The point was, too many days since he had last seen her.

George had attempted to organize another lesson for the following day, but it was not to be. Though he could hardly imagine what Dodo had been doing that could keep her from him.

You fool, he thought darkly as his attention tracked her progress across McBarland's. *You're acting as though she owes you something—as though she has to check her movements with you. You aren't her father, or her brother.*

Though the fact that she had no guardian with her in Bath *did* awaken some sort of protective instinct in him, whether it was his right to feel that way or not.

The candlelight poured over Dodo as she stepped past a candelabra, shining on her shimmering, dark-black hair. George's manhood stiffened.

Definitely not her father nor her brother.

But if there was one thing he was starting to learn about Dodo, and it had been a hard lesson to accept, it was that she did not appreciate being crowded. She had her own mind, her own opinions, her own plan as to what should be done.

George watched carefully as Dodo approached a table. It was true he had encouraged others not to play with her, but that had been weeks ago, and she might find opponents more willing to accept her as a player this time. But at that table… "Not that one."

He had been unable to help the murmur that had slipped out, but no one had been close enough to hear it. Dodo certainly hadn't, and she was being welcomed with open arms to the table at which sat—

He groaned. "Not that one."

It was well known throughout Bath—*at least, by most people*, he corrected himself with dismay as he watched Dodo remove her pelisse and incline her head at the two men at the table—that Mr. Gregory and Mr. Gillingham were not good people. Not good at all. Since their arrival in town, they had done nothing but make trouble.

And they were good at cards.

Far better than him, anyway, though George was starting to accept that did not mean much.

Anxiety flowing through his bones, he attempted to see what, precisely, was going on at that table. From what he could gather from this angle, it appeared that they were attempting to coerce her into playing a game of poker.

A slow smile crept across George's face.

Well, it wasn't as though he didn't know how impressive Dodo was at that game. And as he watched, though he could not hear what was being said thanks to the loud chatter in the room, the raucous laughter of other tables... He saw it clearly.

Dodo attempted to decline, then allowed herself to be persuaded. Eventually, she removed her gloves and allowed herself to be dealt into a hand, showing nerves from every inch of her face.

George's smile grew larger. *The minx.*

He should have noticed before—but then, had he not been taken in by just the same trick? The woman had pretended she had no idea what she was doing at the table, then all of a sudden...

He hadn't lost too much then, though he had certainly lost a great deal since. He would have to slow these lessons if he wanted to keep his coin where it belonged, in his pocketbook. But he could not resist her.

George did not have to wait long to see the consequences of Dodo's cleverness. With her mouth puckered into an "O," feigning surprise that she had been so fortunate as to win, Dodo clasped a hand to her breast and blushed prettily.

Very prettily.

A roaring anger that she could blush at someone who was not him crept across George, and he started to rise from his seat.

The very idea of leaving Dodo there to—

But no. George forced himself to sit. Dodo would hardly thank him for getting in the way of her game, would she? And the men, Gregory and Gillingham, would not believe him, even if he told the truth.

No man liked to believe he had been conned out of money.

The next ten minutes, however, demonstrated just how swiftly Dodo could work. She took the subsequent three hands, gaining a greater sum each time, and the charmed expressions of the two men started to fade.

George's chest puffed out.

It was remarkably odd. Dodo was nothing to him, at least on paper—yet he felt such a strange sense of, well… Pride. Ownership.

Perhaps 'ownership' is not the right word, George thought as his gaze lazily moved along from her delicate hands to her delightful wrists to the softness of her arms, to her neck…

Possessiveness. Perhaps that was more accurate.

Whatever the right term, it was ridiculous. This was not some young widow he had picked up at a ball or a dinner party, could have his way with, and never seen again.

Bath was too small a place, for a start. But it went beyond that.

He knew almost nothing about her.

The thought was unpleasant, but George could not deny it, despite the sinking feeling. He could list the facts he knew about Dodo on one hand and still have a few fingers to spare.

She was a woman. She played cards well. She was clever enough to travel to and continue to stay in Bath without a chaperone…

And that was essentially it.

A ripple of uncertainty plagued him as George watched the two men at Dodo's table get more and more irritated. One of them, the squat man with a glistening temple he knew to be Gregory, offered a piece of paper which they both wrote notes on. An IOU, perhaps? It appeared more like a bet, an agreement, a shaking of hands. Making a bet to consider the outcome of the debt?

I really shouldn't be doing this.

Not sitting here at a gaming hell, though it was hardly polite Society. No, it was worse than that. He was an earl, a Chance. His brother, William Chance, the Duke of Cothrom, certainly would not appreciate his younger brother getting involved with a woman with a dark past.

Assuming it *was* a dark past.

It had to be, did it not? Why else keep so much a secret? Why else show up in town alone, no guardian to see to her safety? Why else ensure he could discover nothing about her?

"No more personal questions. That's an order."

"You know, you are the only woman to even consider ordering an earl about."

"And will you obey?"

George swallowed hard as Dodo won another hand and tilted her eyes, ever so slightly, to meet his own.

And in that moment, he would have decried his own family, denied his name, and walked away from everything that meant being the Earl of Lindow.

Anything, for her.

You're being ridiculous, a voice at the back of his head whispered. *She's just a woman!*

The lurch in his stomach, and a tad farther down, proved that. He was most definitely having the reaction to her as a man to a woman.

But it wasn't anything more serious than that, was it? Surely not. He wasn't the sort of man to do something so foolish as to develop feelings for a woman. That was the sort of thing that happened to other people. Like his brothers. Both of them this year had been so foolish as to be entrapped by ladies.

George blinked. So lost had he become in his thoughts, he had been staring without seeing. Only now did he realize that the two men, Gregory and Gillingham, had departed from the table with scowling faces—leaving Dodo alone.

It took him less than half a second to make his decision.

"You know," George said conversationally, as though they were continuing a chat they'd started only moments ago, "you're not going to make yourself popular if you never let a gentleman win."

He sat opposite Dodo and grinned.

She returned his smile. "Once I meet a gentleman in this place, I shall be sure to remember that."

George chuckled, crossing his legs and hoping to goodness he was going to be able to control himself.

There was something about this woman—something that made it difficult to keep one's head. Just when you thought you had everything under control, she went and said something like that. It was most disobliging.

His pulse skipped a beat, causing physical pain. It was all George could do not to grasp at his waistcoat buttons.

He was being ridiculous. It wasn't as though he were, oh... *in love*, or anything like that.

Heaven forbid.

"You appear to be doing well," said George aloud, forcing himself to concentrate on the table before him, instead of the most inconvenient thoughts whirling through his mind.

Dodo shrugged, causing him for a moment to see far farther down her light-cream gown.

George swallowed. *Hell's bells, man, keep a hold of yourself.*

"Two pounds, so far," she said, placing her reticule in her lap as though it could be taken by a cutpurse at any moment. "Not a bad beginning to the night, I think."

He nodded, though he said nothing.

And there was another one of Miss Dodo Loughty's enigmas. This fascination with money.

No, he could not call it a fascination, for it was more than that. An obsession. He had never heard anyone speak about money as she did—certainly not someone from the gentry. Her interest in it went far beyond that which he would expect from a polite and genteel young lady.

Which either meant she was not a polite and genteel young lady... or...

Well, what could he lose by being direct? "Your lack of escort aside, you don't look like a woman short of money."

As it turned out, there was a great deal that he could lose. The cordial expression faded from Dodo's face, and she crossed her arms, becoming closed off in an instant. There was something in the curl of her shoulders, her entire demeanor: it told George very clearly that this was not a line of conversation that Dodo was going to accept.

Damn and blast it.

Cursing silently did not appear to change the situation, but it certainly made him feel better.

What was this woman truly about? He could not begin to solve the riddle she was—or the equation, which was perhaps a more accurate descriptor.

Try as he might, George could not understand her. And he understood people—was famous for it. The Earl of Lindow was a charmer, a man who always managed to coax people into doing what he wanted.

It was how he had managed to keep solvent all these years. Most older brothers wouldn't happily hand over the chunks of cash that old Cothrom had. And as for all the ladies George had managed to bed...

Strange. None of them stuck out, now. In fact, he could not recall a single one of their faces. All he could think of was—

Dodo glared. "I said, no personal questions."

"It's not a personal question," George said quietly. "I didn't ask a question, for a start."

"But you were thinking one."

He had to shrug at that. "Is it a crime to think?"

She bit her lip, evidently unwilling to declare it was so yet clearly wishing she could.

George wished to goodness he had chosen to sit closer to her. From this side of the table, there appeared to be a gulf between them that he simply could not cross.

Why must they spend all of their time together trapped on opposite sides of a table? When he was so desperate to be close to her, to feel her softness, to know the scent of—

"Why do you need to earn so much money?" George asked softly.

The question had been dancing on the tip of his tongue ever since they had first met. It was not a very personal question—that was, any question about money was personal, even he would admit. But it was not the most personal thing he could ask.

It most definitely wasn't as personal as what he wanted to ask. *Has anyone else kissed you? Was I the first? Has anyone touched you in a way that made you shiver? Have you—*

"I said," Dodo said quietly, her voice full of malevolence, "no personal questions."

George did not know what made him do it. He certainly did not plan to rise from his seat, step around the table, and drop into the seat right beside Dodo.

Yet that was precisely what he did.

"I am your friend," he said quietly. "I deserve to know—"

"You are not my friend," said Dodo calmly.

George stared.

By God, this was a turn-up for the books. He was hardly what one would describe as someone who was thin skinned, most definitely not. He'd received his fair share of critiques in his time, and jests at his expense. Old Aylesbury couldn't see him for laughing, and Cothrom had at times been very cutting.

And as for Pernrith…

George pushed aside the irritating memory of his—of that man. He certainly wasn't his brother.

But nothing anyone had ever leveled at him had the potency of what Dodo Loughty had just said.

"You are not my friend."

It would have been George's instinct to make a jest of such a remark. To say she had injured him most grievously, and he would need the kiss of life to be returned to health. Something of that nature. Something better, if he only had a moment to think.

But somehow, he could not laugh about such a thing. Her words had hurt him, deeply.

Could she see that in his looks?

"Ah," George said helplessly. "Well… What am I, then?"

It appeared that was a most difficult question. Dodo hesitated, glancing at the reticule clasped tightly in her hands before saying, to the reticule, "I don't know."

And he did not know what he wanted her to say.

The room was heating up, bodies pressing in, desperate to gamble and win. Laughter, and smoke, and the sloshing of ale and arguments in the corners.

And despite all the distraction, George could do nothing but look at her.

Dodo Loughty. No, they weren't friends. They couldn't be. A lady and a gentleman—it was rare indeed that such a friendship could grow between two such people. It would be inappropriate in the extreme, unless they had known each other while young—sometimes even then.

And yet where did that leave them? What were they to each other? It couldn't have been nothing but teacher and pupil, though there was a rather exhilarating and seduction direction that could take.

George watched Dodo swallow and tried not to think about her lips as they parted.

"I don't... I don't want to talk about myself."

"But you are the most interesting woman I have ever met," said George impulsively.

It had been the wrong thing to say. He flushed immediately at the sudden regret that poured through him, but his cheeks were surely nothing to the flaming pink on Dodo's cheeks.

He was leaning so close to her, their knees were almost touching. *Almost...*

As though startled into openness by his inappropriate revelation, Dodo peered closely. "Truly? You think I am interesting?"

How could she ask that? "I have never met a woman like you. You... You are so different to anyone I have ever met, in truth, man or woman. You... You bewitch me."

The words were perhaps far too dramatic, but George could not help himself. He was not usually given over to the dramatics, but Dodo made it impossible to be anything else.

There was a suspicious furrow across her forehead as Dodo's fingers fiddled with the reticule in her lap. "Truly? That is not an exaggeration, is it?"

George exhaled slowly. At least, he had intended to. All that seemed to happen was a jagged breath that revealed far more of his consternation than he wished.

"It is one hundred percent the truth," he said quietly. "I... I don't know what to say, Dodo. I don't know what we are to each other, what we could be. I know what we should be—polite, aloof, like Society expects. But you... I want to be your friend."

I want to be a hell of a lot more than that, George thought silently, managing to crush the words under his tongue. *But I'll settle for friend. For now.*

Dodo was examining him closely, as though attempting to spot the lie amongst the truth. Try as he might, he could not entirely hold her gaze, for it was piercing and far more prescient than anything he had ever encountered.

Gone were the days, it appeared, when the Earl of Lindow could say whatever he liked without being questioned about it afterward.

Then she inhaled deeply, and his pulse skipped a beat.

"I... I am sending money home. To my parents."

George opened his mouth, hesitated, then closed it again. There had to be more than that, surely? Elegant ladies of Dodo's caliber did not turn up mysteriously alone at places like Bath merely because they needed to earn money.

A woman, earn money?

"What of that necklace you wear when at the gaming tables? The one with the shiny, blue baubles?"

"Glass." She swallowed.

So that men, like him, would assume she was rich.

"They... They are sick. My parents."

Dodo had not really spoken, more whispered. It had been all George could do to hear her words over the chatter of McBarland's, but he could not be mistaken.

Sick. Ah.

And something George rarely felt, and would have laughed at Aylesbury for feeling, swept over him. Something he was sure he should have felt for others all the time, but no one had ever elicited it from him like this.

It was compassion. "Why the devil didn't you say so?"

Dodo looked up with fierce eyes. "What, as an introduction? Introducing myself would already be quite forward. But add that on? 'Good evening, my name is Doris Loughty, and I have two sick parents'?"

George cursed himself for his inopportune critique. "I apologize. My choice of words was not—"

"Besides, it is not ladylike to wish to earn money," she continued, holding her head high as though she were admitting to stealing the Crown jewels.

A soft smile slipped across her lips and all the desire he felt for her... Well, it did not disappear, not exactly. It was still there.

But in this moment, this delicate moment between them, there was something more important than his own needs.

It appeared he could surprise even himself.

"It may not be ladylike to wish to earn money," George said softly. "But it is very daughterly to be caring for them."

For an instant, it seemed as though Dodo were getting fired up and ready to shoot a retort back to him—but as she turned in her seat to glare, she paused.

Perhaps, George thought with a jolt, *she can see I am in earnest*. It was a strange thought, and no mistake. When was the last time he had been truly earnest about something?

Heavens. He could hardly remember.

"They are getting better?" he asked gently.

And saw immediately that he had gone too far.

The openness in Dodo's expression altered very swiftly. Mayhap if he had not been examining her carefully at the time, he would not have noticed. It was delicately done, her lips moving into a thin line, her chin lifted.

The frankness he had managed to coax out of her, God knew how, was no longer there. The mask had returned, a distance had come between them despite neither of them moving.

And that was it. George could see that he was going to get little else from Dodo this evening.

"There," she said briskly, a false grin plastered across her face. "Now you know something about me."

"And is that all?" George asked, knowing he was pushing his luck.

"What else is there?" Dodo asked airily.

He bit his lip.

So much else, he wanted to say. *I want to know about your parents, what ails them, what can be done. What siblings you have—surely, you cannot be bearing this burden all alone? Why has no one come with you to Bath?*

I want to know what you read, what you love, what music you loathe. I want to watch the sunshine pour onto your face, and the rain wash away your tears, and laughter fill you up. I want to make you laugh, Dodo Loughty.

George swallowed. He could not say any of those things.

He may not have had a full understanding of Dodo, but he knew well enough now not to push his luck. Not if he didn't want to risk completely pushing her away.

"A hand of cards?" Dodo asked with a bright and stiff expression.

George wavered.

He could stay. He could remain and attempt to winkle a few more details about Dodo from her. He could stay and hope she warmed to him, try to tease her into getting into bed with him—though now that he knew the reason for her desire for funds, he thought that would take priority over any chance of her ruining herself with him.

But staying would also mean punishment. Being close to her and not touching her. Wanting to be intimate with her and seeing her close herself off again and again, refusing to let him near.

And that was before one considered just how much money he'd lose.

George forced himself to rise, shaking his head. "No."

"No?" Dodo repeated, her voice full of surprise.

It was painful, but he had to do it. He couldn't stay. Not today—though he would see her again, he was sure of that. It was impossible to stay away. "No, I think… I think I'll go. I'll see you soon, Miss Loughty."

Chapter Nine

October 4, 1812

"Honestly, I don't know why you brought me here," said Dodo awkwardly.

It was the question that had been playing on her mind ever since the note had arrived. After their, well... awkward parting at McBarland's, she had presumed their lessons were at an end.

Which meant the end of a perfectly good source of income, too. Just when her mother's letter had arrived, scolding her for her mad idea of staying in Bath all alone, but making no mention of sending her aunt or anyone else after her, instead decrying the vast number of bills which had arrived. How they were supposed to pay it, only God knew...

But the subsequent post had brought another missive. This one was shorter, far more to the point. It warmed Dodo to a much greater extent.

> *Miss Loughty,*
>
> *You would do me a great honor if you would give me the pleasure of your company tomorrow at the Bath racecourse. Meet me by the North Gate and wear sturdy boots. 11 o'clock?*
>
> *Your friend,*
> *Lindow*

Dodo had swallowed hard when she'd first read it. *Your friend.*

"I am your friend. I deserve to know—"

"You are not my friend."

It was a tease, of that she was certain. But at the same time, there appeared to be no malice in the note. No hatred toward her, no anger as there had seemed to be days ago. He truly seemed to wish to see her.

It had taken her five minutes to read the blessed thing, ten minutes to find paper, then almost an hour to think of a reply. Which was pitiful, when she considered what she'd managed to come up with.

My lord,

That sounds agreeable. I will see you there.

Doris Loughty

Fortunately, Mrs. Bryson had proven less of an obstacle to meet up with George than Dodo had expected. The landlady, though ostensibly there to act as chaperone for any of the young ladies in the boarding house, had enough to occupy her that Dodo's continued insistence that she was visiting a lady friend in town never seemed to draw further inspection from the woman.

That, or she was glad enough of Dodo continuing to make rent and would not ask questions, even when handing off letters clearly written by gentlemen.

An *invitation* from a gentleman.

Even now, as George beamed at her and Dodo attempted not to slip in the mud that had been churned up by the hundreds of people present at the Bath racecourse, she was finding it difficult to work this man out.

What on earth did he want with her?

Not just here, but at all. There had been no mention of lessons in the fifteen minutes since he had met her at the North Gate, coat pulled tightly around himself against the cold. No mention of cards, or mathematics—more's the pity. That was solid ground.

And so, she asked the question. Not that she'd received a reply yet.

"What was that?" asked George politely.

Dodo forced herself to ask the question again. "I don't know why you brought me here."

He grinned, a swooping in her stomach making it almost impossible for Dodo to remain upright. "To put your theory into practice, of course!"

Precisely what theory he meant, she was not sure. He most definitely could not mean anything about her very basic knowledge about horse riding. She could ride—every genteel young lady could—but her family had not owned a horse for... goodness. Far longer than she could remember.

If George were so foolish as to place her on the back of a horse, she would promptly slip off the other side. It would be the only way to stay safe.

It simply couldn't be horse riding. So... what?

From what she could see, attending the races was more a social event than a sporting one. A sharp, pricking sensation gnawed at the back of her throat as she realized she was brazenly here in the daytime with a gentleman, without a chaperone in sight. She ought to have pretended to be a widow when she came to town to allow for greater movement without fear of staring eyes. Everywhere one looked, there were members of the *ton* in their autumn finest. A few were wearing winter coats, as the temperature had dropped so dramatically overnight.

Perhaps she could suggest an aunt was seeking shelter from the cold in the nearest building should anyone ask. Yes, that would have to do.

The white fences that lined the racecourse glittered in the low autumn sun, and excited chatter surrounded the whole place as horses were led this way and that, coats gleaming, jockeys with serious faces. She could even see—

"I must say, you look... you look... you look," said George softly.

Dodo blinked. "I look?"

"Y'know," he said vaguely, waving a hand. "Good."

Heat suffused her cheeks as she looked down.

She really shouldn't have done it. She never would have done, if she had not won ten guineas—ten guineas!—on that bet she'd made in McBarland's with Mr. Gillingham. Dodo had never expected it to come off, not really, and to have such riches so suddenly...

Well, as her mother would have said, it had gone to her head.

And so while Dodo had carefully exchanged the guineas for a five-pound note—five pounds!—and sent it on its merry way back to Croscombe and her parents, she had kept the rest of the money. And spent it. Just a little of it.

"I've never seen such an elegant pelisse," George said, his face flushed for some reason. "Very... very pretty."

Dodo nodded weakly.

It had cost an entire pound. *What I was thinking...*

She knew what she'd been thinking. She'd been thinking, she'd reasoned with herself as they'd continued along the racecourse, other spectators eagerly watching for the next race to begin, that winter was coming. She did not have a proper winter pelisse. That was it. That was all. It was merely a matter of practicality.

The fact that the velvet-trimmed, fur-lined, elegantly embroidered pelisse was beautiful...

Neither here nor there.

"George—my lord, I mean," Dodo said hastily, casting a look about them. No one seemed to have noticed her slip-up. "You mentioned my 'theory,' but you still haven't properly answered my question."

"Which is? Oh! Careful now," said George, grabbing her hand as her foot slipped. "Better take my arm."

It wasn't a question and he did not act as though it were one. Instead, George casually slipped Dodo's hand into his arm and continued walking along.

And he still, she thought with a heat spreading through her arm that had absolutely nothing to do with the proximity of the earl, *hasn't answered my question. My theory of what?*

Strange. It hardly seemed to matter now.

"I suppose you don't know anything about racehorses?"

George's voice was light, but the question struck pain into Dodo, which she hoped was not visible on her face.

The pain was guilt. *And it is quite right that I should feel it*, she thought wretchedly. After what she'd done.

She'd betrayed him.

Well, not exactly *betrayed*. Dodo was not the sort of person to risk a person's life—that would be outrageous. And it wasn't impossible to do what she'd done without the information George had so unknowingly bestowed upon her.

"It's a shame Scandal of Lancelot isn't doing too well. My jockey tells me the beast has a weak left flank, though I don't believe it."

"To be sure—as long as Scandal of Lancelet doesn't lean to the left as he always does..."

It isn't as though he asked me to keep information a secret, Dodo thought woefully as they turned a corner and started around the racetrack. So, she'd used the information with the assistance of Mr. Gregory and Mr. Gillingham to bet against George Chance, Earl of Lindow. She'd won ten guineas. Fine.

It wasn't his money! It had been what's his name—the man, from McBarland's. He hadn't been too pleased to be shown up by a lady, to be sure, but Dodo had received her money, and George was none the wiser, and...

And surely, that was all that mattered?

Any feeling of shame had not stopped her from making the bet again. And again.

Even after she'd realized George was betting on his own horses, so she was, in effect, taking money from the earl himself.

"Dodo?" George said gently.

She looked up into his face and knew that it was wrong. Betting against—he was not a friend, and she still had no idea what to consider him, but he had trusted her. He had spoken before her with no thought to the consequences, a particularly Lindow trait.

And she had used that information to win, gambling against his horses.

Her father would have been mortified. But then, Dodo knew, he was happily receiving the efforts of her winnings—the sight of the money she'd sent home had apparently overridden any objections he might have had over her bold plan to travel to Bath alone. Almost one hundred pounds in the last few weeks, all thanks to George's accidental insights. Little snippets here, a little detail here—it all changed the odds. And someone with a mathematical brain may just be able to work it all out.

With the help of two other men. Men most eager to earn their money back and then some after she'd trounced them during that first game.

Dodo swallowed.

One hundred pounds, she told herself severely, *is nothing to an earl, and everything to my family*. A proper doctor would no doubt finally be called, not one of those quacks who charged through the nose for salves and potions that didn't do a thing. Debts could be paid. The roof fixed. A second maid could be hired to help her mother. Life could return once again, for a time, to normal.

"Are you feeling quite all right?" asked George softly, placing his hand on hers as it rested on her arm. "You look... You don't look well."

They had stopped walking. Dodo hadn't been aware of that, she had been so lost in her thoughts, and as she looked up at George, his brows drawn together and pursed lips—all concern and care—guilt twisted within her.

And the worst of it is, she thought dully, *I am falling in love with him.*

It was most inconvenient. Though she'd be the first to admit her trip to Bath and continued activity without a chaperone will have destroyed any chance of a suitable marriage should it be discovered, there had been a time when she'd imagined marriage as an inevitability. And every time she'd imagined that inevitability, love was supposed to come after marriage, once a suitable suitor had been suited up—it shouldn't be sprung upon her without warning.

He was a good man.

George smiled, his light-blue eyes crinkling and a frown on his face. "Perhaps I made a mistake to bring you out here. Why don't I take you back to—"

"No!" Dodo said hastily.

It had only been when he had walked away, that night in the gaming hell, that she'd realized just how much she'd enjoyed his company. His closeness. His touch…

Definitely not his touch.

George squeezed her hand.

Fine, his touch. But the point was—the point, Dodo attempted to grasp on to, was that George would never speak to her again with such friendliness if he found out what she had been doing. He might never speak to her again. At all. Ever.

And if that occurred…

How was it possible that it would be a wrench to her very spirit never to know him again? What would she do, if the man she was growing to love saw her for what she truly was?

A liar?

"You asked me what I knew about horseracing," Dodo said, attempting to distract him from her momentary panic. "Pretend like I don't know anything. You will have to be the teacher today."

Yes, she had pitched that just right. George's chest swelled with excitement and importance as he stepped forward, pulling her along with him.

"Right. In that case, we'll start right at the beginning. Each of these races look the same, perhaps, to the untrained eye, but there are subtle differences in both length and jumps that alter them greatly. First, consider…"

Dodo had spent a great number of years of her life being bored by men.

Oh, it wasn't their fault. Probably. It was just that they chose interests in life that she found incredibly dull, and without any way to integrate with mathematics at all, so what was the point of them?

Fishing? Hunting? The watching out for specific birds that migrated? Dull, dull, dull—and those were just her father's pursuits.

And so, like many ladies, Dodo had learned how to keep a subtly vague expression on her face for just such an occasion. Enough interest to make the gentleman in question believe she was still listening, but nebulous enough so she would not be required to answer questions later.

The instant George had started speaking, Dodo began to arrange her features in just such an expression… and discovered to her great surprise that it was unnecessary.

George was… interesting.

"There, you see?" he said passionately, pointing as a herd of galloping horses raced around the corner where they were standing. "Because of the breeding line of the forerunner, he'll tire before he reaches the last bend. It's the stamina of the Arab line—it's vastly different from…"

Dodo attempted to pay attention and found to her astonishment that she wanted to. And could. George was an excellent conversationalist at the worst of times, but she had never seen him like this. Overcome with excitement, full of passion, he seemed to be more and more alive the longer they stood here.

He was dazzling.

"—so that's why it interests me so much," he finished, then he appeared to realize he had been lecturing for nigh on fifteen minutes. "I, uh… I hope that wasn't too dull for you."

"'Dull'?" repeated Dodo.

His face fell. "Well, it's not to everyone's taste, but—"

She interrupted him. "It is fascinating." She was rewarded with a brilliant smile. "I can see what you mean. Without any knowledge, it does indeed look just like horses going around and around. But there is so much more than that, isn't there?"

So much more, she attempted not to think, *that I can now use when it comes to betting on the horses. Betting against you.*

"Come and meet them," George said impulsively, pulling her away from the racecourse and toward what appeared to be a series of wooden buildings.

Dodo blinked. "'Them'?"

"The horses, of course!"

It was probably only because he was two of the horses' owners, Dodo was certain, that they were allowed to do it. No one attempted to stop them as they stepped into the stable yard, people running about here, there, and everywhere. Trainers and feeders, jockeys and footmen, men in livery and girls bringing out bowls of steaming hot stew and mugs of ale. There was excited chatter everywhere, bitter arguments in corners, and a few jockeys eying her up in a way that made Dodo feel most uncomfortable.

Her grip tightened on George's arm.

"It's quite all right," he said quietly, as though immediately understanding her concern. "Nothing will happen to you. They're quite safe, really, even if they are a tad bold in appreciating a lady. Besides, you are with me."

No further explanation appeared necessary. Dodo opened her mouth to ask, but then she saw the way people treated the Earl of

Lindow as he walked through.

With... respect.

It was most unusual. She had presumed as a horse owner, George would have received nods and stares, but nothing else. He was, after all, not a horseman himself.

At least, that was what she had presumed. But as George approached a particular pair of stalls, a few of the stablehands and jockeys approached him with grins and proffered hands.

"Lord Lindow, sir! Wonderful to see you, did you get my note about—"

"—changed over the feed as you suggested, m'lord, and as you can see—"

"—never saw anything like it, those rogues must have done something to their mares. It's something astonishing how they—"

And as he shook hands, and nodded at people's words, and inclined his head at those who bowed, Dodo clung on to his arm and... stared.

This, perhaps, was the most earl-like she had ever seen him. Oh, it was clear that George was a reprobate of the best kind, and the little he had spoken of his family proved that he was the black sheep. The outsider.

But here? Here he held court as only a prince could, and Dodo could see that it came as naturally to him as breathing. He probably didn't even realize how spectacular he was.

Something lurched in her stomach.

She realized.

"Here he is," George said, disentangling the two of them from all those who surrounded them with a simple jerk of the head. The jockeys, stablehands, and trainers all melted away as George and Dodo stepped into the stable, away from the stares of others. "Honor of Guinevere."

Dodo looked up into the wise eyes of a magnificent horse, who had stuck his head out of his stall to see what all the fuss was about. He was beautiful, a fine beast with impossibly long lashes and a hint in his eyes that spoke of true intelligence.

The little stable was really nothing more than a lean-to. The two stalls opened out onto the courtyard where the horses could poke their heads out, but they currently faced inside the stable, which was covered and walled in. The door shut softly behind them.

They were now enclosed in warmth and the smell of hay and darkness. And alone.

"So... So this must be Scandal of Lancelot," she said softly, slipping her hand from George's arm to walk over to the second of the two stalls. "How is his flank?"

When she glanced back, George was beaming. "Goodness, you remembered! You're the only person I discussed that with and I thought I'd bored you to tears. But you remembered!"

Dodo smiled weakly as self-reproach crept through her. "Well. You know. I listen to everything you say."

He grinned. "Just as long as you don't tell anyone his secret—that if he gets overtaken on the first corner, he loses all hope and gives up! My word, it's pleasant to have someone to talk to about this sort of thing."

"Yes, very pleasant," Dodo said as blandly as she could.

Especially when I am using it against you in the betting pool, she thought but did not say.

How could she? How could she reveal the treachery to which she had sunk, just to get a little coin?

It wasn't a *little* coin, though. And the amount would make far more of a difference to her and hers, than him and his.

"You're the first person I've introduced him to, outside of his jockey and the stablehands," George said fondly, reaching up to rub the beast's nose. He nickered softly, pressing his nose into his master's hand.

Dodo stared first at George, then the beast. "What... Truly?"

He nodded. "I haven't trusted anyone else."

And a sense of connection, a togetherness Dodo had only experienced once before in her life, swept over her. It was the same sensation she'd experienced when George had kissed her in his smoking room. A sense that in all the world, there was no one who understood her, except him. The thought that she had seen a part of George Chance, Earl of Lindow, a part he had never permitted anyone save herself to see...

George's eyes, blazing with something she did not understand, met hers. Then he had moved, taken three strides across the small stable, and was pinning her against the wall.

"I know you said no kissing," he said in such a low voice, it was almost a growl. "And I will hold myself back, Dodo, if you want me to."

"But—But you don't want to?" She gasped, hardly knowing what she was saying as a rush of desire flowed through her.

Oh, this was heavenly: to feel herself pressed up against the wall, to know that mere feet away there were people milling about, not guessing what was occurring in this tiny stable...

George leaned his head to press his forehead against hers. When he spoke, it was with a desperation she had never heard. "I want you, Dodo. I want you."

And that was when she entirely lost her head.

Before Dodo knew what she was doing, she was obeying the instincts in her body rather than the frantic thoughts in her mind. She had leaned forward and lifted her lips to his.

The instant they'd touched, she knew she never wanted to do anything but this ever again. It was exhilarating, his hands clasping her arms, his lips worshipping hers, the two of them standing in a stable where they could be discovered at any moment.

At least, that was what Dodo probably would have thought, if she could have thought anything at all.

Pleasure was pouring through her body as George's tongue teased upon her mouth and delved into its depths, shooting greater ripples of desire through her body. Her stomach had dropped, or melted, or something—all Dodo knew was that there was a scalding sensation between her legs that was burning, burning for something. George's fingers slipped from her arms to her waist and swiftly moved lower, cupping her buttocks and pulling her against his hips.

Dodo moaned, unable to help herself, and somehow, the sound sparked something in George. His kisses grew more passionate, his tongue teasing out exquisite shivers of sensation, and—

The door to the little stable banged open. George sprung back.

"Ah," said an amused voice. "Another one of your—"

"This is my friend, Miss Loughty," said George darkly, glaring at the man.

Dodo blinked, a cacophony of shame, remorse, and the final fading ripples of desire making it most difficult to think. She could, however, speak. "Good day." She recognized the man. The similarities between him and George when so close together were even more obvious.

"This is my arrogant and ill-timed brother, the Marquess of Aylesbury," George said with a wry laugh. "Whom I am sure has an excuse for his terribly irritating interruption."

Heat blossomed over Dodo's cheeks and she wished to goodness there was somewhere to hide.

The marquess who had sent her to McBarland's. At a party she had intended without a chaperone, though she wasn't sure that faux pas had been discovered then. What awful luck he should discover them not only alone, but...

Well. Kissing.

If the marquess chooses not to be discreet, we will be forced into... into an engagement.

The thought rocked Dodo's body so soundly that she lost track of the conversation for a moment. When she was able to focus, it was to see George's brow furrowed and an unmistakable look of irritation in his eyes.

"—make him think he can come here?" he spat.

The Marquess of Aylesbury shrugged. "He is our brother, after all. There's a concert at the Pump Rooms later in the week Florence and I will be attending, assuming I can encourage her out the door, though he couldn't get tickets. He probably just wanted to see you—"

"He's no brother of—he knows full well what I think of him!"

Dodo glanced between the two men in curious astonishment. Was this, perhaps, the answer to why there appeared to be conflicting reports on the bastard Chance brother?

"You don't have to see him, naturally. I'll take him home for luncheon," Lord Aylesbury was saying, albeit coldly. "I just thought you'd like the opportunity to—"

"I don't want to see that man, and that's the end of it," George said flatly. "Go on, tell him for me that if he wants to make a scene by shaming me with his presence, he can do so elsewhere."

Dodo watched the marquess bite his lip.

"You don't have to be so harsh on—"

"Pernrith knows how I feel about him," George repeated. "Now be off with you."

His brother sighed. "Fine. Just don't give away any tips to the ladies, Lindow," he said with a wink at Dodo. "I'd hate to see you lose even more coin on the betting!"

He left the little stable with a laugh that echoed around the stable yard. Dodo's heart raced. It was not the laugh of a man who'd been scandalized, who was about to announce his brother's engagement to the *ton*. The marquess had never even asked after her chaperone.

George turned to her with a grimace. "I do apologize. There was no need for you to hear—"

"Pernrith," Dodo said curiously. "Who is he?"

For a moment, a shadow passed across his face. Then he smiled, though it was a tight one. "My brother—my half-brother, if you must know. He... My father..."

His voice trailed away into an awkward silence.

Dodo nodded wordlessly. Well, it happened everywhere, didn't it? Old Mr. Michaels in Croscombe had *suffered an indiscretion*, in the words of her father. The boy had been raised with the family, but there had been discomfort in the whole village. There was no reason why it couldn't happen to dukes just as it did to butchers.

"And you don't like him," she ventured.

George snorted. "No. No, I don't."

It was on the tip of her tongue to ask further questions, but before Dodo could speak, he drew himself up and smiled more naturally.

"Now, come and watch a race—Honor of Guinevere will be heading out in less than an hour. And if you want to make things more interesting, you could always bet on it!"

Guilt tore through Dodo as they stepped out into the blinding light of the stable yard and started to make their way back to the racecourse.

It appeared they were not going to discuss the kiss. The heavenly kiss. The kiss that had awoken desires in her that she had never... that she could never...

"Come, you must make a bet. It is a part of coming out to the races, and I certainly know you to be a gambling woman," George teased, perhaps mistaking her silence for nerves.

"I suppose I could bet a... a small amount," she said quietly.

He grinned. "Will you use your mathematics to win?"

Dodo's smile faded. "Yes. Yes, my mathematics. That's what I'll use to win."

Chapter Ten

October 7, 1812

"AND IS IT *true that you are courting a Miss Loughty?"*
"*What business is it of—*"
"*Courting a woman?"*
"*Miss Loughty? I've never heard of her! Who is—*"
"*I am not courting Miss Loughty—I'm not courting anyone.*"

Now George came to think about it, if he saw someone swanning about Bath after a woman like he was swanning over Miss Dodo Loughty, well… he would come to the same conclusion.

That he was… involved.

It was vitally important he not give that impression. And not just because the woman could not produce a chaperone if asked. Better no one took note of them together. After all, only bad things could come of it. He would not wish to raise hopes where hopes could not be raised.

It wasn't as though he was—well. Going to offer marriage, or anything. He'd never considered marriage in his life. Why would he?

And that was precisely why George decided, when he woke up the morning after taking Dodo—taking Miss Loughty to the races—not to see her that day. Or the day after. He knew he had been reckless with Miss Loughty's reputation to begin with, just being seen with her without a chaperone present. But he'd been so eager for her to experience what he loved about the races, he'd gotten too lax.

Far too lax.

He could stay away.

After all, he was fully in control of himself, wasn't he? He was a man, and a man near the age of thirty, and what's more, a man with a title, education, wealth. All the requirements of a sensible chap. All he had to do was not see Dodo. Not write to her, not happen by McBarland's, not accidently-on-purpose meander to the direction where he knew she was staying...

Simple. Stay away from Miss Dodo—Miss Doris Loughty.

By the evening of the third day, though, he was waiting outside the Assembly Rooms nervously, checking his pocket watch.

"She's late," George muttered, heart hammering.

It had been a foolish thing to do. The moment, however, his brother Aylesbury had mentioned in passing when they'd met at the stables that a concert was tonight, he had known what he would do.

Even after all of his stern agreements with himself that morning.

After all, his sister-in-law would be present. At a glance, their party might appear most respectable. Though he wasn't actually sure they would see his brother and his wife tonight, considering he had not told them of his plans.

But if anyone asked, he was not here alone with an unmarried lady. His sister-in-law had extended the invitation to a new friend.

There. That would do it. No need to explain his brother's wife had yet to meet this new friend.

The sun had dipped below the horizon, painting the white stone of Bath a splashy, orange color. It looked beautiful, and perhaps George would have appreciated it, if it had not been for the growing noise behind him in the Assembly Rooms.

The place was packed. The two tickets he had managed to purchase were pressed in his pocket, and if she did not hurry up soon, there would be little opportunity for them to claim the best seats. There would be naught but the very back—though he supposed that wasn't the end of the world.

The end of the world, George was rapidly discovering, was not seeing—

"This really isn't my thing, you know," said an austere voice behind him.

George whirled around, a grin across his face. "I think you'll find it will... will be."

And that was all he could manage. After that, his breath was taken away and he was forced to simply stare.

Dodo was frowning. Perhaps on another woman, that would ruin her beauty, but for some reason, it merely enhanced what was already there.

Elegant, black hair, piled up with pins, a single curl falling on the left hand. Brilliant, dark-brown eyes, flashing with amusement or irritation—he couldn't tell which. A gown that was—

George swallowed. A gown that surely should not have been allowed, not in polite circles. Not that he had any complaints. The thing was a picture of sophistication, sweeping over Dodo's soft skin and making it all the more difficult to keep his hands to himself.

The picture was completed by a single chain of gold around her neck that fell into her—

George swallowed again—hard. *Good God, man, hold yourself together!*

"I don't think I will like it," said Dodo, her expression wary. "A concert?"

He nodded, not yet trusting his voice.

Because the thing was, George knew, it wasn't merely Dodo's beauty that held him captivated. It didn't hurt, certainly, but it was no longer what drew him in.

What *was* drawing him in, he couldn't precisely put his finger on. He knew what he *wanted* to put his finger on, but—

Come on, you rake!

"I can't stay away from you," George said simply. "I had to see you."

Maybe Dodo had expected a long speech about the importance of music, how delightful it was to listen to it played well, the chance to be seen at one of Bath's most prestigious environs—well, for gentlemen and ladies *with* chaperones, in any case.

Instead, she flushed.

And that is why, George thought to himself. Staying away from Dodo was impossible, even when he wished to. Not that he could recall wishing to for a long time.

There was something about her, about the way she saw the world, which was quite different to anyone else he had ever met. The mathematical mind in her was something... well, not unique. She would undoubtedly have something to say about the probability of finding someone on the whole planet who was like her.

But still. They wouldn't be Dodo.

"I thought you were busy," Dodo said, taking George's arm so naturally, it brought a lump to his throat. "You said, at the racecourse, you would have to spend a great deal of time there."

George hesitated as they stepped into the splashing light of the Assembly Rooms hall.

He had said that. And he had meant it—he did need to spend more time at the racecourse. Perhaps then he would be able to track down the leak.

It had been Cothrom who had spotted it, of course. The man had a mind like a Peeler, always looking for the worst in a situation, always expecting a traitor. It was one of the traits George disliked about his oldest brother, though he had to admit it was useful.

"You must have noticed," William had said only last night.

And George had shaken his head, mystified that he had not.

"You may be looking too much into this," said William's wife, Alice, with furrowed brows directed toward her husband. "You do not wish to work up your brother, make him suspect—"

"But Cothrom's right—it *is* very fishy," said Aylesbury with a frown, pointing with his fork. "I mean how else could this person, whoever it is, bet against you so thoroughly?"

"They c-could j-just know a g-great deal ab-bout racehorses," pointed out his wife, Florence.

George had glanced at her. Florence Chance, the new Marchioness of Aylesbury. John had chosen the woman he had said he couldn't live without. He couldn't see it. Aylesbury and he had been the scoundrels, the two Chance brothers who had bought wine and cards and women, and had an altogether delicious time.

Seeing him like this... a husband... and with a wife who was so shy, so insipid—

"The Arabian b-bloodline of Heart of Fire, and her m-mother, have been disp-proven by the 1807 investigation into f-false docummentation in Rome," said Florence softly, taking a sip from her wine glass. "I hope you knew th-that."

Her husband laughed. Only then did George realize his mouth was open.

Good heavens. Well, that would explain some of Aylesbury's attraction.

"So who could it be?" asked Aylesbury curiously.

George bit his lip. "Well, I'd hate to think any of my servants were capable of... but then, I have had so many complaints about Northrup—"

"Your butler?"

He nodded his assent to Alice's question. "He's a rather taciturn man, and to be honest, I've presumed that my footmen's dislike of him was the typical sort of a superior being disliked merely for giving orders. But now..."

He hesitated. It wasn't his place to slander a man's character, but someone was certainly betraying him. Who could it have been?

"What does Pernrith think about this?" asked Cothrom. "Where is he, anyway?"

The table fell silent. All eyes turned to George.

He knew they would and had his answer ready. It was simple. "He was not invited."

Cothrom frowned at his reproach.

"Ah," said Alice lightly.

"But he's always invited to our family luncheons—" began Aylesbury.

"I suppose he is, when Cothrom is issuing the invitations," George had said curtly, heat rising. Why, even when he wasn't here, was Pernrith able to sow such discord between himself and his brothers? *The blaggard!* "Look, forget about him."

"But—"

"The point is, someone is leaking information about my horses—Honor of Guinevere and Scandal of Lancelot—and they're damned well betting against me!"

And it was infuriating. George had never spotted the pattern, but of course now Cothrom had mentioned it, it was impossible not to. Despite the changes he'd made to his steeds' feed, exercise, training—nothing seemed to matter. There was always some man out there who knew better.

The following day, he had attempted to delicately inquire around the stable yard at the racecourse, but any hint of suspicion was vehemently denied.

Naturally, no one would admit it. After a very awkward conversation with the stablemaster, and an even more awkward conversation with his own jockey, George had been forced to throw his hands up in the air and—

"George?"

George blinked.

How on earth had they gotten here?

"You were completely away with the fairies," said Dodo quietly. "What were you thinking about?"

About all this damned money I'm losing, George wanted to say. But he didn't. He'd become so lost in his thoughts that he hadn't even noticed they'd walked the length of the Assembly Rooms hallway and were now waiting in line to show their tickets to the footman standing solemnly by the door.

He was here with Dodo Loughty, he tried to remind himself. *Be present!*

But it was difficult. Thoughts of liars and thieves, traitors in his own midst, and what on earth he would have to do to catch them in the act all flittered through his mind as George wordlessly offered out his tickets to the footman.

Who bowed. "My lord, Miss Loughty."

"We're meeting my brother and his wife inside," George said quickly, ignoring the way Dodo cocked his head up at him. "My sister-in-law invited Miss Loughty."

As his smile never wavered, the footman didn't seem to care, though it was not only for his benefit that George had spoken so loudly.

"Please." With a gesture, the footman welcomed them into the Assembly Rooms.

"Your brother and his wife?" Dodo whispered. "She invited me?"

"Your chaperone for the evening," George said without moving his lips much. "I didn't actually tell them we were coming. We probably won't actually see them."

"Oh. Good idea. I should have thought—" Dodo gasped as they stepped forward, staring about her as though she'd never seen anything so wonderful.

Which, George thought with relish, could possibly be true. Mayhap he was giving Dodo her first taste of… well, what Cothrom put as "how the other half lived." Which was a trite phrase, and it would never catch on.

The initial impression one was given was of space and light. Candles glittered from the remarkable chandelier that glittered above them, and from the candelabra built into the wall scones all around the room. The barreled ceiling allowed the noise of the place to gently echo, resounding much as it would do a cathedral. The best of Bath Society were mingling about as musicians sat arranging music on stands, and there was a presence, a sort of reverence in the way that people were looking around them.

"It's magnificent," said Dodo softly as they walked toward the mass of chairs that had been set out.

George swelled with pride, as though it were his very own Assembly Room. "Yes, the marble columns are—"

"I couldn't give a fig for your columns—look at that!"

Confused, George halted and stared up where she was pointing. At... *the chandelier?*

"It's a chandelier," he said, feeling foolish.

"It's designed around the cascading formula of the Fibonacci sequence," she said in a hushed tone.

George blinked. He looked at Dodo for a moment, her eyes wide and a smile lilting her lips, then back at the chandelier.

It was... a chandelier. Crystals and metal, with candles that flickered as the door closed to the hall. The concert was about to start, they hadn't found their pair of seats, and Dodo was interested in a chandelier because of some Italian man?

"We need to find seats," he hissed.

"But it's a marvel. How did they do it?" wondered Dodo, still staring at the chandelier as George attempted to shepherd her to empty seats near the back. "The complexity alone..."

He glanced at her with a wry expression as they took their seats, her words continuing in a thrumming murmur to his left.

Only Dodo could come to such an exalted place as the Bath Assembly Rooms and notice not the spectacular orchestra, or the impressive people in attendance, *or even,* a small voice wondered, *himself...*

No. It was the chandelier. Because of mathematics.

What a shame he cared for her so.

"—idea why everyone is looking at us?"

George blinked. "I beg your pardon."

"Everyone here," Dodo said, lowering her voice to naught but a whisper as the musicians straightened up and gentle applause echoed around the room. "Even with the conductor now here, people aren't looking at them. They're looking at us."

Opening his mouth to immediately disabuse her of that notion, George glanced about to settle for himself just how incorrect she was.

He closed his mouth. *I really needed to get more accustomed to Dodo being right about these things*, he thought with a chuckle.

"Geor—Lord Lindow!" she whispered.

"Ouch!"

She had grasped his arm too tightly for his liking, but any reprimand that may have poured from his mouth was halted by the uncomfortable expression on her face.

"Everyone is staring."

George shifted in his seat. "Not every—"

Dodo raised an eyebrow, cutting him short without a word.

Stomach lurching, he tried not to think about the multitude of eyes that kept turning to stare at him. At them.

His brother and his wife weren't among them, not as far as he could see. Had Florence changed her mind about the concert? What would their excuse be for Dodo's chaperone now?

"And is it true that you are courting a Miss Loughty?"

Well, he'd known this would happen. Mistakes would be made, after all, and it appeared the whole of the *ton* was about to make another one. After all, he was most definitely not courting Dodo. Miss Loughty. *Damn.*

Because these feelings weren't love. They were... admiration. Yes, that was it—he admired her.

Admired her beauty. And her mind. And her cleverness. The way she teased him, sending jolts of desire mingled with need, with a spice of—

Dodo moved to slip her hand free of George's arm, and he instinctively caught it, holding her tight.

"No."

"But everyone—"

"That isn't going to stop the gossip, not now. It's too late," he said quietly as the musicians tuned their instruments. "We shall just hope enough of them heard me say you're here as my sister-in-law's guest. We'll only cause more of a scandal if it looks as though we have fallen out—or I have offended you."

Dodo's eyebrow was still raised. "And that is likely to help, is it?"

George grinned. "Perhaps not."

And discovered… he did not care.

It was a strange sensation. Oh, not a lack of care. George had spent most of his life moving through the world not caring a jot about the consequences of his actions. Mostly because there rarely were some—who would argue with an earl?—but also because his oldest brother, Cothrom, usually tidied things up for him nicely.

Until William had married, of course. That had been a blasted nuisance.

But this was completely different to the disgrace he'd managed to get himself twisted up in over the years. Somehow, having all this gossip centered around himself and Dodo did not vex him in the slightest.

In a way… he rather enjoyed it.

So long as no one questioned the lady's reputation. He would need to continue to be careful about that.

Not at the sacrifice of no longer seeing her, though.

The musicians halted and George looked over to them. The conductor was standing before the orchestra—at least, he was half-certain it was an orchestra. It looked like an orchestra. How many instruments did you need to make an orchestra?

"Where are your brother and his wife?" Dodo asked quietly, her gaze darting about the room.

George shook his head and put a finger to his lips.

The conductor tapped his baton on the music stand before him and all the musicians prepared themselves. Violins were placed on shoulders, flutes were positioned just below mouths, and a man holding two tiny bells frowned hard at the music before him.

And then it began.

It was beautiful, in its way. George had always liked music, but he didn't love it like—

Dear God, he'd almost thought of Pernrith there.

Still, he could appreciate a well-scored piece of music when he heard it, and he knew a poor set of musicians when he heard them. And these were good. It wasn't long before his foot was tapping, his head swaying to the beat of the—

"I told you," hissed a delicate voice in his ear. "Music simply isn't my thing."

George glanced at Dodo. There was the glare again. It matched the one she'd arrived with, but he was starting to read Dodo Loughty far better than he had when they had first met.

And this wasn't a glare. Not really. This was her sense of inadequacy, he knew it. She felt out of her depth—certainly not a position his Dodo wanted to be in.

George's stomach lurched. *His Dodo?*

"I should be at McBarland's, earning more money."

Guilt seared through where mere worry had been before. "You should?"

Of course she should. How could he be so blind—had she not intimated to him, much against her inclinations it had appeared, just why she needed so much coin?

"I... I am sending money home. To my parents. They... They are sick."

George's chest constricted as contrition continued to pour through it. He was a selfish brigand and no mistake. Here he was, demanding her company greedily, crafting an elaborate ruse to excuse her lack of chaperone, at great risk to her reputation, because he was desperate to see her—he could admit that in the privacy of his own mind, even if nowhere else—and here she was, worrying about others.

"I mean... I suppose I had such luck on the horses that I do not need to tonight," Dodo admitted on her exhale. "But still. I may not be so lucky next week. I need to take every opportunity I—"

"There's an outside chance you won't need to," said George foolishly.

She met his gaze. "Why?"

He hesitated.

Because I don't want you going there any more, he wanted to say. *Because it's dangerous. Because I worry about you.*

Foolish things to say. Far better to say, "I can give you money, if you—"

"I will not be bought," Dodo said fiercely.

"Shh!" muttered several people in the Assembly Room's audience.

George's cheeks were burning at the misunderstanding. "I didn't mean—"

"Shhhhhh!"

He subsided, hating that he had created such a situation. Surely, Dodo could not think... He would never treat her as a—

"Music is completely alien to me," murmured Dodo in his ear as though they had not so recently been shushed. She leaned close and made it difficult, as her breath blossomed over his neck, for him to concentrate on her actual words. "I mean, who can understand this?"

"Ah, but what if you don't think of it as music?"

Dodo stared, her frown deepening. "You... You want me to ignore the concert you've brought me to?"

George stifled a laugh as his pulse skipped a beat. "Not exactly."

It had felt like an excellent idea at the time, but now they were here, he wasn't sure. It had felt so obvious—so logical. But now...

Well, it was so much harder to think, wasn't it? Sitting here with Dodo pressed up against him, her hand in his arm, breathing her in...

Oh, dear. Something discomforting and most inappropriate to happen in a public place was, most unfortunately, happening in a public place.

George attempted to shift his breeches to make the protrusion less obvious, but that merely earned him a glare from the gentleman seated on his other side.

Damned manhood, never behaving when he needed it to!

"Instead of thinking of it as music, don't," he said quietly, taking his turn to whisper into Dodo's ear and relishing the opportunity to get close. "Think of it as mathematics."

Now *that* got her attention. Dodo's frown disappeared, replaced with a look of curiosity he knew well. "Mathematics?"

George marveled at the way he could transfix this woman—though admittedly, only through the promise of numbers and figures. What would it take for someone to capture Dodo's attention with the same depth of feeling on any other topic? What must a man do, for example, to make her smile like that when the calculations she'd worked on came out perfectly?

What, in short, would it take to make this woman love me?

He pushed the thought aside as swiftly as it had arrived. Nonsense. He couldn't think that way!

"Yes, mathematics," George whispered, earning the glare of the woman seated before them but completely ignoring her. "Thirds, eighths. Half notes that split a chord perfectly into two. Music made of numbers that are harmonious together—like a... a multiplication table."

He was scrambling a tad here. Mathematics was not something the master at Eton had relished teaching him, mostly because George had the natural ability with numbers as a goat did with French.

Still. He must have gotten something right, because Dodo's eyes had widened and a look of curious interest had spread across her face.

"I've never thought about it like that before," she whispered.

George watched, transfixed by her own attentiveness as she turned back to the musicians and slowly allowed her eyes to close. Her lips moved silently, as though calculating something complex in her mind.

The music faded. At least, it faded as far as George was concerned. How could he listen to a concerto when something far more spectacular was occurring right beside him?

Dodo was smiling.

Admittedly, she was almost certainly smiling at the numbers the music suggested instead of the emotions the melody was supposed to stir—but she was smiling.

Affection poured through George. He'd never experienced anything like this before: joy from her joy, happiness from seeing someone he cared about being happy.

Had anyone else discovered this, he wondered? Was it possible he was the first person in the world to have unearthed that giving one's partner something that would make them extraordinarily happy was, in a way, far better than being pleased oneself?

Partner, a small voice in the back of his head pointed out. *Did you just consider Dodo your partner?*

Dance partner, George thought hastily.

You're not dancing now, came the irritatingly unhelpful thought. *You and she never have danced.*

That was true. But over the last few weeks, it had become impossible to go a few days without seeing Dodo. Without experiencing her company.

Dear God, he was in far more danger than he'd thought.

"I like this," Dodo said quietly, slipping her hand into his and entwining her fingers with his own, as if there were no reason to fear prying eyes at all.

George grinned inanely. The intimacy was not lost on him, and nor was the sensuality of having her so enmeshed within him, even if it was only through his fingers.

In great danger, indeed.

Chapter Eleven

October 10, 1812

DODO'S PULSE THUMPED so wildly as she strode down the pavement in the blustery air, she suspected those who passed her could probably hear it.

Thump, thump, thump...

And it shouldn't. Polite young ladies should not be getting so excited to see a gentleman. Most especially entirely on her own. She had been raised to know such things, was aware of how her stay in Bath flouted Society's rules, and she felt these things, deep within herself.

If only her heart were listening.

It had been days since she had last seen George Chance. *No*, Dodo attempted to correct herself, *it's been days since I last saw the Earl of Lindow*. And that was important, wasn't it?

Remembering my place, Dodo thought as her skirts were swept up by the breeze. Her place, that was, apart from George.

But staying away from him was impossible, particularly when he sent invitations like the one she had received that morning.

A walk? L

It was intriguing. It was mysterious. It was... short.

If she knew anything about the man who had sent it, then he likely as not wished to discuss something. Or merely wished to see her.

She should not be getting her hopes up, as her mother would say.

The trouble was, her hopes were already up, whirling wildly, so swiftly, she could hardly tell what she was hoping.

You cannot keep this up much longer.

The thought was so unsettling, she wobbled as she turned a corner onto the street where Lindow House could be found. Putting out a hand to the wall, the cool of the Bath stone steadied her.

Dodo swallowed. Not just the whole of this Bath madness, staying in lodgings by herself, pretending her chaperone was always around the corner whenever out and about. But stealing from George—because that was what it was, even if she could attempt to sweeten the betrayal with phrases like "inspired by" or "informed by" or even "accidentally learned."

The point was, the Earl of Lindow was spilling his secrets to her, and she was using that information to bet against him.

What was that, if not stealing?

This week will be the last time, Dodo told herself firmly as her legs strengthened and she felt able to continue along the pavement. Just a few more bets, higher now that she had a greater understanding of the system—Mr. Gregory and Mr. Gillingham would advise her there, she was certain—then she could put this to bed.

The mere thought of "bed" so close to "George Chance" caused heat to scald her cheeks. By the time she reached the front door, she was positively pink.

Dodo frowned at her reflection in the spectacularly shined bronze knocker. After wrapping smartly on the knocker that was so inconveniently demonstrating just how rosy she was, she did not have to wait long before the door was opened by a footman who stepped aside.

The butler, Northrup, scowled. "No."

"I—" Dodo blinked. "I beg your pardon?"

It was definitely not the response she had been expecting. True, the butler seemed to have little admiration for her, which was to be expected. She was nothing but a woman, and turning up unaccompanied as she did so often, spending so long alone with the Earl of Lindow in the smoking room...

Well. What must he think?

Still. He was a servant, and she had done nothing wrong. At least, nothing wrong in her eyes. Society may not have appreciated her gallivanting about with an earl and a distinct lack of chaperone, but Dodo had always thought those rules rather tiring. Certainly not wrong—nothing wrong that George needed to worry about.

Nothing that he knew about, anyway.

"I said, no," said Northrup dryly. "His lordship is not at home."

"Not at—"

"You heard what I said," sneered the man. "Go away, miss."

The door slammed in her face.

Dodo's mouth fell open. *Well!* Of all the insensitive, arrogant— Northrup had no right to treat her like that! It wasn't as though he knew she was cheating his master out of a small fortune...

Did he?

Pulling herself together and reminding herself no one knew, that it was impossible for them to know, Dodo knocked again on the door and ensured this time she was ready to speak.

"I have an appointment," she said swiftly, the instant the door opened.

Northrup frowned. "If that is true, the master evidently did not think it important enough to keep. Go away."

The door slammed again.

This time, Dodo took a few faltering steps down the steps back to the street. Not important enough to keep? So George... He truly wasn't at home?

She had presumed, from the rudeness of the butler that it had been some sort of order that the servant had misunderstood. Perhaps George had wished to spend time with her, and her alone, so had asked his servants to turn away anyone else—and that had been misconstrued.

But surely, Northrup would have realized the order had only been given so George—so the Earl of Lindow—could spend time with her without risking anyone else in town discovering them?

It was difficult not to feel rejected. Dodo glanced up at the many windows that were part of Lindow House. She could see no face peering out from any of them, no indication the master was indeed home. Though what sort of evidence she expected, she wasn't sure.

Well. Perhaps he did forget.

It was an unpleasant thought. No one wished to feel a second priority to anyone, particularly when you—

Dodo caught herself just in time.

She was not going to fall in love. She just wasn't. She couldn't permit herself to do such a reckless thing, particularly not when the man in question was an earl, for goodness's sake.

"—trumped-up little thing, hanging around that poor man—"

The words were being spoken by a woman who had a friend, or perhaps sister, looped in her arm. They passed Dodo without giving her a second glance.

"—Earl of Lindow will become a laughing stock if he's not careful, the way that Loughty woman apparently carries on. Have you ever *seen* this supposed aunt of hers?"

"Aunt? I heard it was a family friend who was supposed to be chaperoning her."

"Or the earl's own sister-in-law. But I heard..."

Their conversation continued, but so did their footsteps, so Dodo was unable to hear the rest.

It did not matter. The merest snippets which she had heard were enough.

"*... the way that Loughty woman apparently carries on...*"

Heat rushed through her, pouring through her veins and making her stockings and boots uncomfortably tight. The idea that people were gossiping in the street about her—about her and George! About her lack of a chaperone. As though she were a harlot, desperately attempting to attach a gentleman to herself in such a manner...

Dodo could not deny they had spent a great deal of time together. Much of it alone. The rest of it in public, her chaperone supposedly always being just out of sight and their obvious preference for each other clearly causing comment.

She bit her lip.

For a woman who prided herself on her ability to see sense, to calculate possibilities and understand the likelihood of various events, she had not been smart.

Smart would have been pretending to be a widowed woman with another name entirely, free to roam without a proper guardian in her shadow at all times. Smart would have been holding back from becoming too intimately acquainted with a gentleman who would never... who could never...

Dodo's cheeks still burned, so she was almost certain the trio of gentlemen passing her on the pavement were staring purely for that reason. It had to be that reason. What other reason could it possibly be?

Try as she might, she could not meet their eyes with equanimity.

Was the whole of Society watching her—watching them? Was the Earl of Lindow truly presumed to be courting her? Perhaps they guessed who she was, had realized she was in town alone, and were trying to ascertain what possible hold she had managed to gain over such an eligible bachelor?

The thoughts burned through her mind, bitter and confusing. Dodo could not understand how she could have been so foolish. The concert had been a bad idea. Turning up here, as though she belonged here, was a bad idea. And staying here—staying here would be most foolish, indeed.

She had turned and started to make her way back to Milsom Street when a voice called out.

"Dodo!"

Her very ears were burning now, she was sure.

"Dodo, wait!"

Footfalls were racing after her, getting closer and closer. Whirling around and hoping to goodness the gentleman sprinting after her had somehow become invisible to everyone else around them, she glared at the Earl of Lindow.

"I thought it was you," said George with a lopsided grin. "Apologies for my lateness, I—"

"Do not," Dodo said as calmly as she could manage, "shout my name in public."

George's eyes glittered. "I wish I could make you shout my name in private."

And the world stood still.

She stared, hardly able to believe what had come from his mouth. From how George looked, top hat, impressively cut jacket, highly polished boots, one would take him for a gentleman. But a gentleman did not say such things! Those words were not just wild, they were offensive, they were scandalous, they were...

Precisely what she wanted to hear.

Dodo swallowed. Something had gone wrong here, very wrong. This was only supposed to be a gentleman who was paying for her services. *Her mathematical, card-playing services*, she scolded herself silently. *Not like that!*

Yet here she was, trading quips like that with a man who made every inch of her cry out for him, and some parts of her... Well.

In fairness, it appeared she was not the only one astonished by what he had just said.

George's cheeks reddened. "I can't believe I said that!"

Though he had blurted out the words, it was clear he regretted in part what he had done.

What size of his part, Dodo could not help but wonder. A third? A fifth? How much regret did he feel compared to… desire?

She knew she should have been shocked. *Young ladies should not suffer hearing such things.* She could almost hear her aunt in York saying that. And yet she felt more shocked at how natural the words sounded as they met her ears.

As though George should have told her that a long time ago. As though they should know, not just speak, of what they wanted to do to each other…

Ladies do not think such things, Dodo thought determinedly. *Not even ladies who flout convention and travel alone.* They may have—well, desires. Hopes, for what kind of gentleman may be in their future. But they don't go around imagining a certain gentleman of their acquaintance was in their bed, utterly naked, whispering such things…

Oh, bother. I must look like a tomato.

"Why don't we take a walk?" George suggested, pointing along the pavement toward Sydney Gardens.

Dodo grasped at the suggestion with relief. "Yes—yes, a walk. Yes."

A sedentary, calm, public walk. A walk during which no such scandalous utterances could be made. A walk that would be sedate and… and dull.

Dull. As though any time with George Chance could be dull.

It was only when they stepped silently into Sydney Gardens after a short walk of about five minutes that Dodo realized she had slipped her hand into George's arm. Without thinking. And she was in public view again, with an unmarried man and no chaperone present.

Her instincts told her to remove her hand, but as she shifted ever so slightly, George took a tighter hold. He met her gaze, and a teasing, mischievous look told her he knew precisely what she had attempted to do.

And he had purposefully prevented it.

Well, it was not so very intimate, Dodo tried to reason with herself, surreptitiously glancing at the other couples promenading around the small gardens. After all, there were plenty of other people who were walking arm in arm. They couldn't be the only ones.

Though perhaps they were the only ones unmarried without a chaperone.

"You look well."

Dodo's attention snapped to her companion. "I do?"

"You do," said George lightly, as though he complimented the looks of everyone he came across. "Very well."

And what did that mean?

It means, Dodo told herself sharply, *I should not be looking for additional meaning where there is none. It means keeping a calm head, and not...*

Not allowing her heart to do that pitter-patter thing it always did whenever he looked at her like that. It meant not swelling with pride when he said such delightful things to her, things that made her head swim and her stomach lurch and her legs tremble and—

"Dodo? Are you well? You look a little... flushed."

Dodo forced herself back to Earth. If she wasn't careful, there was a high probability George was going to realize she was starting to have feelings for him that weren't exactly—well. Proper. More than a high probability. Almost a certainty.

And yes, he had kissed her. Twice. And yes, he had been quite dejected when she had not described him as a friend.

But he was George Chance. A rake, a scoundrel, a man whom Dodo knew had bedded and most definitely not wedded quite a few ladies.

He didn't fall in love.

He fell into bed. Then swiftly out of it.

Wasn't him helping to put her reputation at risk time after time, being seen with her without a chaperone, proof enough of that?

"I am quite well, I assure you," she said aloud, when she realized she hadn't replied. "And yourself?"

George beamed, and her stomach did that irritating little swoop it only ever did for him. "All the better for seeing you."

Dodo looked away swiftly. She needed to find some neutral ground. A topic of conversation that wouldn't lead her to think about George Chance leaning over, ignoring everyone else in Sydney Gardens, and—

"The concert was most pleasant," she said hurriedly, forcing away all thoughts of kisses and seduction. "Most agreeable. Thank you for inviting me. It was *you* who invited me and not your sister-in-law, correct?"

"Of course. Thank you for accompanying me," he said generously. "I believe I had the better end of the bargain, too."

Dodo frowned. "You did?"

George nodded. "I was able to enjoy the music, and enjoy you enjoying it."

His expression was steady, and there was something in his eyes...

Something in his eyes Dodo did not understand. Something that asked a question she could not answer, not even for herself.

What was going on here?

If she were asked such a thing, Dodo would reply instinctively that nothing was. But she was no fool. Eight times out of ten—perhaps more—when a young lady said that there was nothing going on, there was *everything* going on.

Sometimes even more than that.

"I am your friend. I deserve to know—"

"You are not my friend."

Dodo hesitated as they gently meandered around a corner, but the conversation had been playing on her mind for too long. It was time to say something. "A few weeks ago, you asked me... I mean, I told you that... that we were not friends."

Her hesitancy overwhelmed her and she halted, unsure what to say next.

It appeared, however, that George knew precisely what she was attempting to say. Or at least, his serene expression made it look as though he did. "And have you worked out what we are yet?"

Dodo shook her head, not trusting her voice.

Because she did know now. Or at least, she knew what she wanted this to be. She knew how she felt, even if the name of that particular feeling was not one she could utter in public.

She had never fallen in love before. Never felt the emotion that meant home, and safety, and danger all at once. Never kissed a man before, but even so, she knew kissing George was unlike anything else she could experience. Never been so certain that the separation she and George would have to undergo would bring her great suffering.

Separation, a mean, little voice muttered at the back of her head, *would be all the swifter if he knew what you were doing...*

Dodo swallowed. She should tell him the truth. But how could she? That Mr. Gregory and Mr. Gillingham were... "in on it" made the whole endeavor sound so sordid, but there was no other way of saying it.

Ellis would know what to do. But Ellis was the reason she was in this mess in the first place. If it hadn't been for Ellis's death—

"Dodo?"

She blinked and looked into the kind, understanding, and desiring expression of George Chance.

"What are you thinking about?" he asked softly, steering them along a path almost devoid of people.

Well, that wasn't a question she was going to answer...

"Oh, someone I know. Someone whose opinion I do not trust," Dodo said lightly.

It was perhaps not a kind description, but it was an honest one.

George's smile was perhaps too knowing. "Well, now. That puts me in a mightily difficult position."

"It does?"

"I had hoped you were thinking of me," he said lightly, as though he told ladies such things all the time. "But now that you've answered my question, I am rather hoping you were not."

Dodo chuckled as she tightened her grip on his arm.

This man. He was full of contradictions. Bluster and banter and blatant cheek when she had first encountered him, but quieter and more sensitive than she could ever have given him credit for. Here was a man who knew himself to be a fool at times, but instead of punishing himself, he embraced it.

He truly was an enigma. If she had been faced with him as a calculation on paper, she would not have been able to solve him.

"Come, let us sit." George gestured to a nearby bench, recently vacated by an elderly pair tottering off along the path.

Dodo nodded.

It was as they approached the bench that she made her decision.

Not because George had said anything. He was silent as he released her arm and without asking, without comment, removed his handkerchief and placed it on the bench before sitting beside it.

"For your gown," he said by way of explanation as Dodo looked at him with a raised eyebrow.

And that was when it happened.

Dodo sat and felt the closeness of him, the affection of his regard—for it was surely nothing more than that—and his leg brushed up against hers.

Well. His breeches brushed up against her skirts.

His care for her, given without a thought or expectation, was what made her decision.

I have to tell him.

True, it would end all things between them. George would hardly wish to spend another minute with the woman who had used him, taking the information about his precious horses and using it against him. He may even attempt to reclaim the money, though Dodo had sent most of it off to Croscombe by now.

But she owed him the truth. Besides, it would be better than having to live with this guilt.

"George," Dodo said quickly, certain if she didn't get the words out now, she never would. "I have to tell you something."

"Well if it's time for confessions, I suppose I should go first," he said quietly, not looking at her.

Dodo blinked. *Confessions?* Surely, George could not have anything to confess.

"You are surprised," he said quietly, turning to her.

"Well, I-I am, a little. I would not have expected—"

"Do not concern yourself. It is not a particularly sordid confession," said George with a snort.

There was something in his manner that made Dodo look closer. There was... well. If the pinched expression had appeared on anyone else's face, she would have said that he was...

Nervous.

"It's merely to tell you that you have made me a better person," he said in a rush.

A furrow puckered Dodo's eyebrows together as she attempted to make sense of this bizarre confession. "I... I don't understand."

"You make me look at the world in a completely new way," George said, and it was definitely nerves that made his voice shake. His hands clasped and unclasped together in his lap. "Not to say that I was a bad person before, naturally—"

"Oh, I don't know," said Dodo weakly.

This cannot be happening. The Earl of Lindow was telling her—*her!*—that her presence in his life had made him a better person.

She was stealing from him! Robbing him blind!

"No, really, you have—you are," George continued with a firmness in his voice that told Dodo he would brook no opposition. "You have a way of looking at the world, through numbers, through the way they are ordered... I don't know how to describe it. You've made me think about my place in the world. What I am doing with my life, what I should be doing with it. It's funny, my older brother Cothrom calls me a liability—"

"Which you are," Dodo said halfheartedly.

After all, he was foolish enough to spout valuable racing information to her without a second thought.

George chuckled. "Probably. But you have made me wish to be better. To learn more. To understand mathematics."

Dodo could not believe what she was hearing. "Considering an occupation in cards? Or trade?"

"Trade? Goodness no. An earl couldn't go into trade," George said dismissively, waving a hand. "No, I meant—well. The business of my estates. The responsibilities I have, as a landowner, as a master. I don't just want to play with horses anymore, though I admit I do love them."

Tension spread across Dodo's shoulders and up her neck.

Now. Now was the moment to say something. To admit she was—

"Thank you." George exhaled.

Had he ever thanked another person? She could not help but wonder. Did earls typically go around thanking people? Probably not.

And a whole cascade of emotions threatened to overwhelm Dodo.

She wanted to kiss him. Love him. Confess to him. Run from him.

All these instincts and more warred within her, her chest constricting as each one of them fought for air.

She couldn't do everything. She couldn't do anything. And every moment she sat here, in indecision, he was waiting for her response.

"George," Dodo eventually managed, her voice quavering. "I—"

She broke off. A gaggle of people was approaching them along the path.

Telling him here, in public, where anyone could overhear her—no, it simply wouldn't do. She couldn't put off the truth for long, though, she couldn't. She mustn't.

"Yes?" George said hopefully.

Dodo hesitated. "Would you do me the honor of dining with me tomorrow? At… At my rooms?"

His eyebrows rose. "At your rooms? Is that wise?"

She nodded. That would be the best place. Mrs. Bryson was ostensibly against unrelated male guests without a chaperone present, but the landlady also did not pry too deeply when suitable excuses were offered. "It will have to be. There's… There's something I need to tell you."

Chapter Twelve

October 11, 1812

GEORGE LOOKED AT the scrap of paper upon which he had written Dodo's address and glanced up and down the street.

It was not a part of Bath he knew. At least, he had seen it on a map once or twice. It was there, and if someone had asked him whether Johnson's Buildings existed, he would have said *yes*. Probably.

But as he looked up at the paint-peeled walls and the cracked panes in the windows, George realized he was quite a distance from Lindow House. Perhaps not geographically. But metaphorically.

The people he passed as he approached the house watched him curiously, plainly wondering what someone with a greatcoat as finely tailored as his own was doing in a place like this.

For a while, George had wondered himself.

Oh, not why he was agreeing to meet with Dodo here. He was far beyond the question of whether or not he would acquiesce to anything Dodo asked—no matter how ridiculous the suggestion of visiting a lady's boarding house was—though he wasn't yet ready to admit to such a thing.

The question was, why?

George rapped on the door to the building. Nothing happened.

He bit his lip uncertainly, glancing about him as though there were something obvious he had missed. There probably wasn't a butler, or a footman or some sort, was there? So who kept charge of the door?

Who decided who entered, and when?

A woman older than him, her face wrinkled with time, was watching him from the other side of the street. Leaning against a wall as though she had naught better to do, a smile cracked across her face as she watched him.

George attempted to smile, then turned back to the door.

It was all most confusing. Oh, not the door—well, the door, but mostly Dodo.

"There's... There's something I need to tell you."

She had been most obtuse when issuing the invitation. Though George had pressed her for more details, she had been unwilling to reveal anything. She had given no purpose for the meeting save the thing she had to tell him, whatever that was.

"But I want to know—"

"And you will, when you come for dinner at Johnson's Buildings. Trust me, George."

And he had. Though he could not explain particularly why everything in him was drawn to this woman, George knew she was worthy of his trust. Considering all of the times they'd brazenly been seen in public without a chaperone for the lady, daring wagging tongues to doubt the idea her guardian was just around the corner, there was bound to be little more harm, he supposed, turning up for dinner could do.

Even if he was having a little difficulty with the door.

"What y'waiting for?"

George turned. The woman was still watching him, a puckering frown creasing her forehead.

"I await the door to be opened, my good woman," he offered across the street.

Darkness had been threatening for a while, and as the sun dipped below the horizon, the street was getting murkier with every passing second.

The woman grinned. "I think it awaits y'hand to open it, sir."

Heat flushed his cheeks. Dear God, was he being that foolish?

He turned back to the door, partly to avoid the woman's look of mirth and partly to examine the door. Well, he had knocked, hadn't he? And no one had come—but he was thinking like an earl. Like a person with a staff, a set of people to open doors for him. Now he came to think of it, when was the last time he had opened a door?

Dear God, he was getting soft. He would have to have a word with Northrup. His footmen had to stop opening doors.

George reached out, grasped the handle, which was cold even through his gloves, and turned. The door opened.

The laughter behind him increased in volume as he stepped through the door and into the building, but it quietened the instant he'd closed the door behind him.

The hallway into which he had stepped was unpleasant, to say the least. Dust had become dirt a long time ago, though there were few ornamentations for it to cluster upon. Pale squares on the walls suggested paintings had once hung here but had been removed, and the only stick of furniture in the place was a hat stand, which was empty. Clearly, the residents of Johnson's Buildings had little faith that their personal belongings would be safe.

George took a step forward, a step that echoed horribly in the emptiness. It was sufficient, however, to attract the attention of someone. Footfalls approached.

His hopes leapt. Dodo had never been one for personal questions, but surely this evening was going to be one of revelations. Even a small detail about her past would be lapped up after the drought of information that she had kept from him.

"I... I am sending money home. To my parents. They... They are sick."

Perhaps she had news of her parents—good news, he hoped. Though if it were good, would she not have told him in Sydney Gardens?

A door to his left opened and a woman wearing last decade's fashions with spectacles resting on her nose peered at him. "Yes?"

"Madam," said George easily, bowing low and slipping into the tried and tested Chance charm. "I had been seeking a"—*he had been about to say friend, even if Dodo had, to his consternation, said he wasn't one, but then he remembered her instruction*—"my cousin, but I find myself distracted by your beauty. You are?"

The woman gaped, then a gentle pink suffused her cheeks.

As it always does, George could not help thinking. Aylesbury was right. There was little that could not be gained by a smile and the pitter-patter of—

"Very clever, m'lord. She said you would be," said the woman with a dry chuckle. "She's upstairs, second floor, first door on the left. You'll like the pie."

She had turned before George could untangle his tongue and say anything.

Clever? She? Pie?

Well, he wasn't going to wait here and attempt to decipher the mysterious code the woman had used. If Dodo was upstairs, hopefully all his questions could be answered within minutes.

It took but two minutes to wander upstairs and find what appeared to be the right door—though George was not foolish enough to take the woman from the street's advice on this one.

He knocked.

Movement on the other side of the door—someone hurrying over to it, then halting before opening it.

A smile crept across George's face. She must like him, mustn't she? She'd accepted his kiss—a kiss he had been too afraid to attempt again.

Well. Not afraid. Afraid is a strong word. Hesitant. Cautious—

The door opened and there she was.

"Dodo."

He had not intended it to be such a heartfelt murmur, but he couldn't help it. His affections were rapidly getting entangled with this woman, no matter what he attempted to do. Just when he was starting to realize his responsibilities to the estate, when he should be trying to discover the traitor in his midst leaking information about his horses... He was here.

Having dinner—alone—with a woman who did not consider him a friend, and who made his pulse race most disobligingly.

"Good evening," said Dodo, her face pink.

She stepped aside and welcomed him in. George stepped forward and saw...

Well. Not what he had expected.

Perhaps the general dilapidation of the building itself should have been enough of a clue. As it was, the decay and the neglect had washed over him as a general sense, rather than suggestive of what was to be found inside.

He was standing in a room that served, as far as he could tell, as both drawing room and dining room. It was not large, perhaps the size of his breakfast room, and there was little furniture. The fireplace was lit but with wood, not coal, and there was a sofa and one armchair beside it. A small table, probably sufficient to serve four, was pushed into a corner. It had a covered platter and silverware upon it that was most definitely not silver; two plates; and two forks. Neither plate had a knife. There were only three dining chairs.

And that was almost it. A small travel writing desk sat upon a dresser that appeared to hold all of Dodo's possessions. No paintings, no ornamentation. No clock, no vases, nothing. Very little at all.

"Come, sit by the fire," Dodo was saying, gesturing toward the motley collection of places to sit. "In a moment, we can eat our pies."

Pies?

George nodded instead of trusting his voice and moved to sit on the sofa. It creaked and was most uncomfortable.

None of this made sense.

Oh, he wasn't expecting luxury. It was clear Dodo had never lived the quality of life that he had as a son of the late Duke of Cothrom.

Few had. Even now, as the Earl of Lindow, George was conscious that most people never had the experiences he had, the fabrics for his clothes, the silver for his cutlery, the disposable income to walk past a jewelers and say *that one*.

But Dodo was a lady. She had admitted that beautiful necklace was glass, and perhaps, now that he thought of it, those delightful gowns were few in number. But she was always beautiful in whatever she wore, exuding a sense of grace and elegance.

He had never truly thought things had been this dire.

Now the fact that she needed to send money home made sense.

"You are very quiet," said Dodo softly from the other side of the room.

George looked up. She was pouring red wine into two glasses—one chipped glass, and one intact glass. *Can it really be this bad for her?*

"Pies," he blurted out.

His stomach churned the minute the word was out of his mouth. Dear God, she would think him a complete ninny!

"Yes, pies," Dodo said as she stepped toward him and offered the unchipped glass. George took it wordlessly. "I did not know if you had a particular favorite, so I asked Mrs. Bryson to make up three for 'my visiting cousin' and me. That way, you'll have a choice. I like all the pies she makes."

George blinked up at her, totally at a loss. They weren't—surely, they weren't going to have pie for dinner?

He took a sip of the wine and grimaced, attempting as best he could to cover up the instinctive movement. God, this wine was awful. Where on earth had she found it?

"Yes, Mrs. Bryson cooks for all her lodgers," Dodo was saying, moving about the room and doing nothing as far as George could see, but remaining very busy while she was doing it. "Her pies truly are the best I have ever tasted, and…"

George allowed her words to wash over him for a moment, attempting to get his bearings.

Well. Dodo—Miss Doris Loughty was perhaps not the sort of woman that he had taken her for. Glass sapphires notwithstanding, she had spoken and held herself like a lady who would have been in respectable accommodations. He had thought her address being in this area of town had been a mere cover to hide the fact that she was in Bath without a chaperone, and he'd imagined a ladies' boarding house of a better class. George was astonished to discover that the truth of her living circumstances was not the sort of thing he had imagined.

Not… Not this. Genteel poverty.

With all the money that Dodo could win, was winning at cards, why on earth was she sending so much to her parents? Did she not deserve to have some of it herself?

"—fortunate to get this place. Mrs. Bryson only takes on lady lodgers, and so we're safe here, very safe. The last time I heard of anything untoward, it was… "

George nodded, not really taking anything in. His gaze was flickering about the room, attempting to discover any clues, anything at all, about Dodo's past or present.

But there was nothing. The only personal possessions, as far as he could see, rested on the small, wooden dresser just to the side of the window. Upon it was a candlestick that looked too fine to belong to the room, a small painting of four people, and a box which could have been a jewelry box. Perhaps holding the glass necklace?

"—don't you think?"

"Yes, indeed," said George vaguely as he rose to his feet. "Go on."

"Well, I told myself I should be fortunate to find anything for an unaccompanied woman," continued Dodo, evidently thinking he was listening to every word she was saying. "When I got here… "

George stepped nonchalantly over to the dresser. Was it a jewelry box?

When he reached it, he could see swiftly that it was. It was just the size and shape for necklaces—he'd seen old Cothrom purchase one for Alice. But the jewelry box was no longer the item that caught his attention. It was the small painting in a wooden frame beside it.

Four people were in it, and one of them was most definitely Dodo. Few women in the world had that imperious expression paired with that ebony-black hair. Beside her stood two people, a man and a woman. A generation older, and connected. The gentleman had her nose, and the woman, her eyes. Her parents, then.

George's attention slipped to the fourth person in the painting. A man.

Dark-red hair, a haughty expression, and a sense of possessiveness about him. He shared no features with any of the other three yet had been positioned in the painting close to Dodo.

Very close.

Bitter anger rose, unbidden and uncontained. He knew what this was—had seen similar in the drawing rooms of the *ton* wherever he went. They did not usually include the parents of one of the party, but...

This was an engagement painting.

"—chicken, and I think—yes, I think this one is ham—"

George couldn't believe it. An engagement painting. They had become fashionable a few years ago, and he could see a small date, 1810, in the corner.

So. Was Dodo engaged? Why on earth hadn't she bothered to tell him her heart was already—

George caught himself just in time.

He wasn't interested in her heart. He couldn't have been. It would be too painful to admit it, now that he had evidence her heart had been given to another long before they had ever met.

His hands were shaking. He quickly clasped them behind his back, attempting to force down the fury that rose in bitter waves, cresting over him and making it impossible to stop looking at the painting.

At the evidence of her deceit.

Was this why Dodo had always been so reluctant to share any history of herself—to answer any personal questions? Why she had always held herself out at arm's length, never permitting him to get any closer?

"I am your friend. I deserve to know—"

"You are not my friend."

Was this why?

Good God, what was wrong with the man? His betrothed was in Bath, entirely on her own, and he had not even had the good sense to send at least a maid along with her?

Did he even *know* where she was?

Had she deceived him as well as George? Only did she intend, once she had collected enough money, to run home to him?

Would the man still have a woman who'd been seen with an earl all over half of Bath?

Perhaps he had been *fine* with the idea. Perhaps he'd been unwilling to marry her without a dowry, and knew, like George did, how clever and charming and resourceful Dodo could be—

"George?"

He spun around. "What?"

Dodo was staring curiously. "Well? Which pie do you want?"

She lifted the platter lid and revealed... three pies. The sort one could purchase from a seller on the street, if one was wont to do such a thing.

George's stomach curdled. The idea of eating right now was unpleasant, but he couldn't avoid it. Not without storming right out of the building, which he was still in half a mind to do.

"George?"

"Whichever, I care not," he said vaguely, mind spinning.

Should he leave? He knew now there was no possibility of... of a future.

There. He'd finally admitted, even if it was only to himself, that he had wanted something permanent with Dodo. Something meaningful.

Something that was most definitely precluded now that he knew she was already engaged.

"Come, sit," said Dodo with a broad grin, patently ignorant of the rushing pain roaring inside her companion. "They're best warm."

How George found himself on the other side of the room, seated at the small table with a pie before him, he did not know. But he was. What on earth was he going to do?

For Dodo had made him no promises. Given him no hint of understanding that he could presume for her hand. In fact, she had been most clear she wished to share little of herself.

So how had his affections become so tangled?

"You're very quiet," Dodo commented.

George swallowed. He had to say something. He could not go on like this, sitting here as though his chest weren't tight with the pain of her secret.

"How is your pie? Is it—"

"It's fine," he snapped, poking at it with his fork. He still had yet to take a bite.

Silence fell between them for a few minutes, then finally, Dodo placed her own fork on the table. "I don't understand."

George looked up. "You're not the only one."

His curt comment clearly hurt Dodo—he could see it in her eyes.

"I invited you here," Dodo said uncertainly, "to—"

"What, to tell me that you are betrothed?"

Dodo's mouth fell open. "I beg your pardon?"

George swallowed. Dodo was not a person to hide her thoughts, nor her emotions. Everything she thought and felt was played out on her features, and it could not have been more obvious, with her gaping mouth and her stiff shoulders, that she was genuinely astonished by his words.

So… what did that mean?

Was it possible he had this wrong?

"What on earth are you talking about, George Chance?" Dodo said insistently, staring at him, unblinking. "Engaged? Me? You must be joking!"

Try as he might, George could not help it. His gaze flickered past her and toward the painting on the dresser.

It was clearly Dodo and her parents, and a man. Why else would the man be included, if not for that?

"I saw the painting," George said heavily.

Dodo looked over her shoulder for a moment, then turned back with a raised eyebrow. "You did?"

He nodded. Words could not encapsulate the agony he was feeling.

Well, it had to end somehow. He was not her friend, and they were hardly mere acquaintances. They were entrapped in a strange limbo, one which may have ended in... If he had hoped for more...

It did not matter what he had hoped. The point was, she was someone else's future wife. And no matter what the *ton* said, what Society muttered, what the scandal sheets gossiped, he was not one to take another man's wife.

A widow, or a working man's daughter, if she was of age and was eagerly consenting... Well. That was different.

But Dodo was not his Dodo. She was someone's betrothed.

George's stomach churned. *And he had kissed her.*

"The painting of myself, and my parents, and—"

"I don't want to know his name," George growled.

This possessiveness he knew he should not have felt was rising, making it impossible to think. He had come here tonight hoping—

What he had been hoping, he would never now articulate.

Dodo was inexplicably smiling. "Why wouldn't you want to know my brother's name?"

"I said, I didn't... I beg your pardon?" To George's great surprise, she was laughing. *Actually laughing!* "Did you say... *brother?*"

"Oh, come on, George," Dodo said with a chuckle, picking up her fork and taking a mouthful of pie. She swallowed it and continued. "What is the likelihood that the man there, in a portrait of me and my parents, no other set of parents present, is a sibling? Surely, two to one. Perhaps even odds."

A brother. Dodo's brother.

He was an idiot. George could have curled up into a ball and hidden away under the small dining table, he was so embarrassed.

Here he was with two, arguably three brothers, and he hadn't even considered the idea.

He scowled. "Well, how was I to know? And why are you still grinning?"

Dodo's smile was indeed far too broad. "I'm happy."

"And why is that?"

"Am I not permitted to be?" she countered.

George shifted uncomfortably in his chair. He'd had... perhaps not high hopes for this evening, but certainly greater hopes than what he was currently experiencing.

"You... You really care about me, don't you?"

Dodo's voice was gentle now, with no mockery or mirth. When George looked up and met her gaze, there was softness there. And warmth. And... And something he could try to name but would surely be disappointed if he were wrong.

Trying to take a deep breath and calm his swirling mind, George was certain there was only one way to play this. One way an earl should play this, definitely.

Calm. Detached. Aloof.

He wasn't desperate for this woman to care for him. He hadn't been heartbroken to think of Dodo as out of reach. He was the Earl of Lindow. He was one of the Chance brothers, always being outrageous, always scandalizing the *ton*, always having a laugh, always on top of the world.

And when it came to this woman, he fell apart.

George could not understand it. Dodo brought out his panic, all his desires, his needs, a contentment he had never known before, everything. Her dedication to her family had helped him see his own duties to his brothers. Her love of mathematics had reminded him what he owed to those who depended on him.

And she was so... intriguing. And clever. And beautiful.

George inhaled and pushed his pie away. "I really care about you. Perhaps too much."

Dodo's eyes were wide, cheeks faintly pink, but she did not look away. "Too much?"

"For example," he continued, knowing what he was about to say was reckless but past the point of caring. *It was time to be open.* "I am not hungry. Not for pies, at any rate."

"Not—Not hungry for pies?" Dodo asked softly. "Well, I can run down to Mrs. Bryson, see if she has something else—"

"I don't mean that," George said with a wicked expression. By God, he was going too far. But was anything too far for this woman? "I'm not hungry for food. I'm hungry for you."

Chapter Thirteen

For a moment, Dodo merely stared. *Hungry for me? What on earth does that mean?*

It was embarrassing, when she finally realized what the man meant, that it had taken her so long to understand.

"Oh!" Dodo said, hands rushing to her mouth as her cheeks burned.

How could he say such a thing? It was outrageous! It was appalling! It was…

Intriguing.

Dodo pushed the thought aside immediately. There was absolutely no possibility of—of that happening. After all, the very idea—her, and George?

She had realized he cared for her, beyond the bounds of a typical acquaintanceship. It was starting to become so obvious, she was rather surprised he continued to associate with her. The gossip in Bath was only growing each time they were spotted in public unaccompanied together. If the *ton* knew he was having a private dinner with her tonight, in her own rooms… That he had suggested such a thing…

George was laughing. "Oh, indeed."

The heat burning Dodo's cheeks did not let up as his gentle chuckles filled the room.

Hungry? He wished to… to bed her, then. To engage in amorous congress with her.

And before she could stop them, images arose in her startled mind that absolutely should not have been there. Images of herself, being kissed heartily by George. A George without his jacket, his waistcoat, or even a shirt. Strength lay in the arms that held her, and his lips—

Dodo pulled herself out of the image, pulse racing and lungs tight.

No, that absolutely could not happen. It would be a bad idea—a very bad idea.

Or would it?

The little voice she had always attempted to ignore whenever it came to George Chance, Earl of Lindow, was back, whispering hints of pleasure and delight that the man before her could offer.

Dodo swallowed. She could not deny, even to herself, that she had not greatly enjoyed George's kisses. The way he knew precisely how to touch her, the way his lips teased sensual delight from her, giving and taking in equal measure...

She could never have imagined such a thing.

And she had just finished her courses. Her knowledge on such matters was perhaps not as it ought, but her mother had always said it was nearly impossible to get with child just after a lady's menses. So had been her mother's own observation, at least, and it had worked to keep the number of her pregnancies to two, so Dodo felt that sufficient evidence to believe her theory.

She would not be a candidate for marriage afterward, but she had abandoned the idea of a suitable marriage when she'd decided to come to Bath on her own. Her mere presence in this city without a chaperone already ruled out marriage for her now. She had figured she would never leave the city with her deception, the escort just out of sight at all times, intact.

She had taken that risk. Her family's need had been too great. A gentleman would be unlikely to marry her now no matter what, so...

If she allowed herself... If she allowed George to...

Dodo swallowed and looked up at the man who had made such a delicate suggestion. Heat soared between her legs.

Oh, if there was any man in the world who would know how to please her, it would be George. There was expertise in those fingers and she could not pretend he was not handsome.

But what was she thinking? She could not permit an earl to bed her! She was not that sort of woman!

Was she?

Dodo met George's eyes and flushed at the intensity within them. Why she had not guessed he wished to bed her before, she did not know. It was perfectly obvious now, painted across his face. But it wasn't just desire.

Gazing deep into his blue eyes, Dodo saw desire, yes. But there was more. A cordiality, an affection, even. Perhaps she was being too bold. Perhaps she was seeing something that simply was not there.

But it appeared to be. Was that enough?

Dodo cleared her throat and George straightened with evident excitement. She permitted herself a small smile. It was delightful to seemingly have this much power over a man. Over an earl.

"Tell me three things about yourself," Dodo said quietly, "and I'll do the same."

George blinked. "I beg your pardon?"

"You mean to have me? In sexual intercourse?"

Perhaps that had been a tad stark. George spluttered, his mouth seemingly unable to construct a response to a comment so bold.

"Is that something you're telling me," he said weakly, "or asking me?"

Heat once again scalded Dodo's cheeks. *Goodness, but this is difficult.* People were always difficult. If this had been a discussion about multiplication of fractions, she would have been calm and collected. As it was...

"Look," Dodo said firmly—far more firmly than she felt. "You want to—and I... I am open to the option."

"'Open to the—'"

"Open to venturing... there. Yes," said Dodo, hoping to goodness her cheeks were not too pink. She rose from her seat as she spoke, slowly removing the pie platter, plates, forks, and glasses of wine and placing them on the wooden dresser. "But before we... Before we approach that, I rescind the order that we cannot talk about personal things."

"No more personal questions. That's an order."

It had been a foolish thing to say at the time, but it felt even more foolish now. The little George had shared with her had only made her like him more. Was it not possible, perhaps, that he would feel the same?

"'Personal things'?" George echoed blankly as she returned to her seat at the table.

"I-I need to know more."

It was a hard thing to admit. Dodo was not the sort of person to wish for such... such intimacies. On the rare occasions she had attempted to befriend another, the women had rebuffed her. *Dull*, they had called her. *Boring. Insipid.*

Just because she had wished to discuss whether there was an end limit to the number of pi. It was a fascinating subject. She didn't know why no one in Croscombe had been willing to discuss it with her.

George cleared his throat. "I suppose you want dark, deeply personal intimacies?"

There was a pause as Dodo attempted to think what to say. Then she saw the smirk, the arched brow. He was teasing her.

She shoved him on the arm. "*George!*"

"Dodo," he quipped with a smile that made her stomach lurch.

"Look, you asked me. I mean, you said you wanted to eat me—I mean..."

Oh, lord.

"Fine, fine, I understand," said George, raising his hands in mock-surrender, though he looked a little warm himself. "You want greater intimacy before... before we consider that. And that makes sense.

Right. Where shall I begin?"

His expression softened, becoming more serious.

Dodo folded her hands in her lap, her heart racing. This wasn't a test, though she could see how someone on the outside may presume as such.

The fact was, she had never opened herself up to anything like this before. Prior to sharing everything, baring everything with George... they needed to bare something else first.

Their hearts.

"I've told you about my brother Pernrith."

Dodo nodded, her pulse hammering.

"My brother—my half-brother, *if you must know*. He... My father... "

George's throat bobbed. "I've... I've always struggled to get on with him. I can't even tell you when it all began. It seems to have been a part of me for... for as long as I can remember. Right, that's one thing."

If her pulse did not slow soon, she was going to find it almost impossible to breathe. There was something so intimate about this—about the way George was speaking. Unburdening himself. Revealing himself. Almost as vulnerable as taking off his clothes...

Almost.

"I play the fool sometimes," George said with a lopsided grin. "But it's a habit that's backfired on me, I must say. It hurts, when people underestimate me, and they do. Far too often."

Dodo's sympathy went out to him. She was perhaps in that group yet had never intended to be. George was bold, yes, and brash, and reprehensible at times. But he also clearly had a deep conscience, and a need to be loved, and—

"And I am desperately in love with you," George said lightly, as though admitting to nothing more interesting than a favorite color. "Is that three things?"

Someone gasped. Only when Dodo realized her hand was on her

breast, astonishment roaring through her veins, did she realize it was herself.

He loved her? He was desperately in love with her?

Three things about himself. That was what she'd requested, and goodness, he'd had delivered.

Shimmering anticipation was flowing over her body now. They were one step closer...

"Your turn," said George gently.

Dodo hesitated, but after he had been so open, so exposed, she could hardly demur, could she?

"And I am desperately in love with you."

"I am cleverer than people think, and though I know I should hide it, hide what is unbecoming in a woman, I can't help it," admitted Dodo, her stomach wrenching.

He was looking at her. No judgment, no appraisal, just interest.

Dodo's voice was hoarse as she spoke again. "I never feel more at home than when I'm alone, even though I know I am supposed to desire company and revel in the presence of others."

It was hard to reveal that one. What lady of good breeding would prefer to stay home with an abacus than go to a ball?

"And..."

Dodo's voice failed her. She knew what she wanted to say, knew what she needed to say—but the words did not come naturally. She had never spoken them before, knowing that once voiced, they would never be given to another.

"And..."

George stared at her, all kindness and affection and desire.

Dodo's stomach lurched as the words spilled out. "And I-I'm desperately in love with you. Exponentially. At least fifty times more than I could have expected."

Something glimmered in George's eyes. "You are?"

Dodo nodded, hardly able to believe she was going to do this but knowing there was no turning back now. Not after having revealed such things to him, not after knowing so much about him.

They knew each other far better than she had realized. Slowly, without the intention of opening up to each other, they had. And now...

"Weren't you saying something," Dodo said shyly, cheeks burning but determined to continue, "about being hungry?"

He did not appear to need any additional invitation. Moving more swiftly than she had believed a man could, George had risen from his chair and reached for her hands, pulling her upright.

The instant Dodo was on her feet, her legs were quivering. Whose wouldn't be, if they were being kissed by George?

Because this wasn't George Chance, Earl of Lindow, who was preventing himself from giving into temptation. Dodo had not realized it at the time, but both times he had kissed her before, he'd been holding back.

Desperately holding back.

His tongue ravaged her lips until they parted, unable to resist the delicious assault, and Dodo sighed with heady bliss as his kiss deepened, becoming more sensual, cascading flickers of carnality down her spine.

His hands were not idle. Though they had both started on her waist, pulling her close into him, one had already meandered to her buttocks, cupping her even tighter to him.

Dodo moaned, unable to help herself, yet George did not appear offended by her admission of desire. Quite to the contrary, it appeared to spur him forward, both hands now on her buttocks, cupping her to him so tightly, he—

"George!" Dodo gasped, breaking the kiss to stare.

As well she might. The strength in his arms had always been something she had supposed, but now she had been given proof. George had lifted her by the buttocks, her feet dangling in the air, and moved to place her on the dining table.

Sitting on a table? What next!

"Dodo, you can stop me at any time," George said, his words hurried and his voice winded. "Do you understand? At any time."

Dodo blinked, unsure precisely what he was attempting to tell her. "Of course, but I trust you, I won't need to—"

"You might, once you know what I want to do to you," he said with a wicked look, the corner of his lips raised in a tight smirk. "Lie back."

She stared. What on earth did he want her to do that for? "Lie... Lie back?"

"Lie back," repeated George, his voice still ragged and his expression full of desire. "I told you. I am hungry."

Not sure how lying on the dining table would solve his hunger issues, and wondering whether she should have sent down to Mrs. Bryson for a different pie, Dodo slowly lowered herself onto the dining table, her knees at the edge of the surface and her lower legs dangling.

It was a most unusual position to be in. The ceiling had a damp corner she'd never noticed before, and—

"George!"

All thoughts of ceiling—though not of dampness—disappeared.

He halted, his fingers on her knees.

And not her knees through her gown. No, he had already swiftly pulled up her skirts and pushed them up, untying her garters and pushing down her stockings so that her knees were bare.

And he had been... parting her knees.

Dodo swallowed, still lying back on the table. He couldn't mean what—no, that was just an appalling thought she'd once had about what might feel nice. But he wouldn't actually... Surely, no man would—

"May I keep going, Dodo?" George whispered.

His breath was on her thighs, his head must have been right—

Dodo closed her eyes, almost unable to bear the thought of what a sight she was. Then she said, "Y-Yes."

She was unable to say anything more for quite a few minutes. Slowly, inching leisurely up her thigh, George was kissing her. Kissing her thighs, first one, then the other. Incrementally, he was moving closer and closer to…

"Oh, God," Dodo moaned.

She was unable to help herself. No one could have prevented themselves from crying out to a deity of their choice with that sensation running over them.

George's fingers were on her thighs now, pulling them apart, and his mouth—oh, God, his lips were on her secret place, and he was lapping at her.

As though a thirsty man had discovered a life-giving stream.

The pleasure he was creating was crackling through her body, sparking parts of her to life that she had never encountered before, never even known had been there. And she was quivering, quivering with the delight that surged as George darted a tongue inside her.

Oh, it was heavenly. His hands moved to her hips, holding her down to prevent her unconscious squirming from shifting her on the table, and Dodo could do nothing but twist and sigh as George's tongue swirled slowly around her nub, inching her closer and closer to—

Her hand shot down, her fingers swiftly entangled in his hair as the tempo of his tongue quickened, the waves of gratification roaring through her body.

"George," Dodo whimpered. "Please—please, George, yes, yes—oh, George!"

The crest broke over her without warning. Every inch of her body was on fire, shivering with the ecstasy she had never felt before. Dodo's body shuddered against the table, her concentration focused entirely on the way George's tongue was edging her over the cliff.

It was subsiding. The waves were slowing, though her whole body still felt incredible.

When Dodo believed she would be able to see after opening her eyes, she did so. The damp patch was still on the ceiling, but she was fairly certain it would be nothing compared to the damp patch before her on the table.

With shaking hands, she propped herself up on her elbows to look over at George.

He was straightening up, licking his lips with languid delight as he met her eyes. "You taste wonderful."

"Is there... Is there a possibility I could feel like that again?"

Something swept across George's face. "You—You mean that?"

"But I want you to enjoy yourself," Dodo whispered. "I cannot be the only one to—"

He arched a brow. "You think I did not enjoy myself?"

Heat splashed across her cheeks. "You know what I mean. You... Your... You know."

Her attention drifted down. Down to the very prominent bulge pressing against the material of his breeches, desperate to be released.

George followed her look and grinned at the sight of how obvious his desire was. "Now do you believe me when I say that I enjoyed doing that? I could do that to you every day."

Closing her eyes for a moment as she attempted to collect herself—the idea of George doing that to her every day was a very heady one—Dodo opened them again. "I mean it. Take me, George."

"Don't tempt me," he growled.

"I *want* you to be tempted," Dodo said, and it was true. There was something aching still within her, something that hadn't yet been satisfied. "I need—I need you to finish... I can't explain, but I want—"

George crushed his lips onto hers and prevented her from speaking, but it appeared he had understood. As he worshipped her mouth, his tongue slowly lingering along her lips until she opened for him, she could sense his hands were elsewhere.

And then she gasped.

He was standing between her legs, on the edge of the table—and was without breeches. The soft skin and rough, wiry hair were a cacophony of new sensations, and Dodo knew she wanted them all.

"I want you," she breathed, breaking the kiss for only a minute.

Her hands scrabbled at his shoulders, pulling him closer, not sure how to convince him to take her—but George had been right. He did not need much to tempt him.

Dodo huffed with shock and delight as he roughly grabbed her hips and pulled her toward him. Now her buttocks were right on the edge of the table, and George was grasping at—at himself.

His manhood.

She only had a moment's glance before George was slowly easing himself into her.

Dodo's back arched against the table, her breathing halted, and he immediately ceased.

"Dodo?"

It wasn't pain, exactly. No, that wasn't the word—it was pressure, and tension, and an odd tautness she had never encountered before. But it wasn't unpleasant, and as Dodo's breathing resumed, it was remarkably delightful to have the sense of George within her. Closer, more intimate than they had ever been.

Than she had ever been with anyone.

"And... And is that it?" Dodo asked softly. "That was intercourse?"

George chuckled, and only then did she notice his own voice was a mite ragged. "It? My darling, I'm not even all the way in yet. There's so much—so damn much I want to show you."

"You're not all the way—ohhh." Dodo moaned, lying back on the table and gripping hard to the edges as George continued to push his way deeper.

And deeper. She could hardly believe there was so much of him, but her body kept welcoming him in, eager for him, hungry for him, and waves of new sensations were starting to roar in her ears.

He halted. "There. I'm all the way in. Are you—Dodo, are you—"

"You feel good." Dodo moaned, shifting her hips and feeling a thrill of decadent sensation. "Oh!"

George groaned. "God, you're perfect, Dodo. Just perfect."

A hasty kiss was crushed against her lips, but before she could pull him closer, George had straightened. Then he was removing himself, and Dodo almost cried out with the loss of him. She had wanted to hold this moment forever—

Then he thrust into her.

"Ohhh," Dodo moaned, her secret place throbbing with the sudden jolts. "Oh, George, that was—"

"I know," he said softly, starting to build a rhythm now, in and out, slowly, ensuring he fully sheathed himself within her with every thrust. "Just lie back and experience it, Dodo."

How could she do anything else?

Because the aching was building again, and this time, Dodo knew the destination he was taking her. She clung on to the table as though by letting go, she would float to the ceiling. Her breathing quickened and her pulse raced as she heard George's panting in time with her own.

Every thrust, every movement shot pleasure through her body, building, building to a peak as he sped up, the pace moving faster and faster, and just when Dodo thought she couldn't take any more hedonistic bliss, George slipped a thumb into her and circled around her nub.

And Dodo exploded.

"Oh, George!"

Her whole body quivering, shaking with the uncontrolled ecstasy that overtook her, Dodo could just about hear George over her own screams.

"Damn—Christ, Dodo, yes, yes!"

And George was shouting as well, and shaking, and something hot was streaming into her and Dodo knew she would never be this close to another person again. Never feel so one with another.

Never love another like this.

George collapsed into Dodo's waiting arms, and she knew, she knew. He was the only one for her.

Chapter Fourteen

October 12, 1812

GEORGE WOULD NEVER say he was a particularly luxurious person. He had standards, like any gentleman. His standards may, in fact, have been higher than the average gentleman's being, as he was, an earl.

But he was hardly one to complain about small irritations. His butler, his valet, his housekeeper—he was sure none of them had received an unmerited cross word from him. He was rarely cross with them at all.

Yet despite all of that, George thought with his eyes closed and a small furrow across his forehead, he was going to have to speak to someone about this bedlinen.

It was awful. Scratchy, uncomfortable, and most unpleasant to sleep in. Why, George could not recall ever having slept in bedding so terrible.

He couldn't understand it. His staff had always been given carte blanche to buy the very best of whatever they needed. George liked the finer things in life and had never begrudged a bill that was sent his way.

Not that he actually looked at his bills, of course. That was another thing he was going to have to change if he was going to take more responsibility of his own life, his own estate.

So how on earth had anyone who worked for the Lindow household thought buying this sort of abrasive linen was acceptable, he did not know.

George opened his eyes, disgruntled and uncomfortable. Then he blinked.

Well. That would certainly explain it.

He was not in his bed at Lindow House. In fact, from the little he could see in the dark, early morning glow of the room, he wasn't in Lindow House at all.

He blinked again. Then the memories from last night started to flood back.

"There. I'm all the way in. Are you—Dodo, are you—"

"You feel good. Oh!"

"God, you're perfect, Dodo. Just perfect."

The disgruntled sensation melted. George rolled over onto his back and looked up at the ceiling, his mind full of happy reminders of just what he had enjoyed the night before.

Amorous congress. A true, lustful union between two, body and soul.

He had never understood the term before. Oh, he had bedded women, plenty of them. And most of the time, he had felt satisfied.

But never fulfilled.

George grinned up at the ceiling. Not like he had been last night. No, what he and Dodo had shared last night—it went beyond physical satisfaction. After their antics on the dining table, it had not taken long for them to… Ah. *Get hungry again.*

Taking off all their clothes and trying out the small bed in the other room she had taken had seemed like the best way to solve that problem. And they had. Several times.

George glanced to his left. His smile broadened.

There, curled up on her side, black hair flowing out around her and a peaceful, contented, and most of all exhausted look on her face, was Dodo.

Miss Doris Loughty. The woman he loved.

"And I am desperately in love with you."

"And I-I'm desperately in love with you. Exponentially. At least fifty times more than I could have expected."

He could hardly believe he had admitted it to her. Having never felt that intensity of emotion for anyone before in his life, it was a challenge to understand how it had managed to flow straight from his heart to his lips.

But he had, and perhaps just as importantly, Dodo felt the same way. It was astonishing—he could not understand how he was so fortunate.

After such longing, such restraint, it was a strange sort of happiness to suddenly be so open. To find that sharing one's emotions, one's affections for the other person, was infinitely more pleasurable than keeping it inside.

And speaking of infinitely pleasurable...

George shifted in the bed, trying to keep the stiffness in his manhood to a minimum. It was difficult enough at the best of times in the morning, but with the recollections of what he had so recently enjoyed and the woman with whom he had enjoyed it all lying in bed beside him...

His eyes drifted over to her once more. Ignorant of his gaze, Dodo shifted in the bed, the cover falling down to her waist.

George swallowed. And she was naked. So was he, but that was different.

God, he had never felt this way about anyone before. He had laughed openly when his two older brothers had found themselves entangled with ladies to such an extent that they had to marry them. The idea there could be that sort of connection, one that was wanted, one that was reciprocated...

It had never occurred to him.

And now here he was, lying beside a woman he would cut off his own leg for, and he had no idea what to do with all these feelings, all this energy. This sense that if he didn't do or say something to her, he would explode.

George shifted in the bed, wondering whether Dodo would wake if he pulled her close. If he curled her into him, his body protecting hers, keeping her safe…

Somehow, even the mere thought was enough to disturb her. Blinking in the growing sunlight of the morning, Dodo stirred.

"George," she whispered, still hazy as she got her bearings.

George's pulse skipped a beat. Even sleepy and not quite awake, the first thought that had entered Dodo's mind… had been about him.

"Good morning," he said softly, reaching for her.

Instinct made him do it, and when he brushed her hair from her face so he could see her more clearly, George's stomach lurched.

Natural. That was what it felt like. As though this should be part of every morning.

Dodo's smile was open and lethargic—then her eyes suddenly widened and she hid her face.

George laughed. "Now, then, don't—"

"I can't believe we did that!" Dodo cried out into her pillow.

His chuckles grew in volume. "Dodo, come here."

"I can't believe we—"

"Yes, I know," George said fondly, reaching out with greater certainty this time and pulling her toward him.

His manhood twitched as his hands stroked soft skin, pulling her into him as he lay on his back. *Just think of the emotional connection you shared*, he tried to tell himself. *Don't think about how desperate you are to bury yourself into her once again…*

Dodo placed a hand on his chest as her face nestled into his neck. "I can't believe we did it," she whispered.

George tried not to laugh. "All of it, you mean."

"George!"

"I'll be living in those memories for the rest of my life," he said mercilessly. "You honestly think I'm going to forget the way you—"

"George!" Dodo attempted to playfully place her fingers across his lips, hushing him.

George responded in the only way he knew how—by kissing those fingers fiercely, pulling one of them into his mouth and sucking it.

Judging by the sudden gasp and the way Dodo's leg was immediately hooked around his middle, he was doing something right.

"We mustn't," she said softly, though with what sounded to George like a hint of longing. "Not again. I'm sure Mrs. Bryson fell asleep early, as she does, and I can tell her when I see her next that my 'cousin' left after dinner, but if we make too much noise... No, we can't."

Privately, he quite disagreed. He wasn't sure Dodo actually believed what she was saying, anyway.

All roughness of sheets forgotten, George shifted and tightened his grip around the woman he loved. "In all seriousness, though. Thank you."

"Thank you?"

"For trusting me. Being so open, letting me—"

"Pleasure me with your mouth, and your fingers, and your—"

"The pleasure was all very well," said George swiftly, knowing he would never get that particular image of Dodo being railed on the dining room table out of his mind. And he never wanted to. "But it was the *closeness* I truly valued, Dodo. The... attachment."

The words did not come naturally to him, but George knew he had to say them. They were true. He had never said them before, not to anyone.

George swallowed. *Just to her.* "I'll never forget. I'll... I'll treasure those memories forever."

"Does this mean," Dodo said, peering up with a teasing expression, "you don't want to repeat the experience?"

A jolt of need shot to his manhood—which, most inconveniently, was pressed against Dodo's hip.

George swallowed. "I didn't say that."

This was not precisely what he'd had in mind when he'd arrived at Johnson's Buildings yesterday, though he would be a liar indeed if he didn't admit he had hoped.

Expected, however? Quite a different thing.

He really shouldn't permit himself to continue being riled up like this. With every passing moment, his body was getting more and more primed to sink his most delicate self into the warmth of Dodo Loughty. If he stayed here much longer, he would be walking like a crab back to his home.

George's focus flickered to the window.

Soft light was pouring through the thin curtains. Though he had no idea what time it was, the hour could not be any earlier than eight o'clock.

He would need to leave soon, if he had any hope of returning back to Lindow House without being spotted by the somnolent landlady or someone of the *ton*. The last thing he needed, with all this gossip that he was courting Miss Loughty and how her chaperone was ever just out of sight, was the suggestion that he had in some way taken her honor.

Even if he most definitely had.

That was something he... he *would* rectify. Shortly. But not immediately.

"So you do want to repeat the experience?"

George swallowed. *Damnit.* "There is a ninety-nine percent chance I want to repeat it *right now*—"

Dodo leaned forward and kissed him, softly, on the neck just below his ear.

Closing his ears to fortify himself for the decision he knew he must make—and immediately realizing he could smell the delectable scent of Dodo even better by doing so—George forced himself to say the words he knew he must.

"I have to go."

Dodo nodded, kissing him again on his neck. "Stay."

One word, just one word. It cut to the core of George's restraint as nothing else could.

A simple request. *Stay.* An order, a command. A request. Visions of Dodo begging him to stay flickered through George's mind, as nothing was so erotic as having a naked Dodo wrapped around him, nuzzling into his neck and breathing her desperate need.

Nothing, as a matter of fact, was more erotic than what was happening right now.

George growled and lifted her chin with a finger. *One kiss. What damage could that do?*

As it turned out, it could utterly wreck him and make him unsuitable for human company. The instant his lips touched hers, George knew he could no longer restrain himself.

Why should he? The sweet hunger on Dodo's lips was matched only by the way her fingers drifted down his chest toward his—

George lost all control. The desires welling up inside him could no longer be ignored, and with Dodo so warm, and so soft, and so eager in turn for his touch...

An hour later, or two, perhaps more, George lay back, panting.

"Dear God," he blew out.

"I think I should be the one getting credit for that," breathed Dodo heavily, falling back onto the bed. "I didn't realize a lady could do that."

George swallowed. He was introducing Dodo to the very worst—or very best—of what two people could share together. If he wasn't careful, he was going to find himself trapped here, in Dodo's rooms, in Dodo's bed, for a significant portion of the day.

"What time is it?" she asked muzzily from his side.

George heaved a sigh. "Late, I would imagine."

When he swung his legs over the side of the bed, she groaned in protest, but she wasn't able to reach him. He rose, legs slightly unsteady after such a heady bout of pleasure, and found his pocket watch in his waistcoat.

Then he swore quietly.

"George?"

"It's almost ten o'clock," he said ruefully, turning back to her and trying to promise himself he wasn't going to get back into bed with her. Lord knew what time it would be when he would leave it. If he ever left it. "I have to go."

"I suppose you do," Dodo said, sitting up in the bed and fixing him with a shy smile. "Despite how much I would like you to—"

"Don't even say it, or I may have to move in here permanently and never leave," George warned with a grin.

"You say that like... like it would be a bad thing."

His stomach lurched.

It wasn't supposed to be like this. A man was supposed to bed a woman, bed her again in the morning if he were lucky, then leave. That was how it was done.

At least, that was how it had always been done. What he had done—though never before with an unwed lady of his class.

The thought of staying here with Dodo, being here, being allowed to be here, be anywhere, with her in the eyes of the *ton*... never having to part with her, sharing her bed every night as well as her days...

George swallowed. *This was madness. Madness!*

"I need to get dressed," he said decisively.

It was not difficult to find his clothes. He had not dropped them far and Dodo's two rooms were not large. Pulling up his breeches and buttoning them, he tried not to notice how Dodo was examining him curiously.

He could hardly blame her. He'd had a remarkably good look at her before she had awoken.

"Men's clothes are so much simpler than ladies', aren't they?"

George snorted. "Much simpler."

It had been an absolute headache, trying to get her out of those stays.

"About a third simpler, I would say," mused Dodo from the bed, pulling the coverlet up to her waist and allowing her breasts to remain uncovered. "Perhaps three-quarters simpler for children."

George smiled to himself as he pulled on his shirt, fingers fumbling with the buttons. There was still so much about Dodo he did not understand. Her need to categorize everything, to reduce things to numbers…

She made his hopes so full, yet he still did not understand her. And that meant, his affections soaring, there was more of Dodo to discover. More of her to relish.

Every time he found out something new about her, he had a vague feeling he would fall even more in love with her. Which would be most inconvenient. He would do anything for her now: what on earth would he do if he loved her more deeply?

"You have to go, I suppose."

George looked up as he pulled his waistcoat on, every inch of him quivering at the pain of leaving her. Dodo's face was resigned, a light smile on her face but sadness in her eyes.

"I have to go," he said quietly, feeling wretched.

It was only Society's rules and expectations forcing him away. If Dodo did not have so much to lose, he would spend the rest of the day here, seeing just how much bliss one person could endure.

But as it was…

"We took a calculated risk yesterday," George said quietly, stepping over to the bed and sitting on the end. Far from Dodo's questing fingers.

"A calculated risk?"

"I don't think anyone will suspect that I stayed here last night," he continued softly. "If you tell your landlady your 'cousin' left after dinner and I manage to sneak out the door without anyone noticing, we should be fine in that quarter. I did not tell anyone about my visit, and my servants will presume I stayed out all night."

Dodo raised an eyebrow. "Something you are wont to do?"

George hesitated.

Yes, was the answer to that question. Odd. He had never been ashamed of his antics before. What he did with consenting adults was between them—he had never felt any sense of discomfort or regret.

He did a little now. The thought that he had shared this with others, before her…

But no, it wasn't the same. As George's gaze took in the delightfully pink lips; the bright, shining eyes; and the pert nipples peeking out from the coverlet, he knew this was different.

Dodo and him, what they had shared… He had never professed his love for anyone before. He had never *felt* love for anyone before.

"Some risks are more calculated than others."

George's head jerked up from the sight of her breasts. "What do you mean?"

Dodo's cheeks were pink. "I mean that I… I finished my courses the day before yesterday. The likelihood of a child… I think it's very low."

He nodded. Was that true? He'd never heard that before, but he certainly had never had cause to discuss such matters.

There were other precautions he took—ones that he had not taken with Dodo. He had never been so overswept with desire for a woman before that he had not used a protective. That was something he would have to remedy for the next time.

Oh, God, the next time…

"And the risk of your reputation?" George said. "If I am spotted leaving here—"

"After all of these weeks of pretending I'm here with a chaperone, I am not sure my reputation is something I care much about losing any more," said Dodo, her expression affectionate. "Not to you."

Joy sparked across him, splashing into his lungs, pouring through him. This woman, she was—she was everything.

Everything.

He didn't want to leave. What was out there in the world he could not find here? Nothing else would satisfy. Nothing else would give him the security he had with Dodo.

"I don't want to leave," he said, his voice breaking.

And in a movement of bed linens, Dodo leaned forward and kissed him swiftly on the mouth. "I know," she said, pulling back with a wry expression. "And I want you to stay."

George groaned as his head dropped. "Damnit, woman, could you stop being so—"

"So what?" she said, her cheeks immediately flushing.

He saw his mistake immediately. "So wonderful."

Dodo's smile was shy. *I must never forget that*, George told himself sternly. Just because she was willing to give herself freely when it came to amorous congress, that did not mean Dodo's reticence, which was a core part of her character, had gone.

And it was part of the reason why he loved her. This woman, brilliant, clever, outstandingly loyal to her family, had no need to be admired by the world. She only wished to pass through it quietly and calmly.

Perhaps not the sort of woman he had presumed would attract him. But Dodo was so much more than a list of characteristics.

He groaned. "Why are you making this so difficult?"

"Me? I'm just sitting here!" protested Dodo, mythic beauty whose breasts shifted as she inhaled.

Gritting his teeth and knowing he would regret this the moment he did it, George rose to his feet. "I have to go."

"Stay."

"Dodo Loughty!" George half-laughed, half-scolded her as Dodo beamed. "You are doing this on purpose!"

"Of course I am," she said softly, eyes glittering. "I want to make it as difficult for you to leave me as possible."

The sense of loss hit him the instant George stepped out of Dodo's bedchamber, and it only grew worse as he stepped across the room that was part dining room, part drawing room. The table drew his eye, the place where he had first given Dodo a taste of ecstasy.

Now do you believe me when I say that I enjoyed doing that? I could do that to you every day.

Resolve weakening, George forced himself out through the door and onto the landing. If he was swift—

"Did you like the pie? Mr. 'Cousin'?"

"Wha—Oh, yes, very much, good day," he gabbled at the woman who had to be Mrs. Bryson.

Cheeks burning and wishing to goodness he had been able to resist the welcoming arms of Dodo that morning, George hastened down the stairs and out onto the street.

It was bustling. The people of Bath were out in full force sharing the last of the bright days, and it was thankfully easy to slip into the crowd and pretend he had come from his own home.

Even if, George knew, his hair was undressed and his clothes were rumpled. That was what happened when one's clothes were unceremoniously dropped onto the floor.

It did not take long to hail a hansom cab. The idea of walking home like this was not to be borne.

"Where to?" asked the squat driver.

"Charlotte Street," said George, clambering inside. There was no need to give away his identity, after all. Saying "Lindow House" was certain to draw attention.

"Right y'are." The driver clicked at the horses.

Only when George leaned back in the carriage did he take a breath, and think back to what—to whom—he had left behind.

And a thought fluttered into his mind. A good one. One he had to act on.

"Actually," George said, poking out his head toward the driver, "take me to Milsom Street. I have… I have some business there that must be taken care of immediately."

Chapter Fifteen

October 14, 1812

Dear Mama and Papa,

You have probably been wondering why I have not written to you in the last few days. And that is because I have been greatly distracted ~~by a gentleman by a man~~ by an opportunity to earn more coin.

I know you disagreed with me when you learned I had come to Bath, but I hope I have proven over the last few weeks that I know what I am doing. I have come to no harm, and Mrs. Bryson is taking very good care of me.

But as I was saying—I have found an opportunity to earn more coin.

And yet I admit to having a moral quandary about it. I know I have not told you before because I did not wish you to worry, but I think I'm ~~doing something wrong know I'm doing something wrong cannot extricate myself from this situation and~~

Dodo stared at the piece of paper under her fingertips, a furrow across her forehead.

She had been attempting to write this letter to her parents for over an hour, but whatever she wrote down, it did not seem to fit. There was so much she could tell them—so much that had happened during her short stay in Bath.

So much she would never have believed.

Attempting to explain how happy she was, without giving the

specific details of why she was so happy, was turning out to be a great challenge indeed.

Dodo picked up an earlier version of the letter, skimming through it to see if there was anything there she could use.

Dear Mama and Papa,

You have undoubtedly been waiting for a letter from me for some time, and I must apologize for the tardiness. I have, however, an excellent reason for being delayed in my correspondence.

I have met a gentleman. I met him weeks ago, actually, and though I believed at first that he was a rascal and a rake—he is, of course, but he is so much more. Oh, the way George Chance makes me feel! I wish you could be introduced to him. I am certain you will be as charmed by him as I am.

He is actually the Earl of Lindow. I know, an actual earl! I do not believe an earl has ever come to Croscombe, and I can tell you now, in a way there is nothing much different between an earl and any other man.

Except that George is like no other man.

He is the most wonderful, the most excellent

Dodo placed the letter down. No, it would not do to tell her parents about George in that manner. *Neither,* she thought as a smile crept across her lips as she picked up another discarded draft, *is this appropriate.* Though in fairness, she had never intended to send this one to anyone.

I can't believe it. I have been bedded, thoroughly, by the Earl of Lindow. And he was so kind, so loving. I have never experienced such—

The pleasure, oh my goodness! Words cannot describe what he makes me feel. I have attempted to calculate the percentage increase of my happiness since George Chance entered my life, and I believe it to be at least a four-hundred-percent improvement.

Nothing makes me feel like he does. When he touches me, my whole body seems to come alive. It's like I've been dead, or asleep, waiting for him my whole life.

Enjoying amorous congress with him was like losing myself completely and finding myself all over again. He knows how to touch a woman to exact the utmost pleasure. If he asked me to stay in bed with him for a week, then I would.

The way he has with his fingers—and his tongue—I thought I would die when he

She had forced herself to stop there. Paper was not cheap, and the instant she'd realized there was no possibility whatsoever of permitting a living soul to see it, she'd had to halt.

Biting her lip, she looked at another draft. This one was more serious. She'd been unable to finish it, too.

Dear Mama and Papa,

I don't know what to do. I seem to have managed to get myself twisted up in a situation that is most unfortunate, and no matter what I consider, I cannot find a way out.

I have gained the trust of a good man—a rake, also, though that is not important—and I have been taking the information he has trusted me with and using it to bet against him. He owns horses and bets on them, not very intelligently in my opinion, and I seem to have accidentally created a gambling ring... against him?

I don't know how it happened. Two men I've encountered, Mr. Gregory and Mr. Gillingham, assured me they would only use my information to skim a little off the top, but now the earl is losing hundreds of pounds. I know he can well afford it—he is an earl, after all. The man probably wouldn't notice, except that he has such pride in his horses. And I can see how hard he is working, and it tears me apart to see him so frustrated.

But not enough to stop.

We need the money. Your illness has entirely changed the family, and Ellis—

I promised I would not write about him, but do you not think that never speaking of him again is only going to prolong our pain? Ellis would never have wished for us to pretend he had never existed. I've kept the painting you commissioned for my twenty-first birthday, and I look at it often.

The earl saw it the other day and gained quite the wrong impression. He was hurt, and it pained me to see him feel so despondent. And I'm doing worse to him, far worse, and he does not even know.

And one day, he'll discover that it's me, and I don't know what to

No, that one could not be sent, either. Dodo was not sure what her parents would think of the manner of her earning. They had not pried as to the source of the money she'd sent and she did not want to give them any more reason to send her aunt to collect her.

They think me genteelly playing whist at the best houses, Dodo thought with a dark smile. They had no idea that she had been to the notorious McBarland's. That she was betting on horses—betting with clandestine information. That she had been ravished by a handsome earl…

She permitted herself ten minutes of daydreaming about George. There weren't enough minutes in the day, in all honesty, to spend thinking about George. Every moment without him was a chance to think of him, so Dodo was having to ration herself. Ten minutes in the hour was more than enough.

Sighing happily at the thoughts she had indulged in, Dodo turned back to the letter. Or in truth, letters.

She really just needed to write a letter and send it. The fifty-pound note in her reticule, a frighteningly large amount of money, needed to be sent forthwith.

But what to say about George?

Dodo bit her lip. To disregard him and not include him felt wrong, somehow. He was such a part of her life, to have nothing about him in the letter to her parents seemed a huge injustice.

But nothing of the future had been spoken between them. No promises.

She had not asked for any, to be sure. But what would her parents say if they knew what she had already done...

Dodo held her head up high. They didn't need to know. Not yet.

Picking up her pencil, she wrote the shortest letter she could manage, while still being polite.

Dear Mama and Papa,

I hope you are well, and I apologize for the lateness of this letter. I have found myself incredibly busy here in Bath, and I hope you will forgive me.

Please find enclosed a fifty-pound note. It is probably the largest sum I shall send you, and I hope it will pay off the final debt to Doctor Hollister. Will he mix your medicines now? Is the mortgage still very pressing?

I have spent time at the racecourse with an acquaintance, George Chance, the Earl of Lindow. There is much to learn about horses and racing, with some fascinating opportunities to calculate speed alternating on corners and straights. Most satisfying.

I will write again soon, I promise.

Your loving daughter,
Dodo

Tilting her head, Dodo read back the letter and considered whether there was anything in there that was amiss.

No, not as far as she could see. She had mentioned George, but without the hint of intimacy that earlier drafts had included.

The fifty-pound note was a wonder to behold, and Dodo found herself distracted for a few minutes as she stared at the thing. She'd known they existed, of course, but to actually see one...

Then she folded it carefully right into the center of the letter. She would have to hope, as she sealed the note with a dab of wax, that no one would guess that the small, insignificant letter held something of such importance.

It would be a miracle if it arrived unscathed at Croscombe. The idea of that much money going into a letter, handed to some stranger who promised it would be delivered to her parents... It was a very odd concept, when one came to think about it.

The safest way to deliver it to her parents would have been to go herself.

A slow smile crept across Dodo's face as she leaned back in her chair, overlooking the decrepit conditions of the rooms she had taken.

But she couldn't waste that sort of money, could she? Going back to Croscombe just to hand over money would in and of itself be a waste of money. Not to mention she couldn't be sure her parents would allow her to leave on her own again, the promise of more money or not.

She rose, leaving the sealed letter on the small desk, and meandered over to the window. If the doctor's debts were paid, that left only the ongoing cost of her father's medication, and her mother's spectacles, and the mortgage.

Dodo's stomach churned as she looked out onto the street below. The mortgage. Why hadn't they told her they'd raised money on the old place? It was half falling apart at the best of times. To take out a mortgage on such a property, one the new vicar wouldn't dream of taking from her family, when her father was too ill now to perform the duties he once had as the parish vicar—

Her gasp caught in her throat.

There he was. George. He had just stepped out of a carriage, one with the Lindow livery painted on the side, and had glanced up at the window. Their gazes had met and that had been enough to expel all the air from her lungs.

Without giving a thought to how it may appear to others, most especially Mrs. Bryson, who had inquired after her "cousin" with what Dodo could only describe as a twinkle in her eye, Dodo darted down the stairs and out of Johnson's Buildings.

"Dodo!" George cried with evident delight. "I won!"

Dodo's eyes widened. "Won? You didn't. You won a race?"

It wasn't that she had no faith in George's horse-rearing abilities. The more she had gotten to know the man, the more she could see his passion. He had an interest in his horses most owners never had, and he spent far more time than any of them at the stables on the racecourse.

That did not guarantee, of course, that he would be any good at it.

But the idea that Honor of Guinevere or Scandal of Lancelot had actually won a race...

"Oh, we didn't win the race. That's a little far-fetched, even for me," said George, his grin wide.

Dodo tried not to laugh—she really did. It was most indecent for a lady and a gentleman to be laughing so openly together, in the street—and her, as ever, unchaperoned!

But she could not help it. George's open, affable features were spread into a knowing grin, his ability to laugh at himself one of the most attractive traits in him.

And there was a lot to be attracted to.

"No, I meant I won a bet," George said confidently, tapping the side of his carriage. It pulled away without him needing to say another word. "I was certain Scandal of Lancelot would come fourth, and he did! And that smarmy man who is always betting against me, whoever he is—he must have forgotten to bet!"

Evident delight was pouring off him, so strong, it was almost as though his horse had indeed won a race.

Dodo tried her best to reciprocate the obvious excitement George was feeling. "That... That's wonderful!"

It was a sharp reminder that she had completely forgotten to bet against him yesterday.

"*And that smarmy man who is always betting against me, whoever he is—he must have forgotten to bet!*"

Hearing herself described that way at all would have been rather unpleasant, but it was agonizing to have George say those words straight to her face.

He did not know. He certainly would not have used such strong language if he'd had any idea she was the one who had been "guessing" at the deficiencies of his horses the last few weeks.

"—absolutely certain he would do far better on a shorter distance," George was saying happily. "I spoke with my jockey and he agreed. It didn't appear to have paid off at first; we were a tad worried he'd overshot himself. On the third corner, you know the one, he peeled off to the left..."

Dodo swallowed, tasting only bitterness as her stomach twisted itself into knots. With all that had happened between them the last few days, the intimacies they had shared, the confessions of love they had exchanged...

"*And I am desperately in love with you.*"

"*And I-I'm desperately in love with you. Exponentially. At least fifty times more than I could have expected.*"

She had completely forgotten to speak with Mr. Gregory and Mr. Gillingham. They would undoubtedly be irritated with her—this may have been an excellent chance to win significant funds from George.

"—but I knew better than that, and the beast did marvelously right at the end," George was still speaking, rapture on his face. "There's nothing like it, honestly, Dodo. I imagine it's like you and your numbers—when it all comes together and it just works, there's no feeling like it in the world. Well. Not quite."

Dodo glanced up at her rooms in Johnson's Buildings. In there lay a letter for her parents that held fifty pounds. Fifty pounds she had won because she had betrayed George's trust.

And it was her lack of attention these last few days that had helped him win this money—that had made him so happy.

"Isn't it wonderful?" George was saying.

He reached out to embrace her, but the sudden passing of an elderly gentleman, his cane tapping along the pavement, forced them apart.

George grinned, sweeping his hair from his eyes. "I almost forgot myself there for a moment. Almost forgot we were out in public. That I can't... I can't touch you as I wish."

And perhaps those words would have enflamed Dodo's body, making her crave his touch even more—but she was still locked in a private battle of her own.

Whether or not to tell George the truth.

She had to, did she not? Whatever this love was going to become, she could not continue with any sense of honor. Could not use him, take the insight he so happily shared with her and use it to win coin against him at the races.

It was cruel. It was unfair.

And it was the only thing, short of begging for money, standing between her parents and ruin.

"Dodo?" George's voice was soft, and gentle. Just like him. "Are you quite well?"

Dodo managed to smile, but she could not make herself speak. She was being torn in half from the inside, knowing she should speak, admit everything to him... and at the same time, terrified that it would mark the end of whatever this was.

"*I am your friend. I deserve to know—*"

"*You are not my friend.*"

She had been right when she had spoken those words, and they would still be true now. What they were to each other, she did not know. What George wanted from her in the long term, she could not tell.

But if there was to be any hope of them finding happiness in the future, of being together in the future...

Well. She would just have to tell him and hope he would understand.

"George," Dodo said, her voice breaking.

He nodded. "Yes?"

A pair of ladies walked past them on the pavement, running past so hurriedly that Dodo was buffeted about in their wake. When she looked back up at George, it was to see a gentle grin and mischievous eyes.

Her heart skipped a beat. How could she do it? How could she hurt him?

But telling him wouldn't be the hurting, would it? She had already done that. The damage had already been done. Now all that remained was for her to confess.

Something she had vowed to do yesterday, before she had been so delightfully distracted.

Dodo took a deep breath. "George, I have to tell you something—"

"I don't suppose," he began at the same time. "Sorry. Go on."

"No, no, what were you going to say?" said Dodo eagerly.

It was cowardly of her, she knew. She should persist, persevere through the pain that the conversation would undoubtedly create, and tell him.

But the chance to put off the inevitable, if only for five more minutes, was too tempting to avoid.

"No, you started speaking first," George said easily. "I really shouldn't have spoken over you. My sister-in-law Florence hates that."

A prickle of curiosity curled around Dodo. Was this the sister-in-law who was to have been her supposed chaperone at the concert? She had never actually met the woman.

She had heard about the Chance brothers, of course, from George. At least, a tad. It had been far easier to get information from Mrs. Bryson, who appeared to know everything about everyone in the *ton*.

The two older Chances had both married this year, and to ladies who on the face of it were not the sort of people to become duchesses and marchionesses. Dodo could not help but wonder about "Florence," or as she would have to address her if she ever met her, her ladyship the Marchioness of Aylesbury.

Her lungs tightened with the very thought. *Meet George's family? Why, I would only do that if—*

"Fine, I'll go first," said George cheerfully, clearly ignorant of the war that had been waging in Dodo's chest. "I wondered whether there was an outside chance that I could come in and… well. Eat."

Dodo blinked. Eat? It was three in the afternoon—did he believe she served herself afternoon tea? Surely not. The man had seen what sort of lodgings she had. He had to know that—

"*I'm not hungry for food. I'm hungry for you.*"

Ah. Eat.

The look on George's face confirmed she had been on the right lines. There was a hunger in his eyes, a lustful yet loving expression on his face, that told Dodo she could be experiencing the delights of the flesh within minutes.

Hot warmth jolted to between her legs.

She swallowed. She really had intended to tell George precisely what she had been doing—to confess. She would have to soon. Attempting to keep these two parts of her life separate was going to become more and more difficult, particularly if his horses started doing better.

And yet the idea of saying *no* to this delectable man…

"I suppose there is an excellent chance my '*cousin*' can find something to eat," Dodo whispered.

George took a step toward her, closing the gap between them and making the air catch in her throat. "And I suppose, if you are very fortunate, you may find something to… to put in your mouth. I hope."

Dodo swallowed. She had wished to repeat that particular experience very much. There was nothing like taking George's manhood in her hands then placing it between her lips. The power, the exquisite pleasure she seemed to create, it was heady.

Her secret place throbbed.

"Right, then," she murmured, ignoring the passersby, who were undoubtedly looking at them curiously as they stood so close together. "A meal it is, then."

She knew her desire shouldn't get the better of her. Dodo had never had to fight off her desire like this before, never had to choose between what she wanted and what she needed to do.

But how could she possibly deny a man when he looked at her like that?

"I've missed you, Dodo," George murmured, taking her hand in his as though the world weren't watching, and pulling her toward Johnson's Buildings.

Dodo's stomach lurched. She would tell him. She most definitely would. Later. "And I've missed you."

"Not," he growled as they hurried upstairs, fortunately passing no others in the hallway, "for much longer."

Dodo wrenched open the door and pushed George through it. He staggered in, already attempting to pull off his boots by the time she'd closed the door.

"No," she agreed hungrily as George's fingers scrabbled at his buttons, dropping his breeches and revealing… "Not any longer."

Chapter Sixteen

October 15, 1812

THE RIGHT PLACE to do it was the smoking room.

That much was obvious to George. They had spent so many happy hours here, after all. Before they had found an understanding, this was the place where Dodo had taught him—fine, *attempted* to teach him about mathematics.

George wasn't sure whether his card-playing skills were any better than they had been before, to tell the truth. It was damned hard to concentrate when someone like Dodo Loughty was talking to you.

It was where they had shared their first kiss. Where she had opened up, just a little. And since they had discovered their mutual delight in taking off each other's clothes and enjoying amorous congress, it was a place where they had retreated when it was no longer acceptable for him to keep turning up at her rooms in Johnson's Buildings pretending he was merely a visiting "cousin."

George knew his servants had guessed at the… at the activities he and Dodo had taken to occupying their time. They had certainly witnessed her turning up time and again without a chaperone. But they didn't *know*. They couldn't *know*.

Thank goodness his great-uncle, the previous Earl of Lindow, had installed such thick paneling around the room.

So when it came to choosing a place to do it, he wanted to choose somewhere private and somewhere personal to them.

The smoking room at Lindow House was perfect.

George sat, then immediately stood up again. His ears were pricked for any indication she had arrived.

He glanced at the grandfather clock. He had asked her to be here at two o'clock, and it was five minutes to. She was not one to be late—at least, he had never known her to be.

That was what was so exciting about Dodo. There was still so much to discover. So much to learn. So much to enjoy.

Excitement thrummed through his body as George nervously paced around the room.

What would she say when she knew?

It was a ridiculous question. George knew precisely what Dodo would say—what she would feel. The only real question was, how would she express her gratitude?

His manhood twitched, but he forced himself to think cool, calming thoughts until the instinct went away. He wasn't expecting *that*, certainly. At least, he wasn't *expecting* it. If Dodo wished to, on the other hand...

The door to the smoking room opened and a flushing Dodo appeared in the door way.

"Miss Loughty for you, my lord," said Northrup with a raised eyebrow.

George ignored him. There was only one figure in that doorway who interested him. "You're here! You're late."

A swift glance at the clock told him she was, in fact, a whole three minutes late.

The color on Dodo's cheeks darkened and she looked, not at himself, but at his butler.

George halted in his tracks. He had been approaching Dodo at speed, intending to pull her into his arms for an embrace the instant Northrup closed the door behind them.

But his servant was still standing in the doorway, and Dodo

seemed... upset.

His jaw tightened. "Why are you late, Dodo?"

He had not intended the question to come across as a barking interrogation, but it had. Dodo was distressed, pressing her lips together in a posture of great discomfort.

And his butler had not departed.

"I was merely informing Miss Loughty, my lord, that there was talk amongst the servants due to her frequent unaccompanied visits," said Northrup blankly, as though informing his master of the weather. "That was all."

That was all?

George halted before them both, trying to slow his breathing and doing a very poor job of it.

The devil take the man! What in blazes did he think he was doing, lecturing a woman far above him in station about her comings and goings? What was it to his butler whether a woman visited him or not?

Glancing at Dodo, he saw her eyes downcast and her hands clasped tight together.

Oh, hang it all. There was only one way to resolve this, and though he may regret it later, he very much doubted it.

This could not be allowed to continue.

True, he had dismissed the idea of the butler being the one to leak information about his horses—the man could not have known enough about them. But there were other things that had bothered him for too long.

"Northrup," George said smartly. "Pack your bags."

The butler inclined his head. "I shall instruct your valet to pack your bags, my lord. Where shall I tell him you are going?"

"*I* am not going anywhere, but you are," said George, his jaw tight and every word an effort. "I said to pack *your* bags. You are dismissed."

The man's mouth fell open. To his right, Dodo's head jerked up with a look of horror.

"I beg your pardon, my lord?" said his butler, his eyes blinking rapidly. "You cannot possibly mean—"

"Please do not presume to know what I mean, just listen to what I say," George snapped. "I'm tired of it, Northrup. Complaints from other servants, having to put up with your inconsiderate nature—then you offend one of my guests? No, it's gone too far. I shall write you a reference, if you wish."

There was a strange sort of ringing in George's ears. He did not regret what he had done—in fact, he felt a tad ashamed he had not done it sooner. The Lindow household would be a great deal happier, he suspected, with a more pleasant butler.

Still, there was a strange sort of giddiness in his head he could not understand.

Perhaps it was because, for the first time in his life, he had made a decision about his duties as master of the house. He'd just left things to Northrup, for years, and to his steward and the rest of the staff in the countryside.

For the first time ever, George had made a change without reference to Cothrom, or to Northrup, or to anyone.

He stood proud, chest puffed up. And it was all because of Dodo. She saw in him something he had never seen in himself. She made him want to be a better man!

Already, a cloud of sullenness had dropped over his butler's face. "Very good, my lord."

"I shall give you three months' wages, as a courtesy, but I want you out of the house by dinner," George said quietly. "Thank you, Northrup."

The man stepped back, closed the door behind him, and left George and Dodo alone.

The silence of the room was almost deafening. George blew out a long, slow sigh. "Well, that was—"

"I hope you have not done that merely for me," Dodo blurted out swiftly, her cheeks still red. "I suppose he thought he was protecting you, protecting your name. I do not wish him to lose his position merely because—"

"It has been a long time coming, I assure you," George said hastily. The last thing he wanted was for her to feel guilt for such a thing. "This is not the first strike against him. Come, come sit."

His excitement was bubbling up again, uncontrolled, unfocused, over another matter entirely.

He was proud of himself. It had not been easy, getting all of this sorted. From the very moment the idea had occurred to him, he had known it would be difficult, but he had never imagined it would be so complicated.

But it was done now—and he could finally reveal to Dodo precisely what he had achieved.

There was a teasing look in her eye as she carefully sat in the seat he had pointed out. *Her* seat, in fact. The seat she always sat in when they were playing cards together.

"Your note sounded as though you had news of some sort," she said, leaning back in the chair and looking more relaxed. "I wondered whether you had done something rash and purchased a third horse."

It certainly was a little rash, George admitted to himself, *at least at first*. But the more he had progressed along the path, the more it had become clear. This was the right thing to do. And Dodo would never be able to stop thanking him for it.

"I have not bought another horse," he said aloud. "Though it is an excellent idea."

Dodo's eyes sparkled. "And you don't think you have enough to be getting on with, with the two horses that you have already?"

He snorted. "Not by half."

And that reminded him—he would have to ask someone to look into that again. There was most definitely someone spilling secrets, someone in the stables. How else would this blaggard, whoever he was, be able to bet so carefully against him?

That would have to be the first thing he did after... after this.

"Well?" Dodo prompted. "What is it?"

George could hardly contain himself with elation but managed to sit in the chair beside Dodo's. He took a deep breath.

Here it was, then. His chance to show her, beyond a shadow of a doubt, just how he felt for her.

And there was no better way than this. Not even the prospect of one day protecting her honor.

"I had a letter this morning," he said, trying to keep his voice level. "From a doctor."

Dodo waited expectantly. "And?"

"From a Doctor Hollister," George said quietly.

He watched her carefully, wanting to drink in every moment of this conversation. He would never be able to have it again, after all. He wanted every heartbeat to imprint itself on his memory, like a painting. He would stroll down this gallery of memory time and time again.

Dodo's eyebrows raised. "Goodness, what a coincidence. That is the—I mean, I know a Doctor Hollister."

George shifted in his seat. "I know. His... His letter to me arrived at breakfast confirming that the final part of my plan had been executed, and I am delighted to say, with success."

She was laughing now, apparently overwhelmed by his exuberance. "Are you just going to tell me what you've done, George, or do I have to tease it out of you?"

Biting back the words that he would very much like her to tease it out of him, George hesitated, just for a moment.

He had rehearsed this. Oh, that sounded far more ridiculous than it actually was, but still. He knew this piece of news would be monumental—would radically change Dodo's life. And he wanted to give her that elation.

The important thing, he told himself sternly, *is saying it.*

"I have paid him."

Dodo blinked, clearly waiting for the rest of his sentence.

Blast. That didn't explain it at all. "What I mean to say is, I have paid him for your parents' treatment."

The laughter on Dodo's face started to quiet. Her smile started to fade.

She's clearly overcome by shock, George thought triumphantly. And she didn't even know the best part yet!

"And he informed me your parents had built up quite a few debts in—Crumbscome, I think it's called?"

"Croscombe," whispered Dodo.

It was more of a wheeze than a whisper. George congratulated himself on such a perfect way to tell her. *Oh, she will never forget this.*

"So I paid them," he said promptly, his grin widening. "And I paid off their mortgage, too—you never mentioned they had to mortgage their home, so awful—and I have given Doctor Hollister a thousand pounds, against any future needs they may have!"

George ended on a jubilant note. As well he might. It was an absolute coup, the perfect way to show Dodo just how much he loved her. The best gift he could offer before asking for her hand.

Well, of course, there were other gifts, like the things he'd like to do to her again—

Dodo rose from her chair so swiftly, it tipped over onto the floor. The dull *thump* echoed around the smoking room, as did her footfalls as she staggered away from the card table.

"Dodo?" George said hastily, rising to his feet.

This had somehow all gone terribly wrong. Unshed tears stung her eyes. Instead of looking delighted, as he had expected, she looked... mortified. Upset. Almost—no. *She would not be offended at such an act of devotion, would she?*

"I thought you'd be pleased," he said recklessly, not sure whether to start after her or stay where he was. "I thought—your parents, I know you care so much about them, and—"

"That must have cost you a fortune," Dodo breathed, her voice catching in her throat.

Oh, is that it? She was worried, perhaps, that it was going to take a great deal out of his coffers? Well, he could soon put that concern to bed.

"Only about three thousand, I assure you," said George, taking a cautious step toward her. She took a corresponding step back. "And it's really nothing to the Lindow estate, honestly. Yes, I hadn't expected to lose so much on the races this autumn, but—"

There was a sound from Dodo that was almost a groan. It sounded akin to despair, as though she could not believe what she was hearing.

"You should not have done such a thing!"

George stared wildly, unable to understand what was happening. "What do you mean? Why shouldn't I—"

"Earls do not go around paying off debts for women's parents!" Dodo said, her hand at her breast, as though her heart were in danger of launching itself from her body. "Three-Three thousand pounds?"

"It's nothing," George said, his stomach dropping. "I wanted to do it—I wanted you to know your parents were well cared for!"

"*I* was caring for them!"

"I didn't mean—hang it, Dodo, I thought you'd be delighted," he said, irritation seeping into his words.

Because it didn't make sense. Anyone else would have been grateful, would have thrown themselves on him with gratitude. Would have asked him how he had managed to do such a thing, perhaps, and he could regale them with the tale of tracking down all Loughtys—not a common surname—and finding them in Crumbscome. Or wherever it was.

But Dodo?

She was staring as though he had done something awful. As

though he had transgressed some sort of line. Had offended her, wounded her.

And George could not understand where he had gone wrong.

"You should never have done such a thing," Dodo was saying, still keeping ten or so feet away. "It was not your place to—you've already done so much. You shouldn't have—"

"I haven't done anything, except lose a few pounds to you over the card table," George said, trying to laugh. "Dodo, my darling, you're overreacting. Perhaps I should have told you, but—"

"I've taken hundreds of pounds from you already!"

Her words shot out into the silence and she clasped her hands over her mouth.

George stared. "Hundreds… Hundreds of pounds? You can't have."

The lessons hadn't amounted to *that* much. Dodo, his mathematical genius, had miscounted. She didn't know what she was saying. The shock of such a gift, of such thoughtfulness—

"I'm the one who has been betting against you, all this time," Dodo said, eyes sparkling with tears, lowering her hands just enough to speak. "I've lost you all that money—I listened to what you said about y-your horses, a-and I've been betting against you, George!"

And he stared.

No. No, it couldn't have been. It wasn't possible. He trusted Dodo, knew her as he had never known any other woman. He had been more open with her than he had ever been, even with his own brothers.

Even Aylesbury did not know so much about him—did not know the real him.

And now she was saying she had…

"No," George said quietly, unable to say anything else. "No. No—"

"I didn't mean—well, I suppose I *did* mean to, but I never expected it to get so out of hand." Dodo exhaled, a single tear now falling down her cheek. "I thought, a few pounds here and there. It wasn't your money—"

"It... You listened to me talking about Honor of Guinevere and you..." George shook his head, as though that would clarify matters. "No. No, you wouldn't do that to me, Dodo."

Because if she had—if the one person he had trusted, truly trusted with his affections could do such a thing...

Another tear cascaded down her cheek. "I needed the money, and I thought it would be the racecourse that would lose the money, I didn't realize for a time that you were also betting and would therefore lose—"

"But then you did know—I did tell you, Dodo." George's chest was tight, every breath agony. This couldn't have been happening. No.

"And Mr. Gregory and Mr. Gillingham, they said that it wouldn't matter, that a few others—"

"You told other people? You involved them in this—this scheme?" George said harshly.

The pain within him was building and had spiked the instant she had mentioned the names. He knew of those men. He had almost *warned* Dodo not to gamble against them, for fear of what they might do—and to learn she had been gambling *with* them!

The plain fact of the matter was, no matter how much he did not like it, he had to face it.

Dodo had created a gambling ring against him, using his information. His tips.

Oh, dear God. And he had thought it someone in the stables.

"How could you—why would—" George stepped forward, desperate to be closer to her and at the same time, growing in pain with every step. "Why would you do this to me, Dodo?"

"I tried to tell you, before—"

"I didn't ask why you didn't tell me—I asked why you would *do this to me!*" he snapped, his temper finally pushed over the edge. "But yes, as you mention it, why didn't you confess this to me before we—"

He did not need to say it. George could see in Dodo's eyes that she understood.

Before they'd been united, physically and beyond. Before they had confessed their love. Before he had felt closer to her than anyone in the world.

"I trusted you." George had not intended to sound so pathetic, but apparently, he was. He had been thinking marriage—he, the Earl of Lindow, the renowned rake, marriage! To safeguard her honor, after what they had done. Because... Because he had never felt like this about a woman before.

All the trust he had placed in her—he had never dreamed, never considered that there was an outside chance she was using him.

Because that was what it was, wasn't it? Dodo—no, Miss Loughty had used him. From the moment they had sat together at a table at McBarland's, she had calculated precisely what she could get from him.

And he, the fool, had given it to her.

"I trusted you," George repeated, his voice cracking. "And I—"

"I don't know why," Dodo said, her voice suddenly harsh, full of pain. "I never told you that you could!"

George swore under his breath as he turned away, certain he would say something he regretted if he did not.

"You are the most difficult woman to love!" he exploded, turning back to her. "Damnit, Dodo!"

"Then don't love me!" she said, tears streaming down her face now, her expression a picture of sorrow. "Don't love me, George. Don't love me anymore."

"Dodo—"

But he wasn't able to get to her quick enough.

Before George had taken four paces, Dodo had turned on her heels and fled. No one could have run faster. He heard the front door slam moments afterward. And there he stood, in the middle of the smoking room, alone.

All his plans, all his hopes for how this conversation would go. He had never considered it could go so badly wrong.

The spiteful words which that been spoken so recently fluttered around him, reminding him of the disaster this conversation had become.

He had wanted to show her, really show her, how he cared about her. Telling her about the financial rescue of her parents, that had been the first way. And as for the second…

Shoulders slumped, George stepped quietly across the room to the bureau. The key was in the lock and it turned quietly, well-oiled and cared for. In the top compartment was a small box that he pulled out and looked at carefully for a minute in silence.

Then he opened the box. A large pearl attached to a gold band, encircled with diamonds, sparkled up at him.

"Well, hell," George said quietly, his heart breaking. "Now what on earth am I supposed to do?"

Chapter Seventeen

October 19, 1812

DODO LOOKED OUT of the carriage window. The lanes they were now traversing should have been familiar, and in a way, they were. The last time she had seen them, the leaves had been green, newly furled and ready to dazzle in the spring sunshine.

Now they were dead. Oranges, reds, and yellows cascaded from the branches, crunching under the wheels of the carriage that had already taken her so far along the journey.

But not quite far enough.

How long had it been? Weeks? A month. A long time. Part of her had wondered if she would make it back in time for Christmas and now here she was, coming in... in disgrace.

"I trusted you. And I—"

"I don't know why. I never told you that you could!"

The small village of Croscombe appeared as the carriage turned a corner, the low afternoon sun dazzling on the windows. Strange. The village had always seemed so large, full of possibilities, lanes and lanes to get lost in on lazy summer days.

Now it looked small. Bath had seemed huge when Dodo had first arrived, but somehow—she had not noticed how—the place had become small itself. It made Croscombe look minuscule.

How could she have not noticed there were only twenty or so buildings in the whole village?

The coach slowed as it entered the main street of Croscombe, and Dodo leaned back from the window. She didn't need to look out any longer. The place was just as she remembered. Change did not happen to places like Croscombe.

No, if its inhabitants wanted change, they would have to leave and find themselves in new locales. As she had.

And she had found it, even if she had not realized it at the time.

Dodo pushed a strand of hair behind her ear. She had been changed by George—and if she hadn't been so foolish as to prioritize money and wealth over him, then perhaps...

"George, I have to tell you something—"

She forced the thought aside, knowing that it would only bring her pain. Whatever George had been intending to say, she would never know. The man had always acted out of the kindness of his heart, and what had she done?

Cheated him. Lied to him. Beggared him, on some of the larger bets.

It was right, Dodo told herself, *that I should leave Bath*. She'd had enough of pretending a chaperone was around every corner. Of being whispered about. And the idea that she could accidentally run into George again, pass him on the street, see him across McBarland's...

No. She would not be able to bear it. Far better to come here.

The coach slowed, eventually coming to a stop right beside the village green. The driver dismounted, stretching after the long ride, then stepped around and opened up the carriage door.

"Miss," he said with an inclined head.

Dodo tried not to pretend her surprise at the additional cordiality. But then, she had traveled to Bath months ago on the mail coach, sharing the space with two men, a woman who knitted aggressively, and a chicken. Now she came to think on it, she wasn't sure to whom the chicken had belonged.

The idea of waiting for the weekly mail coach that would pass by

Croscombe was intolerable. The instant she had left Lindow House, she had rushed back to Johnson's Buildings, packed up her meager belongings, told Mrs. Bryson she was leaving, ignoring the landlady's gibes about Dodo's "cousin," and gone to the Francis Hotel. A coach could be hired from there, she knew. And she still had a few pounds left.

Perhaps they were not pounds well spent, Dodo thought as she was helped out of the coach by the polite driver. But she'd had to get away. She'd had to leave him behind.

"Thank you," she said quietly.

The man nodded as he dropped her hand, clambering up to the top of the coach to retrieve her trunk. Her only luggage.

"You'll be safe 'ere, will ye?" he said, glancing about suspiciously. She didn't think he was worried only because she was traveling without an escort.

Despite the pain and regret that had been circling it for hours now, Dodo could not help but sigh contentedly.

Her driver evidently had the classic suspicion of country life as a man of the town. *He must consider this some sort of wilderness*, she thought dryly. *Without civilization.*

"I'll be quite fine," she said aloud. "I was born here."

"Ah," said the driver, eyebrows raised.

Well, she supposed everyone had to be born somewhere. Why wouldn't it be Croscombe?

"Thank you for driving me out here so swiftly," Dodo said, hoping he would understand this as a taciturn dismissal.

He did. Bowing his head again and checking quickly on the whinnying horses, the driver closed the carriage door and mounted up to the driver's ledge.

"And you're sure—"

"My parents' house is just two streets over, and there's plenty of light left in the day," said Dodo brightly, as though she could think of nothing better than returning home in disgrace. "Good day, sir."

The man nodded, and within a moment, the carriage was rattling around the green, the horses returning the way they'd come.

Dodo stood and watched as the carriage disappeared off into the distance. Only when the horses had turned a corner, taking their load with them and disappearing from view, did she take a long, deep breath and look at the trunk by her feet.

Well. She had come all this way. The journey that remained could easily be done on foot. No time like the present.

The trunk was heavier than she remembered, and the handle was frayed, digging into her palm. Dodo found herself leaning to the left as she walked slowly around the green toward Vicarage Lane.

There were very few people about. She had expected crowds, but that was Bath. In Croscombe, there were only a handful of people. If half of them were helping bring in the last of the harvest, and the rest were at home, that left very few people to be milling about.

Dodo turned a corner. Everything was so familiar; the streets along which she'd learned to walk, the windows with their leaded panes, the roofs that tilted with moss growing on some, others thatched.

And yet it was all so different. A few doors were painted different colors. Mr. Michaels had decided to cut down the yew tree that had stood before his house.

Small differences that were sufficient to make it unsettling.

You're home, Dodo tried to tell herself. *Was this not the goal? Wasn't it the plan, to earn enough money to get your parents out of debt, then return to the life you loved?*

She took another left and stood on Vicarage Lane. There were only three houses here, and right at the end of the lane was Vicarage House.

Her home.

Dodo sighed as she approached it, though whether with happiness or exhaustion, she could hardly tell. Her trunk was getting heavier with every step, and she was starting to wonder why she hadn't asked the driver to escort her home—and carry the trunk—when a shriek echoed down the street.

"As I live and—Dodo? Is that you?"

Reaching the gate and depositing her trunk there, Dodo straightened up and tried to plaster a smile across her face as a cherub-cheeked woman who looked very like her hastened forward.

"Hello, Mama. I hope you do not mind that—"

"Mind?" Mrs. Loughty engulfed her daughter, pulling her into such a tight embrace, it was a tad difficult to inhale. "Why did you not tell us you were coming? Foolish girl, going off to Bath like that!"

"Mama, you're choking—"

"When your father found out, he wanted to send your aunt to watch over you, but I told him, his sister is not one for traveling, and in any case, look at what dear Dodo is sending! She writes of a Mrs. Bryson, her kind and watchful landlady. Our daughter must be well cared for, well regarded. Well, and what proof we had of that!"

"Mama—"

"If you'd written to tell me you were coming, I could have met the mail coach at the inn at Croscombe over the way. You didn't have to walk—"

"I can't breathe—"

"And in this heat too, what a gorgeous day it is! I am sure you will agree, the place has never been looking better. See, I've—"

Dodo gave out a strangled sigh.

Her mother pushed her back and examined her. "You sound like you're sickening for something."

Inhaling huge amounts of air as her lungs ached, Dodo shook her head. "You knocked the wind out of me, that's all."

It was difficult to blink back the tears. After months of worrying, weeks of receiving letters that boded ill, of hoping she would somehow earn enough money to send back to her parents to pay for a quality doctor, to keep the doctor treating them...

Here Dodo was. And here her mother was—well, and happy, and strong.

Mrs. Loughty cast a careful eye over her. "It is good to see you, Dodo."

Dodo brushed her eyes with the back of her hand. Not because she was about to cry. Most definitely not.

"Come on in. See your father."

"And he's... How is he?" Dodo was almost afraid to ask as she and her mother stepped along the garden path to the house. "In your last letter, you said he—"

"If I'd been permitted to write my own letter, you would have known," said a cheerful, deep voice emanating from the hallway. "What are you doing here, my little Dodo?"

Her tired feet, aching legs, and sore back from being cramped in that carriage all day no longer mattered. Dodo ran forward, her pulse hammering as she saw a sight she had not witnessed in months.

Her father. Standing on his own.

Well, not entirely on his own. As she grew closer and stepped over the threshold into Vicarage House, she noticed that Mr. Loughty was still leaning on a cane.

But he was standing—and not in pain, as far as she could see, and without that breathlessness in his voice that had so frightened them last winter.

Oh, to think that all her hard work, all the toil, the worry, the fears, the risks she had taken... they had all been worth it. To see her father like this, to hear her mother speak so strongly after the fever...

"You look so well!" Dodo exclaimed, hugging her father.

"No need to sound so surprised," said her mother jovially as she shut the front door behind them. "Anyone would think we had been ill!"

Dodo cast her mother a sharp look over her father's shoulder.

Mrs. Loughty had the good grace to look a tad sheepish. "Well, perhaps we have—but that is all a thing of the past now. And you're home."

Closing her eyes and hoping the tears she felt did not fall, Dodo nodded and clung to her father.

Home.

It had felt so far away. She had been determined not to return until every last penny was paid off, and in a way, she had.

"And I paid off their mortgage, too—you never mentioned they had to mortgage their home, so awful—and I have given Doctor Hollister a thousand pounds, against any future needs they may have!"

And a part of her had wondered, had worried, had attempted not to think about the fact that when she did return home, it may be to a Vicarage House devoid of inhabitants…

"You both look—well, you look… *well*," Dodo said as she pulled back from her father and attempted to examine him. There were still bags under his eyes, but there was some color in his cheeks now. His skin, which had sagged with wrinkles, had regained some buoyancy. "You've been taking all your medicine?"

"Like your mother would permit anything else," said Mr. Loughty with a wink. "Come on, let's sit in the drawing room. The light will be wonderful in there."

"And you don't have any pain?" asked Dodo, watching carefully as her father navigated around the coat stand and a chair to reach the drawing room door.

It was a miracle. Yes, he was holding a cane, but from what she could see, he was hardly leaning on it. In fact, she was almost certain that if he left it behind, he could still traverse the space with little difficulty.

"Oh, when you get to our age, Dodo, you'll soon learn that aches and pains are a way of life," said her father heartily, dropping heavily into an armchair.

By a fire, Dodo noticed, that was lit. And with a bottle of brandy on the side, half-empty. The little riches her parents had sacrificed immediately when their health had started to deteriorate.

And now...

She swallowed her relief as she sat on the sofa opposite her father with her mother beside her. Now they could enjoy their middle age in the way they deserved. Comfortably.

"My child, I wish you had not felt the need to deceive us," her father said softly.

Dodo glanced at her folded hands in her lap. "I'm sorry. I did not know how else you might permit me to go. You and Mother were ill. You needed Jenny here. My aunt would never have consented to join me in Bath. I had no choice."

"You had a choice—"

Mrs. Loughty waved a hand in the air. "Now, dear, what's done is done." She beamed. "Just look at her! Look at us all, as a result of our Dodo's little adventure. Though I admit, we are astonished to see you." She rang a silver bell that sat on a nearby console table. "Tea, Jenny," she instructed the maid who poked her head in the doorway.

The maid's doe-like eyes bulged. "Miss Doris! No one said you were—"

"Thank you, Jenny," Mrs. Loughty said, not unkindly.

Dodo suppressed a smile. Jenny had been with the family for as long as she could remember, and her curiosity was a habit her mother had never managed to alter.

"We received your letter only this morning, with the fifty-pound note," her father said, ignoring the coming tea and pouring himself a large brandy. "You did not mention that you intended to return home."

And that was when Dodo swallowed.

She'd had a great deal of time in the coach, on her own, during which she could have conceived of an explanation for this. But she had not. Each time she had considered how to explain it, something would rise and strangle her words.

Mentioning George—mentioning the Earl of Lindow would be a complete disaster…

And yet *not* mentioning him, when he had been such a part of her life, when he had been the one to save her parents, to save her from this constant financial fear…

Did they know the identity of their benefactor? She had not thought to ask George that. Perhaps not. But she had mentioned him in that letter that had apparently only arrived today, had she not?

I have spent time at the racecourse with an acquaintance, George Chance, the Earl of Lindow.

Was there a risk they could ask about him? Only a one in four, Dodo hazarded. She had only mentioned him the once, and in that single letter. There was no reason for them to—

"Tell me about this earl," said Mrs. Loughty genially as Jenny entered with a tea tray. "I want to know—"

"Thank you, Jenny," Dodo said hastily.

Her mother caught her eye and immediately sat back and fussed over the tea tray. That was one of the wonderful things about her mother, Dodo thought. Unlike so many people in Society, her mother could take a hint.

Though it appeared she did not have much patience. The instant Jenny had departed the room and the door was definitely closed behind her, Mrs. Loughty turned on the sofa to face her daughter.

"Lord Lindow," she said firmly.

"Lord who?" Mr. Loughty asked vaguely. So he was not aware of the man who had saved them all.

Dodo's stomach lurched. She was not prepared to have this conversation, so that meant she would need to calculate precisely how much she wanted to reveal. She would need time to do that—perhaps this evening, before bed. Then tomorrow, she could—

"I'm in love with him," she blurted out.

There was silence in the drawing room. She looked into her mother's eyes, who appeared to have frozen in shock. Then she turned to her father, who had halted midway through bringing his glass of brandy to his mouth.

Dodo sighed weakly. "I... He's a complete rake, Mama, and he's careless with his money, and he's overly reckless, a complete charmer, and he bets on horses—without even understanding the probability system. Papa, you would be mortified how he—"

"He's an earl, isn't he?" her mother said, attention darting about the room. "Your letter said—"

"And he doesn't share any of my values, and he doesn't like mathematics, and he's a complete fool half the time and completely wonderful the other half," Dodo continued. It didn't seem possible to stop speaking—the words poured out of her. "And worse, he's overruled me, and argued with me, and made me like music, and..."

The words dried up. They did so the instant Dodo noticed precisely two things.

First, her mother was smiling.

And second, her father was grinning.

"Just what is so amusing?" she asked icily.

It was certainly not the appropriate reaction. Here she had been, pouring out her heart, holding back her tears, and her parents were looking at her as though she were making a quip.

"Made you like music, eh?" said Mr. Loughty, taking a sip of his brandy. "That's when you know you're in trouble."

Dodo's mouth fell open. "Are... Are you laughing at me, Papa?"

"Doesn't like mathematics?" Mrs. Loughty shook her head. "Goodness, I cannot imagine what that must be like."

There was a twinkle in her eye.

Dodo frowned. "But Mama, you hate—"

"Oh, my dear child, I thought you more intelligent than this," her father said, interrupting her in his deep voice. "You must realize that you are describing your mother and I!"

His words rang out in the drawing room.

Blinking, Dodo stared, unable to understand what her parents were saying. Could they possibly mean...? They could not be suggesting she and George were anything like her parents.

Could they?

"Of course, I assume your courtship has been done properly," said Mrs. Loughty, nodding. "Your landlady acting as a substitute for your father and me? Since your father has been ill, it's understandable his lordship might not have made overtures to him first."

Dodo's head sunk into her shoulders, and she swallowed back her answer. There had been nothing *proper* about their courtship—if one could call it that. It was like her mother hadn't heard Dodo proclaim the earl a rake to begin with.

Mrs. Loughty didn't seem to notice, though, and took the opportunity in the break in conversation to thrust a cup of tea into her hands. "Drink that."

"The girl doesn't need to drink tea," said her father. "The girl needs to—"

"I know what's right for our daughter, thank you for your input," said Mrs. Loughty cheerfully without a hint of malice.

Dodo pointed at her mother, glad for an excuse to shift the topic away from the propriety of her courtship. "Yes, that's what he's like!"

"Yes," said her father wryly.

"It's infuriating!"

"She has her moments, yes."

Mrs. Loughty glared good-naturedly at her husband. "I'll thank you to not speak about me as though I'm not in the room."

"Oh, well," said Mr. Loughty, eyes twinkling. "You have your moments, my dear."

"Thank you," said his wife graciously, a grin dancing in her lips.

Dodo looked from one to the other, attempting to follow this most egregious carrying on.

She had always known her parents had wed in a love match. It was rare, indeed, for someone of her own generation, but for couples thirty or so years ago... Well, it was almost unheard of. The odds had never been in Dodo's favor to repeat the feat.

"He does whatever he likes," Dodo said uncertainly. "Whatever he likes, without any reference to me."

"Yes, that's a man's prerogative, apparently, my dear," her mother said dryly.

Mr. Loughty spluttered into his brandy. "Now just what—"

"And I suppose he is the one to thank for the bills paid, and the mortgage recompensed, and the bottle of your brandy your father is doing such an excellent job at emptying?" continued Mrs. Loughty calmly.

Dodo opened her mouth, hesitated, wondered what on earth she could say to that, then closed it again.

Seeing her parents like this—safe, content, happy, healthy...

It had been easy to argue with George in Lindow House when she could not see the results of his actions. Easy to tell him he should not have interfered, that she had already taken so much from him.

"I trusted you. And I—"

"I don't know why. I never told you that you could!"

But here, with the proof of the pudding directly before her, it was much harder to retain her ire toward him. George had done what he had thought was right, and here they were. Her parents. Happy.

"He treated me like a fool," Dodo said, once again blinking back tears. "He didn't tell me he was going to... He just went ahead and did it!"

"I think he treats you like someone he wants to care for," said her mother softly. "Like someone he cares for, deeply."

Dodo swallowed. "Cares for?"

Her father nodded as he sipped his brandy. "Like an equal, but in a different set. Mathematically, you're probably a negative integer, say minus x, whereas he—"

"You cannot reduce this to mathematics!" Dodo said.

"Well, that's a first," said her mother with a chuckle. "Besides, I believe your father would prefer pure algebra. If we take the two of you as constants—"

"Inconstants," muttered Dodo, despite herself.

It was all so infuriating. She had assumed, once she had been able to tell her parents about what had happened with George, that they would immediately be on her side.

It wasn't like they could give the money back, obviously. That was going to be its own delicate problem.

But she presumed they would understand just why the whole situation was impossible. Why George was impossible.

"Fine, let's keep it simple," Mr. Loughty said quietly. "With this earl of yours subtracted from your life, how do you feel?"

Dodo hesitated.

She felt wretched. The instant she had revealed the truth to him, that she had used him for his information and lied about it, used him to gain money behind his back, she had felt dirty. Like a traitor.

Seeing the pain on his face, it was awful. And with every mile that the carriage had taken her away from Bath, away from him, the aching pain had only increased. Exponentially.

There was a heavy sigh. Dodo looked up to see her father shaking his head.

"Let's try it another way," he said, placing his brandy glass down. "What are the odds that you will meet someone like him again?"

Dodo twisted her fingers together in her lap. "An outside chance, I would say. I'd require pen and paper to precisely work out—"

"No, you don't," her mother said. "You know the answer."

The two of them looked at her, nothing but kindness and understanding on their faces.

And it was perhaps that overwhelming kindness that finally pushed her over the edge. Dodo attempted to gasp, but every movement was agony in her lungs. That was when the tears started to fall.

"Zero. There's a zero chance," she said, taking in a jagged breath. "And I betrayed him. He'll never forgive me. It's all my fault… and I'll never meet anyone like him again."

Chapter Eighteen

October 20, 1812

THIS REALLY WAS a new low.
George knew that. Yet here he was, doing the one thing he had always told himself he would never do.

Thank goodness it was dark. He wasn't sure what he would do if someone saw him here, standing outside the one house in Bath he had always vowed he would never enter.

He glared at the door knocker, as though it were the brass implement's fault he was here. George supposed it wasn't anyone's fault but his own, though he still wasn't sure how.

The trouble was, he didn't have anywhere else to go. Cothrom had gone back to London. Apparently, Alice was more comfortable there. She was starting to show now, anyway, so there did not need to be much of a secret about why.

Aylesbury wasn't about, either. George had gone to him first, obviously. The man had always been the Chance brother to come on his adventures with him, and if there was one person who could get him out of his mess, it was Aylesbury.

He had waited almost fifteen minutes in the impressive hall of his brother's Bath residence only to be informed, eventually, that the master was… indisposed. The gaunt servant's eyes had flickered, only momentarily, to the ceiling.

George had left the place as soon as he'd been able. The very idea that he had almost interrupted his brother and his brother's new wife doing—

Well. It left him with few options.

And so despite everything within him telling him this was a poor idea, one he would most definitely regret, George lifted the knocker and allowed it to thunk onto the door.

He did not have to wait long, thank God. The door opened, and George stepped forward, eager to get off the street, where someone might see him.

"Is your master—" he began.

Then he stopped, one foot on the threshold, the other still on the street.

"Dear God, man," George said in wonder. "Since when does a viscount open his own door?"

Frederick Chance, Viscount Pernrith, chuckled. "Since when did you think I could afford both a footman and a butler? Come on in."

It appeared his half-brother did not need an explanation for George's sudden and unplanned appearance. Stepping back and gesturing with his arm that he was most welcome, Pernrith waited for him to enter.

George was in half a mind to leave now. This had been a mistake, most definitely, and one that he could rectify by just… leaving.

But he hesitated.

He had nowhere else to go, no one else to turn to. And though Pernrith was only half a Chance, and someone George himself disliked most enthusiastically, he was a Chance. Even George could not deny that there was something about their father in the eyes.

Swearing under his breath and wishing to God there was another choice, any other choice, George stepped inside.

He'd never been in Pernrith House in London, and he had been forced to ask one of his footmen where his half-brother lived when in Bath. Which was shameful in and of itself.

So George could not help but be curious as Pernrith closed the door behind him, giving George a few heartbeats to look around him.

It was... Well. Not as impressive as he had thought.

Pernrith was a viscount, so it was therefore right and proper, George thought awkwardly, that Lindow House was always more striking. But he was still a viscount. George had expected better furnishings for a man who outranked barons, baronets, and those who were given knighthoods for distinguished and loyal service to the Crown.

But this hallway was... Well, there was no other word for it. Dour.

It was clean, at least, but no amount of furniture polish could make that dresser more impressive. There was a coatrack, but with only two coats. The man surely had more than two coats?

The rug on the floor was not exactly threadbare, but it was approaching that description in some places. The chandelier that hung from the ceiling was not lit. Instead, the place was illuminated thanks to a pair of candlesticks that stood over an unlit fire.

An unlit fire, in October? Surely, the man couldn't be that poorly off.

Not that I would know, George reminded himself as he walked stiffly behind Pernrith toward a door. It wasn't as though he were exactly on speaking terms with the man.

And now you've turned up at his door at near eleven o'clock at night, with no explanation, and he...

He's welcomed you in.

It was a damned irritating thing. Who did the viscount think he was, being so pleasant?

As Pernrith opened the door they were approaching, George saw it led to a drawing room. A smaller one than George had, and without some of the finery he took pleasure in. But at least it had a fire lit.

"Come, sit yourself down," said Pernrith quietly, gesturing to a set of armchairs situated around the fire.

George said nothing but gratefully took a seat.

What was there to say? He couldn't even think how to explain the mess he'd gotten himself into, the tangle of emotions and betrayal and money that was his... his *connection* with Dodo.

"*I trusted you. And I—*"

"*I don't know why. I never told you that you could!*"

He shifted in his seat as Pernrith took a chair opposite him.

Well, this was damned awkward. The two of them had never got on, though that was clearly Pernrith's fault. *He had the audacity to be a part of this family, with no shame whatsoever*, George thought darkly. It was hardly George's fault. The boy had just turned up and—

But that wasn't going to help matters, was it, going over old times? Old grievances, old irritations. The arguments of childhood that had never truly been resolved.

Not when he was here for the man's... George could barely bring himself to think it.

Help.

Pernrith leaned back with a curious expression but said nothing.

His good manners not to start interrogating him exasperated George beyond belief. Trust the half Chance to have better manners than—

But Cothrom had asked George to stop thinking like that, hadn't he?

"Look," he said awkwardly into the silence. "I know we're not on the best of terms." There was more to that sentence, George was sure. He just did not know what it was.

Pernrith raised an eyebrow. "You think?"

George swallowed into the silence of the room.

He was going to make this difficult, wasn't he? Pernrith wouldn't be able to resist, he was sure, crowing over George once he revealed why he was here. The man was a rogue, a villain, a—

"Would you like some wine?" Pernrith asked politely. "Brandy, whiskey, I have a selection here."

It was on the tip of George's tongue to say that the selection would surely be subpar compared to what was in his own cellar.

He managed to stop himself just in time. He wasn't at home, was he? He wasn't at his cellar. He was here because... because he had nowhere else to go.

Dear God, he was pathetic.

"Yes," he said tightly.

"Which one?"

"Which—"

"Wine, brandy, whiskey," Pernrith rattled off in a quiet voice, his gaze never leaving his half-brother. "I can bring them all here, I suppose."

George gave a jerk of his head. "Fine."

They remained in silence as Pernrith rose and walked over to a cabinet on the other side of the room. It was a Japanese carved cabinet, lined with gold and dark mahogany wood, a beautiful-looking thing.

Very beautiful. In fact, it reminded George of something.

It was only when Pernrith had removed three bottles and two glasses and closed the cabinet door, allowing George to see it properly, that he remembered.

"That's from the Japanese room, at Stanphrey Lacey!"

Pernrith turned to him, a strange expression on his face. His nose was wrinkled, his eyebrows furrowed, but his mouth was soft. Belligerent, and at the same time defensive, and at the same time, gentle. "You think I stole it from Cothrom?"

George opened his mouth, hesitated, then closed it again.

His pulse was pumping wildly. That was where he had seen it before—it was a part of home. Their childhood home. Part of Cothrom's home now, he supposed, as their father had died.

But that cabinet had always been a part of the Japanese room, right by the window. He could see it now, the difference in color between the left- and right-hand side. The sun had worn away the finish of the wood, so close to the window.

And now it was here, in this second-rate house, owned by a bastard brother.

George clutched the edges of his chair and tried to think. Permitting an outburst was only going to hurt himself. He did not wish to look the fool.

"Here," said Pernrith. "Drink."

He offered out a glass, and George instinctively took it before he asked. "What is—"

"The finest brandy that can be found," said Pernrith quietly, pouring himself a glass then resuming his seat. "Legally, naturally."

George lowered his expectations as he took a sip. Yes, it was as he thought. The illegal stuff was far superior. But it was far more expensive. And you ran a risk.

A risk, clearly, that Pernrith was unwilling to take.

"So," said Pernrith, as though estranged brothers often turned up on his doorstep late at night. "You are here."

It was not a question, but inherent within it were a plethora, none of which George particularly wished to answer.

Yes, he was here. And if he was going to get the sort of help he needed, there was going to be a significant serving of humble pie to go along with this second-rate brandy.

He took another burning sip of the drink. *Liquid courage. Well, I could certainly use it.*

No time like the present, he supposed. "Look. I'm in a fix."

Pernrith nodded. "I presumed so."

George fought a flicker of irritation. *Of course he did, the smarmy—*

"I could use an outsider's perspective," he said, his jaw tight as he said the words he knew he had to say, but hated. "A... A brother's perspective."

He forced himself to meet Pernrith's expression.

His head tilted, his mouth open, the man was shocked, that much was clear. *And why wouldn't he be?* He and George had never been on good terms, right from the start.

George could not recall what had started it. An argument, perhaps. A disagreement. A fight, most likely when they'd been children. It had grown and twisted from dislike to anger to hatred almost before he'd known it was happening.

And then there had been nothing else to do but go on hating him, this interloper, this evidence of their father's betrayal of their mother, for the rest of their lives.

Cothrom had tried to bring the family together. George had laughed at the beginning, then argued with him, then resigned himself to the fact that Pernrith—despite his better judgment—was going to be a part of their lives forever.

But never before had George resorted to actually seeking the man out.

"A brother's perspective?" repeated Pernrith. "That's new."

George could not tell if the man was pleased or offended. And it was new. And most discomforting.

"I don't want this becoming the latest gossip," he said bitterly. "There are few people I trust in the world, but I think… I know our shared blood is enough to guarantee your silence."

Pernrith said nothing, merely looking at him with that steady, unshakeable gaze of his.

George shifted in his seat again. *The damned thing is so uncomfortable. Why doesn't the man have a decent chair in the place?*

"Why is this place so godforsaken dilapidated?" he asked, the words slipping from his mouth before he could stop them.

Strange. He would never have worried about offending Pernrith before.

Pernrith's smile was taut. "I don't have the money my brothers do. I can't just throw money at furnishings for my third house when I can barely pay the staff of my first."

George swallowed. "You could give it up."

"And disgrace the Chance name by demonstrating that I cannot afford three homes?" his half-brother said lightly. "You know what Cothrom would say to that."

It was impossible to argue with him. He was right. George could well imagine what their eldest brother's response to such a thing would be, and it wouldn't be pleasant.

"No, I merely do not entertain," said Pernrith lightly, as though it had been a simple choice, and one he had not cared much about. "I don't think there are too many broken hearts over that fact. After all, I'm not a proper Chance."

George hesitated, but his stomach churned and he knew he had to say, "You're a Chance."

"Half a Chance," Pernrith corrected.

"The point is, you bear our name," George said stiffly. "You should be... Damnit, you should be treated with the same respect as any of us."

It was difficult to say. How many years had he bickered with Cothrom about having Pernrith invited to family events? He'd argued against giving the man a title at all—it was merely a courtesy, one in Cothrom's gift that would not descend to Pernrith's children.

If he had any.

Pernrith shrugged. "I am accustomed to it. I have always been an outsider."

George had not believed it possible, but the comment made him feel even worse. The discomfort in his chair combined with the agony of losing Dodo and the distress of being in Pernrith's presence for more than five minutes made it remarkably difficult to think.

Damnit, I shouldn't have come.

"Now, are you going to tell me what on earth you're doing here?" Pernrith asked, taking a sip of his brandy. "You don't like me."

"Steady on," George said weakly.

"It is quite all right. You do not need to pretend. You don't like me—you never have. You've made it quite clear over the years, and I have never attempted to force a friendship. And yet here you are."

Here he was. Without options, without good advice, throwing himself on the mercy of the one man in Bath he loathed beyond all others.

George sighed, downed the disgusting brandy, and placed the glass on the mantlepiece before turning his attention to the half-brother who he really just... didn't like. "I think I've made a terrible mistake."

Pernrith's eyebrow rose. "Worse than coming here, you mean?"

He hadn't meant to do it. His intentions had been to say something stern, something cutting. But George was so exhausted, his emotions strung out so tight after his argument with Dodo, after the revelation of her betrayal, that he did the one thing he would never have expected.

He laughed.

His dark chuckles echoed around the room, his head shaking as he was joined by the gentle laughter of Pernrith.

And something seemed to change. He was never going to like the man, far from it. The blaggard was still a stain about the family, the result of an indiscretion that could never be denied.

But he was a Chance. And George already felt like such an outsider in the family, always getting things wrong, always being the one to let everyone down, that at this moment, he'd take any familial support.

Even from Pernrith.

"You're a fool, Lindow," Pernrith said with a look as their laughter died away.

George frowned. "You don't even know what's happened."

"I don't need to," he said bracingly, picking up the bottle of brandy. "You're here. That tells me you had nowhere else to go. Want more?"

Over the remainder of the bottle of brandy, George slowly attempted to tell his half-brother what had happened.

Which was a challenge. There were parts he did not understand, and others he simply didn't know. He couldn't comprehend how Dodo had done what she had.

"And just as I thought it couldn't possibly get any worse," he said, finishing up his tale, "Dodo shouted that I should just stop loving her and stormed out of the place."

Silence fell between them. Pernrith was slowly twisting his empty glass this way and that between his fingers, looking at the dregs of his drink rather than at him.

George felt a flicker of irritation. After he'd spilled his heart out, did the man not have anything to say?

"So there you have it," he said, attempting to prod the man into speech. "Disaster after disaster. And now I'm here."

Pernrith looked up, and George was astonished to see that the man had a look of... *Dear God, is that pity?*

Lord save him from pity from anyone, but from his half-brother?

"You said earlier," said Pernrith quietly, "that you think you have made a terrible mistake. And I think you're wrong."

George's spirits lifted, and he sat up straighter in the uncomfortable chair. "Really?"

Pernrith nodded sagely. "Yes, I don't believe you *think* you've made a terrible mistake. I think you *know* that you have."

The remark gained only a scowl from George. "If that's all the help you can offer—"

"You didn't actually ask for my help," said his half-brother, his voice as ever gentle, but with a sharp steel in the center. "And you haven't thanked me for that drink, either."

George swallowed. It was shameful, to be schooled in manners by—but he was right. "Thank you."

Pernrith inclined his head. "Putting aside the fact that the honorable thing to do after taking certain *liberties* would be to marry the lady—I gather you already knew that. So, we are agreed you have made a terrible mistake. The question is—"

"You do not think it is Dodo—Miss Loughty, I mean, who has made the mistake?" George said hotly. "I was not the one who lied! I haven't been soliciting secrets from someone and using them against that person!"

"Perhaps not," accepted Pernrith with a nod. "But you interfered in her life, Lindow. You went behind her back with her parents, investigated into her parents' finances, made decisions for her, for them all, without any acknowledgement to them. Did you think to ask the brother?"

George opened his mouth, ready to reply with—then he halted.

He had not thought to ask the brother. The man had not come up in any of his research into the situation. Why had that not occurred to him to locate him?

"Or," Pernrith added softly, "Miss Loughty herself?"

George swallowed.

It hadn't occurred to him. He had been so fixated on the sudden change of circumstances he could offer Mr. and Mrs. Loughty, the idea of consulting with their daughter had never struck him.

Only then did he see how Dodo must have felt. Shame, and embarrassment. Hot anger, that she had tried to look after her family for months, desperately doing everything she could—and he had just swooped in and saved the day. Frustration, that she had not been informed until it was all over. He had offered her money once without conditions, and she had refused. He should have known how she'd feel about what he'd done. About what *she*'d done.

Deep, deep regret. He could see that now, now that the initial fire of fury over the betting had subsided. Dodo clearly regretted ever getting involved in betting on the horses, and she…

She had tried to tell him.

"George, I have to tell you something—"

George clasped his hands together. "Oh, damn."

"So. How are you going to fix it?"

He sighed heavily, leaning back in his chair. "It can't be fixed."

Pernrith stared steadily. "You don't believe that."

"Don't you tell me how I feel!" He had not intended to shout, but the frustration of the last few days had been bubbling up inside him, desperate to come out.

And yet his half-brother, despite his tone, did not appear ruffled. "You have shouted at me plenty of times before, Lindow. It does not bother me, not in the slightest—but this is different, isn't it?"

George swallowed. He wasn't about to be lectured on—on love, and feelings, not from a man with whom he could hardly exchange two kind words until tonight.

Pernrith leaned forward. "This is different. You care about her, deeply. Otherwise, why would you be here? Why would you come to me, of all people—oh, don't worry, I am not offended. You love her, don't you?"

Once again, it was not a question. George sighed, dropping his head into his hands.

"So my question remains, what are you going to do about it?"

"I suppose there's an outside chance that she might listen to me for more than five minutes," George said wretchedly, his chest tight. "But how can I explain in just—"

"You would need more than five minutes?" Pernrith interrupted, an eyebrow raised. "To tell this woman you love her?"

Chapter Nineteen

October 24, 1812

DODO STEPPED OUT in front of Lindow House, her pulse racing. Her parents had said they would support her regardless.

"It's your decision, Dodo," her father had said fondly.

"Only you know what's best," her mother had said, with a look that told her precisely what her parents thought was best. "I'm afraid I'm still not up for a trip, so I suppose we must entrust you to Mrs. Bryson again. Unless Jenny might be spared, or your aunt."

But Dodo would do with neither of them. Her aunt would be meddlesome, if she agreed to come at all, and she still did not think her parents should do without their maid.

As to whether or not Mrs. Bryson would act as her chaperone, Dodo was certain the woman would prove most helpful when it came to visiting her "cousin," but there was little reason to involve her now. Though she did not say these things to her parents. She sensed they did not want to know.

And thankfully, she agreed with them. It *was* her decision. She knew best. It was far better to come back to Bath, to see what could be done, to try…

And if she failed?

Well. Then she would know, once and for all, that the attempt she had made was all she could offer. If George did not wish to continue, if he did not believe it was possible for them to find their way back to each other…

The odds were small. Dodo knew that. Had frantically attempted to calculate them on a small sheet of paper in the mail coach, wedged between the window and a snoring woman, evidently exhausted.

Less than fifty to one. Perhaps even seventy to one. Oh, God, let it be better than one hundred to one…

By the time the mail coach had arrived at the Francis Hotel, Dodo herself was exhausted. But there was no time to wait. The small carpet bag that she had brought with her—she would only be staying a day or two at most, after all—hung on her arm, weighing her down.

But she had to move. She had to find out if there was any opportunity that they…

Dodo's breathing was short as she half-walked, half-ran down the Bath streets toward Lindow House.

"Isn't that—"

"That looked like Miss Loughty. It really—"

"Why on earth is she in such a hurry?"

"She's alone on the streets again, I see."

Frantic snatches of conversation caught on the wind, some of them making it to her ears, most of them then stolen away. But Dodo did not care.

Let them look. Let them gossip. There was only one person's opinion that mattered to her anymore, and she was going to find him.

Sooner than she had expected, she found herself standing outside George's house.

Well, at least she wouldn't have to face that horrible butler.

When she rapped on the door, it was swiftly opened by an angular-faced footman in Lindow livery.

"Is George—is the earl at home?" asked Dodo hurriedly. "I wish to speak with him. Please tell him—"

"The master isn't here," the man said, jumping almost imperceptibly. "I'm afraid I don't know where—"

Dodo did not wait to hear the rest of the sentence. She was almost certain she knew where he was.

McBarland's was full of smoke, chatter, and nervous laughter from those patrons who were about to lose all the money they'd entered with. There were a few tables in the dingy darkness populated with people she couldn't make out, so Dodo pushed past the crowds to check every corner, quite aware she wasn't dressed to impress the throng tonight.

When she returned to the center, ignoring as best she could the stares from McBarland's patrons, it was with a sinking heart.

He isn't here?

Why she had presumed he would be, she didn't know. They had spent some time together here, and there were few other places she could think to look. It was possible he was at the Pump Rooms, but she thought it unlikely. He could be visiting any one of the impressive houses that populated Bath. But how would she know? The odds of her discovering him was—

The odds.

It took near an hour for Dodo to walk to the racecourse. She could have hired a hansom cab, she supposed, but the little coin she had brought with her would have to go far at this rate.

She was tired, panting, with aching feet by the time she had reached the stable yard. Men turned to stare as she entered.

Dodo smoothed her skirts and tried to hold her head high. She probably looked a state. And she had no right to be there. No reason to be there, other than to find an earl who probably didn't want to see her.

"The Earl of Lindow?" she asked, as genteelly as she could manage. "I am looking for the Earl of Lindow. Has anyone seen him?"

Men shook their heads. Some just gawped, as though the sight of a lady in this place was utterly impossible.

Dodo swallowed, disappointment rising. She hadn't wanted to let this chance slip through her fingers, but it appeared that was precisely what was happening. He could have been anywhere. He could have left Bath altogether, she realized, and she would never know.

"—doing here? No place for a woman—"

Attempting not to hear the hushed mutter, she looked about for a friendly face. There was not one to be found.

Dodo's shoulders slumped. She had run out of ideas.

Her entire life, she had considered herself an intelligent woman. Clever. She had a parent who truly understood numbers and who had shared that understanding with her, and another who read people as easily as she read equations. They both appreciated the way she looked at the world, and yet here, she had reached an impasse.

All she had to do was find a man.

Admittedly, a specific one, but she had not managed that. She was a complete failure.

Turning away from the stables and attempting to ignore the curious looks she was receiving from the many men standing about the place, Dodo started to walk away.

She would have to find somewhere to stay for the night. Evening was drawing in swiftly, and Mrs. Bryson may have already let out her room. She would have to head straight there to see if—

"Dodo?"

Dodo halted in her tracks. Then she slowly turned on the spot, hardly able to believe she could move.

It was George.

His jacket and waistcoat were nowhere to be seen. At some point, he had discarded them, and he had unbuttoned his cuffs and rolled his sleeves up. There was straw in his chestnut hair.

Dodo attempted not to stare at his forearms. Those strong arms that had held her in such tight embraces. That had lifted her onto the dining table. That had—

She dragged her gaze up to his face and flushed to see such intensity in his eyes.

Well, she had attempted to find him. And now she had. What was she going to do next?

"I..." Dodo's voice faltered. Try as she might, it was impossible to ignore the growing crowd around them.

George jerked his head, then turned, saying nothing.

He did not need to. Dodo understood.

Following him into the small stable that was only inhabited by Honor of Guinevere and Scandal of Lancelot, she shut the door behind her with trembling fingers.

Then she turned to him.

George was standing just a few feet from her. Not that he had done that intentionally—the place was so small that unless he wanted to be pressed up against the opposite wall, he had no choice but to be that close to her.

Dodo swallowed. *Pressed up against the opposite wall.* She really mustn't think of—she could not permit her mind to run away with her and think about—

"I need to tell you—"

"I wanted to say—"

She halted, her mind spinning as their mingled words spilled over each other. George's cheeks were red, which made no sense. She had been the one to betray his trust. She was the ungrateful one—why, she had not even thanked him for the incredible generosity he had shown her family.

And *he* appeared unsure of himself?

"I've got to explain," said Dodo hurriedly, forcing herself on. "I must tell you—"

"No, I am the one who has to explain," said George just as swiftly, face set and jaw taut. "All I was trying to do was—no, I can't start there. I have to—"

But she wouldn't let him attempt to explain such an act of kindness. How could she? What sort of person would she be if he felt defensive over such a wonderful thing?

Dodo launched into her prepared explanation. "The thing was, I was so surprised. You took me completely by—"

"I should have consulted with you. I should have asked you first," said George, his voice low and urgent. "If I had not been so swift to appear impressive—"

"No, I should have seen what you had done for my family for what it was, a huge kindness," Dodo said firmly, trying to barrel along the speech she had practiced. "I should never have been so stubborn as to refuse to ask you for help in the first place."

Could he not see that she was trying to show him how much he meant to her?

She forged on. "I should never have done what I did, and I apologize—"

"No, I apologize. I was wrong to act the way I did. I should have known—"

Dodo raised her voice, hoping George would eventually capitulate and just let her get her apology out. "You did nothing wrong, and yet I—"

"'Nothing wrong'? I was arrogant, and overbearing, and condescending," George said passionately, taking a step forward that shortened the air in Dodo's lungs. "When I should have been listening to you, I—"

"You're not listening to me right now," Dodo could not help but point out.

They paused, the tension in the air growing with every passing second.

Dodo laughed awkwardly, and George was chuckling, and she did not know precisely how she was supposed to navigate a conversation like this.

Was she angry with him? Was he angry with her?

Why did they both feel as though they needed to apologize?

"I suppose that's fair," George said, a rueful expression on his face. "Please, Miss Loughty. I won't interrupt you this time."

Though he spoke with nothing but kindness, Dodo's body went cold.

"Miss Loughty"? Was that what they were reduced to now?

She swallowed as George placed his hands behind his back, evidently attempting to demonstrate that he was going to wait until she spoke.

Which was most inconvenient because she had no idea what to say.

"I... I should never have taken the insight you gave me and... used it for tips." Dodo tried to smile, but every muscle in her face seemed to hurt whenever she tried it. "Those conversations... They were precious to me. I should have respected them."

Guilt once more rose in a wave through her, and try as she might, Dodo could not ignore it.

Why she had thought it was acceptable to do such a thing, she did not know. It was shameful. It was arrogant. And it was something she would have to live with for the rest of her life.

George, however, did not appear to agree with her silent thoughts. He waved aside her words with a casual gesture of his hand. "I should have guessed it was you."

Dodo blinked. "I-I beg your pardon?"

"Well, it was my brothers who pointed it out in the first place. I didn't even notice that someone had privileged information on old Honor of Guinevere and Scandal of Lancelot," he said with a frank honesty Dodo had been unprepared for. "But I should have known it was you. It would take someone truly clever. Someone who understood numbers."

"Far better than I understand people," Dodo muttered.

"I beg your pardon?"

"Nothing," she said hastily, cheeks burning. "It doesn't matter whether you suspected me or not. The point was that I shouldn't have done it."

"I think the point is actually that you were trying to look after your family," George said. His voice was quiet now, gentle. "You did what you thought was best. I should have offered to help you long before it was ever necessary for you to take information from me to earn money."

Dodo swallowed, her throat dry. *The thought had never occurred to her. Should it have?*

"Besides," he added, taking another step closer. "I could have inquired with your brother to ask if there was anything I could do. You didn't even have to know—if I were being truly selfless, then I would have… Oh, I don't know, made it appear that a genteel benefactor wished to help you. All of you. Anonymously."

She had done so well to keep the tears from falling, but now it was becoming impossible. As they stung the corners of her eyes, Dodo swallowed hard.

She had to tell him. She should have told him when he'd seen the paintings.

"Ellis died," she said blandly.

George's jaw dropped. "I beg your—what did you say?"

"He… He died," Dodo said. No matter how many times she said it aloud, it still didn't feel true. "An illness. We spent a great deal of money, but Doctor Hollister couldn't come, and our village doctor couldn't help… Then both my parents caught it. A terrible fever. It went on for weeks, and at the end of it… I hadn't realized, you see, that they'd mortgaged the house. When my father had recovered enough, he'd given the deeds to—that doesn't matter now."

"Your brother—the man in the painting… He has passed on?" George asked, clearly stunned.

Dodo nodded.

And what a sickness it had been. The doctor had said she didn't need to worry, that they would all be quite well, in time. Somehow, she and Jenny had never become ill themselves. It had been a haze of pain, of panic, as exhaustion as she'd sat up each night with the people she loved—the people who appeared to be fading, one after the other, away from this world...

"That's... That's why you have felt you had such a burden. To take care of your parents, I mean," George said slowly, as though finally seeing the light. "You were alone."

Dodo forced back the unshed tears. "I was. But I managed."

"Why didn't you tell me?"

It was an excellent question, and not one Dodo was sure she could answer. After being alone, responsible for her parents for so long... knowing they were sick, wondering if they would ever recover, desperate to have enough to engage the services of Doctor Hollister, whom she knew would be better able to continue to supply their medicine...

The habit of being open had slowly withered away. By the time she had met George Chance, Earl of Lindow, the last thing she'd wanted was for him to pity her. To distrust her, someone so clearly in town for a singular purpose.

Dodo took a deep breath. "I... I'm not good with people."

George frowned. "I don't understand."

Case in point, she thought darkly. Aloud, she said, "I never know what to say, or when to say it, or even how to say it. I blurt things out—"

"I think we both possess that fault," said George dryly. "If you could call it a fault. I see it more as a character trait."

"Men have that luxury, but ladies—we are supposed to be charming, and elegant, and refined," Dodo said, a hint of desperation pouring into her voice. How was she supposed to explain this? "And I don't like people—at least, I prefer numbers."

"That, you do."

"I think in truth that I am a tad hard to be around," said Dodo, knowing she was burning every bridge with George, but recognizing he deserved the truth.

After all that had occurred between them, he deserved some truth.

"But I do... I do care, you know. Deeply," she said quietly, her chest tightening at the brutal honesty she'd forced herself through. "Even if I don't show it."

Her eyes had slipped to her hands, twisting together before her. Forcing herself to look up, she saw George was... smiling.

Smiling? Despite everything that she'd said?

"You are hard to love," he said gently.

Dodo bristled despite herself. *Well!* She was permitted to say that about herself, but she certainly did not want him to think that!

"Fine. Right, well," she said curtly, turning and reaching for the door.

She didn't have to stay to put up with this nonsense! She had lodgings to find, and arrangements to make to return to Croscombe, and—

A hand touched her shoulder. Just lightly, but enough to halt her steps. Enough to spark hope.

Slowly, Dodo turned around. George did not remove his hand from her shoulder, caressing it through the layers of fabric. Her skin burned where his fingers moved. Just the suggestion of his touch was enough to spark desire and need.

"I didn't say that I didn't love you," George said tenderly. "But I spoke the truth. It is hard. I think love is supposed to be hard."

Dodo stared into the sparkling, blue eyes of the man she adored. "But it's so easy to love you."

"Is it?"

She glared. "Increasingly difficult."

His gentle laughter could be felt through the contact of his hand, as well as heard. "I think love is something you work at. It's not something you have to play the odds for. You have to earn it."

Dodo's pulse was pattering so painfully, she was almost surprised it was still beating. "I... Do you mean...?"

"I had been about to ask you to marry me," George said ruefully. "When it all came out. Before."

Marry him?

She had hoped, of course. A part of her had wondered, desperately wished to know whether he wanted to be a part of her life forever. She knew he ought to have offered to protect her honor in the face of what they'd done, but she never would have held him to that. She'd have rather lived an ostracized spinster all her life than force his hand.

Marriage? Marriage to George?

Oh, goodness. Marriage to the Earl of Lindow.

"I don't think I'd be a very good countess," she said weakly.

"Look, I love you, and I am willing to bet that you love me," said George, his face growing serious.

His hand slipped from her shoulder, trailing along her arm and causing gooseflesh to rise under her pelisse. He slipped his hand in hers. It was soft. And tight. And belonged there.

Dodo allowed a flicker of a smile to pass across her face. "You're willing to bet, are you? How much?"

"This much."

And he was kissing her. Just like the last time they had kissed in the stable, it was full of passion and need and desire—but it was also different.

George cupped her face and Dodo leaned into the kiss, holding nothing back. Her fingers curled into his hair, pulling him closer, and she whimpered as his tongue teased delicate, sweet agony along her lips. Parting them to allow him entrance, Dodo grew in boldness, her tongue reaching out to meet his own.

How long they stood there, entangled together, desperately clinging to each other, she did not know.

All she knew was that by the time they eventually parted, breathless, she never wanted to be parted from him again.

"So... what now?" Dodo asked, her chest tight.

"Right now," George said, releasing her and turning away, "I want to give you this."

It was a small loss to have him walk away from her like that, but thankfully, he did not go too far. In fact, he only went as far as the other side of the small stable. His jacket and waistcoat were lying in a heap on a bale of straw, and George rummaged through his pockets before returning to her.

"This is for you," he said quietly.

Dodo's eyes widened. *That couldn't be—*

But it was. George slowly opened up the ring box to reveal a brilliantly shining gold band, a pearl atop it and diamonds encircling the pearl.

"That's... That is beautiful," she whispered.

"I had meant it to give to you that... that day, as a symbol of my affection," George said quietly. "Things got a tad out of hand, in hindsight."

Dodo could not help but laugh. "No, I don't suppose either of us could have predicted that!"

When she looked up at George, expecting him to join her in her laughter, it was to see his smooth, expressionless features very serious.

"Nothing about our lives, I'm getting the impression, is going to be predictable," he said softly, taking out the ring from its box.

Dodo's gasp caught in her throat as he reached for her left hand.

"But I know the odds will be far better for me if I have you by my side," George said, slipping the ring onto the fourth finger of her left hand, just as a groom would with his bride. "And I've put this on here, Dodo, but you can take it off if you want. You don't—you never owed me anything. Helping your parents was an honor for me. And it would also be an honor if you left that ring on and promised to stay with me. Stay with me forever."

Dodo's heart thundering, there was almost not enough air in her lungs for her to reply. "You… You do know there's an outside chance that we'll kill each other?"

George grinned. "It's a risk I'm willing to take."

Chapter Twenty

October 29, 1812

"And there you have it," declared George triumphantly. "Indisputably, and most definitely, the winner!"

With a great smile, he threw down his cards.

John Chance, Marquess of Aylesbury, groaned. "You mean to tell me you weren't bluffing the whole time?"

"I knew he wasn't bluffing," said William Chance, Duke of Cothrom, the corner of his lips tilted up. "I just didn't have the cards to call him out."

"How on earth could you tell he was not bluffing?" asked the Duchess of Cothrom with sparkling eyes. "As far as I can tell, the man wouldn't know how to bluff."

Their combined laughter rang out around the drawing room, and George grinned.

Well, he could take being the center of attention, even if the laughter surrounding him was at his own expense. It was hardly a change in his circumstances—he'd often been the butt of Chance brothers' jokes.

And one change in his circumstance made it even easier to face.

Seated beside him, and holding on to her cards with a sorrowful expression, was Miss Doris Loughty. At least she wouldn't bear that name for long. If that damned special license had arrived in the post today as it ought to have done, they'd be spending the evening putting the final touches for their wedding day together.

As it was, it hadn't, and so they weren't. And so he had been unable to put off having all the Chances over for dinner and a few games of cards.

All the Chances…

"I don't know h-how you p-put up with him, M-Miss Loughty," said Florence, the new Marchioness of Aylesbury, with a teasing look.

George glanced at Dodo, hoping she wasn't too disappointed to have been beaten.

And groaned.

"What's wrong now?" asked Aylesbury, starting to scoop the coins together and pushing them in George's direction.

"It's Dodo," he said with a wry expression. "I know that look."

"I haven't the faintest idea what you mean," Dodo said serenely. "Though I do think your declaration of success is a little… premature."

With great aplomb, and a beaming smile across her face, she laid down her cards on the table. Cards that had far more pictures on than his own hand.

"I think you'll find—"

But her elegant celebration was immediately overpowered by cheers and laughter.

"That will teach you, Lindow!" said Aylesbury.

"My word, I've never seen anyone beat him at his own game!" exclaimed Cothrom.

"You simply have to teach us, Miss Loughty," cried Alice. "We're so tired of the men thinking they're always having their own way!"

George leaned back in his seat and chuckled as Aylesbury bowed his head, pouring the coins into his future sister-in-law's lap.

If it were anyone else, George would have been highly irritated. No one liked being beaten, especially in such a spectacular way. Now he came to think about it, it was only due to his own pride and grandeur that he had managed to set himself up so well.

But it wasn't anyone else. It was her. Dodo, the perfect woman.

Oh, she had her faults. But he could not think of anyone more perfect for him than her.

In truth, he could hardly believe that she had agreed to marry him. Yes, he had taken her virtue, but she hardly seemed the type to entrap him over that. He didn't believe he had given quite the proposal speech she deserved, and from memory, he had told her some rather hard truths.

"I didn't say that I didn't love you. But I spoke the truth. It is hard. I think love is supposed to be hard."

But she had accepted him. The ring, the symbol of his love, he had placed on her finger still sparkled there, catching the candlelight in the numerous diamonds surrounding the pearl.

"Oh, it was easy really," she was saying to a clearly impressed Cothrom. "The mathematics of it—"

"—don't know how she does it," Alice was muttering to Florence with a mischievous look on her face. "I'm glad she's joining the family—imagine what she would do if she *weren't* one of us!"

George grinned, through this time, it was tight.

The one person in the room who hadn't spoken, hadn't guffawed loudly, hadn't congratulated Dodo on her spectacular win... was the one person George would have said wasn't one of them.

Frederick Chance, Viscount Pernrith, had been quiet all evening. He had barely said a word all through dinner and had refused a cigar when George had stiffly offered one. His comments while playing cards had been limited to the requirements of the game, and even now as everyone chattered away, he was silent.

George tried not to notice. He'd done enough, hadn't he, just by having him here? The first time Pernrith had been invited to Lindow House.

Yes, George had played his part. Though it was awkward, having Pernrith here.

"It sounds more complicated than it is," said Dodo, her cheeks pink at all the attention she was receiving. "All one has to do is calculate the probability of—"

The entire room groaned, save for Pernrith and George.

"Don't give away your cleverness," George said with a grin.

"She can give it away all she likes. I still won't understand it," Aylesbury said with a shake of his head. "The way you can make numbers do things for you Miss Loughty—"

"'Dodo,' please," she said, a little shy. "We're almost family, after all."

George's chest swelled.

Almost family. It seemed bizarre that they were not yet married. He considered her his wife, had done since the ring he had chosen had been put on her finger.

The only reason she wasn't staying in one of the guest bedchambers at Lindow House was because her parents had forbidden it.

Well. Not *forbidden* it. Just made it very clear, Mrs. Loughty with a purse of her lips, Mr. Loughty with a gentle frown, that it was not to be done. They'd already allowed their daughter far too much freedom, they'd had to admit.

George grinned as he allowed the conversation of his family to wash over him. It was a good thing he'd found a pleasant, three-bed chambered townhouse three streets over from Lindow House to rent for the Loughtys, or he wasn't sure what he'd have done. Gone to Croscombe, he supposed. Heaven forbid.

Mr. and Mrs. Loughty had dined with them quite happily and then retired early. They were still, Dodo had explained to him in a hushed tone, very easily tired, and she had no wish for them to exhaust themselves. Besides, with his sisters-in-law present, Dodo had them to act as chaperones.

Dodo Loughty with actual chaperones.

Fortunately for him, he knew his sisters-in-law would hardly be up to the task.

That meant he and Dodo could play cards with his family, tease each other in the comfort of their company, and perhaps, if he could manage it, he could steal a kiss…

"I've never seen you like this before."

George turned. His oldest brother, Cothrom, was seated on his right. The man had a severe expression most of the time, and there had been occasions during which their differing personalities had caused… difficulties. To put it lightly.

Not today, it appeared. "Like what?"

Cothrom gestured. "You know precisely what I mean. Like this."

George grinned. "Utterly happy, you mean?"

"Out of trouble for more than five minutes together," his brother said darkly. "I hope you realize you've broken several hearts back in London. Apparently, a few ladies had it in their heads that when they came out this Season, they would, and I quote, 'nab you.' I'm glad you're settling down."

Settling down?

He supposed he was, though George would never have used that term to describe what he had with Dodo.

Settling? He would never have imagined he could win the heart of someone so precious, not in a million years.

Down? It was an upgrade, most certainly, and an improvement of his life in all quarters.

Though now that he considered it, and the thought was a most unpleasant one, he supposed if one took a view from the other direction, then Dodo Loughty was most certainly settling *down* with him…

"You're happy, at any rate."

George blinked. Cothrom's smile was brief, but he caught it. "I am."

"Good."

How could he not have been? Being with Dodo gave him the certainty within himself he had never known before. Had challenged him, made him examine himself in a way Cothrom and all his lectures had never managed.

And now he was able to spend the rest of his life with her?

"William," came a quiet voice.

George glanced over and accidentally caught an intimate moment between Cothrom and his wife. Alice had touched her husband on the arm, just gently, but apparently, that was sufficient.

Cothrom nodded briefly, then turned back to George. "We will have to depart, I am afraid."

"Oh, must you?" Dodo asked, then winced at her indiscretion. "I mean—naturally, if you are tired—"

"More than a little tired," said Alice with a tinkling laugh. Her hand cupped her swelling stomach, just for a moment. "I think it is time we three returned home."

Although it was a very brief exchange of looks, George did not miss it—the moment that Aylesbury looked at Florence. His wife made the same subtle movement.

Oh, hell. Not more Chances. Weren't they having enough difficulties with the ones they already had?

"Besides, I should look in on Maudy," Alice was saying as the whole company rose from the table. "She'll be asleep, I hope—"

"She'll be lying awake waiting for you to return, if I know that girl," said Cothrom with a look George had never seen before.

Well, someone was likely to steal the man's heart eventually. George had just never expected it to be Cothrom's stepdaughter. Maude was just over three years of age, and as far as he could remember, was the very picture of her mother. She had the pair of them wrapped around her little finger.

As she ought, George thought with a grin as he shepherded his guests to the hall and oversaw Cawthorne, his thin-faced new butler wishing them a good evening as two footmen returned pelisses and greatcoats. Maudy was a charmer. She was going to make a gentleman work very hard someday.

"—and please do give our best wishes to your parents again," Alice was saying, her pelisse now around her shoulders and her hand slipped into the arm of her husband. "Such pleasant people."

Dodo was nodding, then murmuring a few words of goodbye to Florence.

George's affection swelled. He had never considered it important to choose a wife who understood and fit in with his family. In truth, he had thought little about getting a wife at all.

But now he had Dodo, and he saw how easily she took to being a part of the family... It was like they'd been made for each other.

The Cothroms had already left as the Aylesburys started walking out the door. Yes, his sisters-in-law had quite forgotten their duties as Dodo's chaperones. Forgotten or *"forgotten."* And that left—

"It was very pleasant to meet you, Lord Pernrith," Dodo said softly, curtseying low.

Lower than she needed to. *Why, she knows the man is just a viscount,* George thought viciously. *She never was so formal to me. There's no need to...*

The thought faded away—or he pushed it away, he wasn't sure. George's jaw tautened.

He didn't like who he was when he was around Pernrith. The man brought something out in him, something dark and vicious and cruel.

And whose fault is that?

"Good to see you, Pernrith," he said curtly.

Then he did something he had never done before and was almost certain was going to confuse the man to no end.

He offered out his hand.

George had been correct. Pernrith stared at the hand for a moment, seeming unsure precisely what to do with it.

A flicker of sadness rushed through him. Had he truly been so awful to the man that he was surprised at the merest modicum of civility?

"Lindow," said Pernrith, taking his hand and squeezing it briefly.

They both let go. Probably too soon.

"Well, good evening," said his half-brother, and with a nod to Dodo, the viscount stepped out into the cold, Bath air.

Cawthorne shut the door. "And will that be all, my lord?"

"It will, Cawthorne, thank you. And excellent work tonight," George said, remembering how smoothly the dinner had gone, how much more cheerful his footmen were. And there's been no complaints from the maids, either. Not to mention Cawthorne's gaze did not even flicker to Dodo, no hint of condoning the social faux pas of allowing his betrothed here alone without a chaperone. "Please consider this a permanent position. I'll raise your salary."

The man blinked, evidently astonished but pleased. "I—thank you, my lord. I-I did not expect—"

"Now Miss Loughty and I have some final business to discuss before she leaves," George said hurriedly, uncomfortable at the man's obvious gratitude. "We'll conclude in the drawing room. Good night, Cawthorne."

"Good night, my lord."

Only when he and Dodo had returned to the drawing room and closed the door behind them did he truly relax. "Too much?"

"I think the increase in salary was a surprise, yes," said Dodo with a knowing expression, dropping onto the sofa.

George smiled. That was another one of the things he loved about her. She just seemed to know what he was talking about, without much of an explanation needed.

"I will have to leave salary negotiations in your corner," he quipped.

Dodo's eyes widened. "Why on earth would you—oh. Oh, I see."

"He'll be your butler in a few days," George pointed out, ensuring the drawing room door was closed. He turned the key, just to be sure.

One never knew with the servants—and he wanted this to be a private audience.

"I am still growing accustomed to your family," Dodo said quietly, visibly swallowing.

Does she think I would be offended by such a remark? "We all are, I think," George said, easing onto the sofa with a sigh. "It's changed a great deal this year."

"You mean the addition of your two new sisters-in-law?"

He nodded. "Yes. And them."

He still wasn't sure what had happened that evening when he had gone to Pernrith for help.

Oh, he knew what had happened. They'd drunk brandy, chatting about how much he was in love with Dodo, and his half-brother had encouraged him to do something about it. And then George had left, round about half past one in the morning.

On the face of it, nothing much had happened at all. If it were any other family, nothing would, by all accounts, have happened.

But they weren't any other family. They were the Chances. Encounters like that simply did not happen—certainly not between himself and Pernrith.

Pernrith, of all people!

"We're a complicated bunch," George said aloud.

A bit of an understatement, to be sure, but—

"There's clearly little love lost between you and Viscount Pernrith," Dodo said softly, drawing up her heels under herself and letting her gown flow to the floor.

George hesitated. "You know, that would have been true a few months ago. A few weeks ago, even, but… things are different now."

What that difference would change, he was not sure. He supposed he would just have to wait and see.

Dodo was grinning. "Because you're in love?"

There was a singsong quality in her words that made it eminently clear she was teasing him.

A flare of heat, a need to have her close, perhaps even stop her mouth with a kiss, overwhelmed George.

But he managed to resist. For now.

"Because," he said, rolling his eyes, "I'm in love. Now come here."

Dodo went willingly into his arms. The kiss was passionate, slow and seductive, and George was certain she knew precisely what she was doing.

Making it difficult to stand without embarrassing himself.

But he couldn't help it. His whole body thrummed with need whenever he was with her, and the closer they got to the special license returning from Canterbury, the more challenging it was getting, forbidding himself from touching her.

The kiss deepened, and Dodo had just moved to straddle George on the sofa when she leaned back, panting.

"We said we weren't going to do this."

George blinked up with lust-hazed eyes at the beautiful woman whose hips were pressing into his rapidly stiffening manhood. "I haven't the foggiest idea why."

Dodo gave a laugh, sweeping back the hair that was escaping her pins. "You do something to me, my lord, that—"

He groaned. "Don't you dare call me that!"

"Why on earth not?" she asked, a teasing lilt in her voice even as her cheeks pinked. "I rather like it. *My lord.*"

George shivered. If she kept saying it like that, he was not going to be responsible for his actions.

"You do know, don't you," he said seriously, "that I am incredibly fortunate to have found you?"

"A lucky Chance."

"I am in earnest," George said quietly.

The thought he could have passed her by at McBarland's... that there was even the smallest of possibilities they would not have found each other...

It did not bear thinking about.

"After all, what are the odds that we would have found each other?"

Dodo's face turned serious, her eyes sparkling. "As a matter of fact, I started working this out! The probability could not be too difficult, I thought, not with a limited number of people in Bath. Then there was the fact that your brother directed me to McBarland's to find you, exponentially increasing—"

George leaned back, his head cocked. "My brother?"

Dodo's shoulders shrugged as she suppressed a smile. "Yes, well, I thought he might have told you about that. The marquess."

Oh, George was going to have a few questions to ask *the marquess*. She had mentioned knowing the man at that first meeting, but he'd only suspected his brother had directed her straight to him.

"He told me you gambled with large sums, and my mind immediately started calculating—"

"Dodo, were you at McBarland's to *seek me out* in particular?"

Dodo opened her mouth, closed it, then opened it again. "That is neither here nor there, in the end. I was hardly there with the intentions of *marrying* you. And besides, I do believe the odds were we would have found one another eventually, considering the path I was on. I calculated the probability. I think I left my workings out somewhere in here, actually, I—"

George pulled her close and kissed her on the mouth.

He had never really been one for words. Partly because Cothrom always misunderstood him, partly because Aylesbury had never needed them to get into mischief with him, and Pernrith—

Well. He hadn't exchanged many words at all with Pernrith, now he came to think about it.

With Dodo, words were not necessary. She understood him on a level that was instinctual, deeper than mere affection.

And George tried to show her just how much that meant to him as the kiss deepened, his hand moving to her breast, teasing the nipple through the fabric of her gown, which was most annoyingly in the way, and—

"We mustn't," Dodo said breathlessly, pulling away but remaining straddled over his lap.

George groaned as he leaned his head on her shoulder.

It was getting more and more hard—*more and more difficult*, he corrected himself with a half-smile—to be around Dodo and not want to seize her.

And they had told themselves they would be good. The trouble was, they were so good in bed together.

"I should probably send you back to your parents," George said, with just enough breath to make out each word. "In the carriage."

"I suppose you should," Dodo said, turning her head to kiss him on the forehead.

For a good number of minutes, neither of them moved. Then—

"Or," said Dodo, a mischievous look on her face as she started to fumble with the buttons of his breeches.

George groaned. "Oh, thank God."

It did not take her long. As his manhood sprang free of the fabric that had been restricting it, Dodo carefully lifted herself up and moved her skirts about to spear herself onto him.

Biting his lip to prevent himself from crying out, it was all George could do not to moan as Dodo slowly lowered herself onto him.

Oh, Christ, she was so wet. So warm. So ready for him—just as eager for him, in fact, as he was for her.

"I do love you, you know." He gasped, holding on to the edges of the sofa cushion to steady himself.

If he tried to touch Dodo, he was in danger of exploding into her before she had her own peak. And he wouldn't be that selfish—not if he could help it.

Dodo smiled down at him, the flickers of pleasure she was evidently feeling burning her cheeks. "I should think so. I'm about to ride you far better than your jockeys ever rode Honor of Guinevere or Scandal of Lancelot."

George did groan at that, and Dodo captured his lips immediately, preventing the noise from echoing through the house.

Slowly, inch by inch, the woman he loved built a rhythm upon his manhood that had George twitching and moaning. Her own climax was taken twice before she looked at him and nodded.

"Come with me," Dodo whispered.

It was not an invitation he was likely to decline. Wishing to goodness she were staying the night so they could see in the dawn experiencing ecstasy like this, George felt his whole body twitching and tautening as Dodo rode him closer and closer to a peak he was desperate to—

"Dodo!"

"Yes, yes, George!"

They came together, their need mingling as he shot himself into her. The pleasure was exquisite, almost painful, and she kept riding him, right to the very edge of the precipice and then beyond.

George's head tilted back over the edge of the sofa as his body shuddered at the end of his release. "Damn."

"Dodo," she corrected, kissing him lightly on the lips.

Blinking up through the haze of requited coupling, George nodded, his hands moving to cup her buttocks. *I will never lose her again.*

"Dodo," he repeated with a grin. "My Dodo."

Epilogue

November 1, 1812

THE PEN SCRATCHED painfully across the paper, leaving an ink splat halfway across that obliterated most of the equation.

"Bother," Dodo muttered.

She scrunched the piece of paper into a ball, threw it indiscriminately behind her without looking to see where it fell, and picked up a pencil.

It was always better, she knew, to start working with a pencil before you were happy with the formula. She should have done that from the start, but it had been her own arrogance that had failed her. The whole thing had looked so easy, so beautiful, so elegant in her mind.

The drawing room of Lindow House filled with the scratching of the pencil as Dodo slowly moved it across the page. From the lead poured numbers. Numbers and letters, a few dates, calculations that grew in complexity the farther down the page the pencil moved.

She'd been offered the use of the study, now it was clear she rather than George could actually make use of it, but she had declined. There was something far more comforting about sitting curled up in an armchair with a large book in her lap, leaning upon it instead of a desk. Something… primal. If mathematics could be primal.

Dodo's eyes focused on the calculation, unable to take anything in. The numbers opened up for her, revealing the truth that she had suspected before she had put pen to paper. It was not nearly as large a number as she had expected, either. In fact, it would be rather soon—

A subtle movement from the corner of her eye. A pressing warmth on her neck.

"Dodo," whispered her husband.

Dodo dropped the pencil and swiftly moved a sheaf of paper over the calculations she had been working on. "George."

She hadn't noticed him come in, which was unusual. Typically, the man couldn't breathe without her noticing—but then, her mind had been distracted by something of great import.

George pressed another kiss on her neck before stepping around her and dropping onto the sofa to her left. "Working on something interesting?"

Dodo pressed her fingers on the paper that was covering up what she had been working on. "Maybe."

"Plotting against me, then?"

"Oh, most definitely."

Heat spread across her, though it was accompanied by a little queasiness. He hadn't asked directly, so it wasn't precisely a lie. And if he really wished to know, he would ask again.

That was the wonderful thing about what had grown between them, though it may have started off slowly and strangely. There were no secrets between them. Dodo knew if George wanted to know something, all he had to do was ask.

But he didn't. Instead, her husband of just three days stretched out and yawned. "Goodness, I'm tired. I've spent all day thinking about it, and I really think Scandal of Lancelot could be far better if we changed the exercise routine."

"You spent all day yesterday thinking about it," said Dodo vaguely, shifting the papers so she could glance at her calculations. She had been right. "And you decided then that the best thing to do was stay the course and stick to the exercise program we already had."

George shot her that delectable, spine-melting smile he always had when he was being annoying. "I did, didn't I?"

"You did."

"Well, I must have been talking nonsense, then," he said happily, crossing one leg over the other. "We've tried changing the food, and some of the training—it's the exercise itself we haven't adjusted."

"Statistically irrelevant."

"Statistically—what do you mean by that?"

Dodo smiled elusively, not looking up from the paper. There it was, in pencil. Gray on white, the answer to the question that had been consuming her.

"Dodo—"

"I mean that statistically, Scandal of Lancelot is only half a head behind his main competitors, and after the changes you have already made with food and training, he hasn't gained in the slightest," Dodo said airily, looking up and laughing at the mock outrage on her husband's face. "Suggesting that he has reached his peak performance, and any other tinkering is merely going to throw him off his stride. You know I'm right."

George snorted. "Doesn't mean you have to always be right, though."

There was such tenderness in his words, she was momentarily overcome.

What had she done to deserve this man? Oh, he was a scoundrel. He was far more accustomed to making trouble than making plans, and some of his mathematical understanding was truly atrocious.

But he was hers. There was no way around it. Dodo knew that she belonged to him in a way that she could not explain. Not even with numbers.

George Chance was the only person she wanted in the entire world. Now her parents were next week to return to Croscombe, to be safe and sound in their own home, something they could never have expected, and with a talented doctor paid in advance to treat them as need be...

Well, that left her with only one thing to worry about.

"—unfair that the jockey should say such a thing. I read it in the newspaper, the outrage!" George was saying. When precisely he had started to speak, Dodo was not sure. "I should have the blaggard raked over the coals for merely speaking to the press, but... you're not listening, are you?"

Dodo cleared her throat and tried desperately to concentrate. "I'm listening now."

That made him laugh. "And when, exactly, did I manage to gain your attention?"

"Just after you lost it," she said sweetly.

Their laughter mingled through the drawing room, and Dodo knew she would never be as happy as this. Never. It felt a mathematical impossibility that she could hold any more happiness.

Yet she would. She knew she would. Her life with George, their life together—it was only just beginning.

And it was all about to change.

"That's when I decided to paint all the horses bright green," George said nonchalantly. "I think it will make it harder for the other competitors to see them, you understand, and so will naturally have an advantage."

Dodo nodded. *Well. It made sense.*

Then her mind caught up with her. "You're going to what?"

"I knew you weren't truly paying attention," said George with a sigh, shaking his head with mock severity. "I don't know. I come in here, distracting you from what you were doing, and you don't have the good graces to dedicate every iota of your attention to me!"

His eyes twinkled.

Dodo had to keep herself from laughing. There was a certain amount of nonsense in her husband's approach to life, and she wasn't sure whether she would ever get used to it. In a way, she rather hoped she wouldn't.

"I was paying you some attention," she said. "I noticed the green paint."

"Eventually," George shot back.

"My point is, I was listening."

Her husband grinned. "Want to bet?"

Dodo laughed, the joy flowing through her body like fine wine: rich, and pleasant, and warming. It gave a tingle to her mind that made it difficult to concentrate, and a fluidity in her body that nothing but George's presence could create.

He was charming—and he was honest. Mostly. He was good to her, and good to those he loved. Even, it appeared, to those he did not love. Dodo could never have predicted, given what he'd said about the illegitimate Chance brother, that Viscount Pernrith would have actually turned up at their wedding.

In truth, she thought Pernrith was surprised to have received an invitation in the first place.

And Dodo's parents adored her husband. *Well, of course they did.* She should not have been surprised that George had been able to charm her mother and impress her father within five minutes of meeting them.

It certainly didn't hurt, after all, that he was an earl...

"Remind me," he said. "When is the big family dinner?"

"Tomorrow," said Dodo, wondering if she needed to share the news before then. It was too soon to reveal in front of her parents. They would wonder when it had happened, since she and George had only been wed a few days. But if she couldn't hide this nausea much longer...

George groaned. "And we really have to have all of them?"

She had to laugh at that. "The vast bulk of them are *your* family!" Though it was *their* family now.

"All four Chance brothers, under one roof," he said forebodingly. "And two wives."

"Three wives."

"Goodness, you know, I didn't count you," he said with a smirk. "And your parents, naturally. A full house. There won't be any room for anyone else!"

Dodo grinned as her husband laughed, though her stomach twisted. They had never discussed it. Oh, she had been certain they would eventually. But the time for that was coming, and swiftly. Soon she would have to tell him—

"What are you working on?" George asked, his gaze flickering to the wad of paper on her lap.

Dodo swallowed.

She had not actually intended to talk to him about it now. Now did not seem right. It was too soon, too early. She did not know enough. She hadn't had enough time to recheck the calculations.

But as her attention flickered up from the gray pencil scribblings on the paper, she saw—

George. Smiling, and happy, and curious. Not a man to push her before she was ready, not someone who would force her to reveal what she would prefer to keep private.

But a man who loved her. Who respected her. Who admired her, without the desire to censure her.

And her core melted.

"I... I have been working on something," Dodo said, finding to her surprise her voice was hoarse.

"Giving you trouble?"

"You could say that," she said. Her fingers shook as she picked up the paper. "Here."

She wasn't exactly sure what she expected to happen as she passed the seemingly innocent paper over to her husband. Fireworks? A chorus of angels? Stars from the heavens?

When George placed the paper on his crossed knee and took a look at it, nothing happened. There was silence in the drawing room, nothing but the sound of a gardener passing the window and a bird singing in a tree near the building.

Dodo swallowed. He would understand, of course. It was obvious. In all honesty, she was rather surprised she had managed to keep it to herself for this long. It was so blatant—

"I don't understand," said George, squinting slightly at the page as he tilted his head, as though that would make the numbers more legible. "What's this bit here—plus nine? Why nine?"

A thrill of excitement rushed through Dodo. *This is it.* The moment she could decide to retreat and not say anything. She could pass it off as a mathematical exercise, just some fun she was having with the numbers. She did that sort of thing regularly enough for it to pass without comment.

But somehow she knew, deep within herself, that this was the moment to confess. That the knowledge, once shared, would be far more wonderful than it would be kept close within her.

"I have been doing some calculations," Dodo said quietly, training her eyes on her husband to watch his reaction. "To work out... To work out when our little one will be born."

And George did not move.

For a few heartbeats, Dodo wondered whether she should repeat herself. He did not appear to have heard her. Surely, if he had, he would say something.

His finger moved over the page. "When... When our little one will...?"

His voice seemed to fail him and uncertainty poured through Dodo. Could she have misjudged this so utterly? After so many years of always getting the calculations right, of never overstretching herself, never worrying about pushing her luck...

Had she finally done so?

And then paper was cascading onto the floor. Not just the piece Dodo had given him, though that had fallen first—but George had grabbed her hands and pulled her upright, causing book, pen, pencil, and reams of paper to stream over the carpet.

"George!"

"Dodo!" he cried affectionately, pulling her into his arms. "Oh, Dodo—you're sure? A child?"

"The odds are—"

"I don't want odds. I want to know how you feel—are you well?" George said anxiously, pulling away and casting a severe look over her. "And here I was, making you walk all day!"

"We walked around the garden. I am quite well," Dodo said, laughing with elation.

"But the baby!"

"Both mother and child are doing well, so I am told by the doctor," she said, fondly stroking George's cheek as his hands clasped her waist.

His delighted expression lessened somewhat as he frowned. "You've been seeing a doctor? Without telling me? Are you ill? You're not—"

"Only to make sure," Dodo said hastily.

And that was the truth. She had been almost certain, as the numbers had seemed to suggest—and when had she ever not been able to trust the numbers?

Flickering emotions scattered across George's handsome face. Joy and fear and laughter and surprise and delight and—

"You know, there's an outside chance they'll be born on July the eleventh," Dodo said, looking hastily for the piece of paper she had been working on. "And I think, if my calculations are correct—"

"Hang the calculations!" George cried. "Sorry," he added hastily, seeing her expression. "But goodness, this is so much more than mathematics!"

Dodo raised an eyebrow. He knew her thoughts on this—there

was nothing more than mathematics.

"You and me," George whispered. "You and me, creating a new person—half of me, half of you, and half themselves."

"That doesn't add up—"

"Maybe not on paper," her husband said quietly, moving a hand from her waist and placing it carefully over her stomach. "But it still does."

Dodo's breath caught in her throat as they both looked at his hand.

There, somewhere underneath his palm, was a life. A child, someone growing who would soon come into the world and meet them. George was partly right, even if his numbers were nonsense. Half of him, and half of her, and completely themselves.

"As long as they are healthy," George was saying, "I couldn't give a fig when they were born. And we'll be happy—we will be happy, won't we, Dodo?"

Dodo looked up and caught his gaze.

And there was desperation there, and love, and eagerness. A need to be loved, a vulnerability in his eyes she knew George had never allowed anyone to see before.

And she smiled. "Happy? There's not an outside chance of that, my love. That is a certainty."

A short letter from the author

Hello! Thank you so much for reading *An Outside Chance*, the third novel in my Chances series. I truly hoped you enjoyed it, and that you fell in love with George and Dodo just as much as I did.

I've always wanted to write a series of brothers, but I could never 'meet' the characters that were quite right. After waiting years to meet them myself, I have had a lot of fun writing the four Chance brothers—and I think Cothrom's, Aylesbury's, and Pernrith's stories are just as much fun. Make sure to pre-order Frederick's story—he's going to get himself into a mighty pickle…

Being an author can be a lonely business, but knowing that there are readers from all over the world who are going to adore my stories makes it all worthwhile. Thank you for your support, and I hope you love reading more of my books!

Happy reading,
Emily

About Emily E K Murdoch

If you love falling in love, then you've come to the right place.

I am a historian and writer and have a varied career to date: from examining medieval manuscripts to designing museum exhibitions, to working as a researcher for the BBC to working for the National Trust.

My books range from England 1050 to Texas 1848, and I can't wait for you to fall in love with my heroes and heroines!

Follow me on twitter and instagram @emilyekmurdoch, find me on facebook at facebook.com/theemilyekmurdoch, and read my blog at www.emilyekmurdoch.com.

Made in the USA
Coppell, TX
11 November 2024